WONKS

My thanks to the following editors
for publishing selections from WONKS:
George Plimpton of *The Paris Review*,
Leslie Wilson of *Review Americana*,
Anna Sidak of *In Posse Review*,
J.T. Barbarese of *StoryQuarterly*,
and Tom Dooley of *Eclectica Magazine*.

And to Carolina Arnal for design and layout.

Eclectica Press Intl LLC
ISBN-13: 9780996883047
ISBN-10: 0996883045

WONKS

WILLIAM REESE HAMILTON

This book is dedicated
to the children of Santo Tomas
and the men of the First Cavalry
who set them free.

For Sam.

CHAPTER 1

When the big historic tale gets told, this might be a part they let fall through the cracks. So let me fill you in. I'm not going to tell it pretty, because it's a war story. And a war story is like a hunk of shrapnel. It's got nasty ragged edges.

The Japanese Imperial Army swept into the Philippines on my twelfth birthday, bombing and strafing and generally laying siege. I was living with my folks in Manila, but after the Yanks pulled out to Corregidor and Bataan and old General MacArthur declared Manila an "open city," the Japs waltzed right in, scooped up all us "non-Asians" and put us in this camp. Internment Camp Number One at the University of Santo Tomas. They told us to bring food and clothing for three days. That's a real belly laugh the way things turned out.

All sorts got trucked into our camp. From rich folks to harbor bums, all jammed together with no rhyme or reason. And just when you figured they must've dug up everybody, living or dead, a fresh batch piled off the rear end of some old Ford truck the Japs'd requisitioned. Mom called it "wholesale dislocation." Lots of people sure did look to be broken up – just trying to find a spot of shade to sit and guard their little pile of portable property, eating their last measly snack food out of tins, lining up long hours to wash off at a spigot, then sleeping in their clothes on the classroom floors.

We'd been yanked out of our homes, losing about everything we owned, without a clue to what would happen next. When that soldier rolled over our garden wall and landed with a thump and a clank in the middle of our bed of bright red canna lilies, it was enough to give me and Mom the walking willies. Especially since Dad wasn't there. That soldier just stood there in the shadows of the mango tree, staring hard from under his helmet, rifle and bayonet at the ready. I had

7

about a million wild and scary pictures running through my head. Most had the "Nanking" label tied to them. If you never heard of the "Rape of Nanking," better check the newsreels. "Nanking" stimulated the imagination. Like that part about throwing kids in the air and catching them on bayonets. Nobody knew what a crazy Jap might do.

But the worst was Dad not being with us. We'd been cut off from him since mid-December. Not a single word since then. He was closing down company mines in North Luzon last we heard and never made it back down to Manila. The Jap invasion split the island right in two. Mom kept telling me not to fret, but I could see she was worried silly herself.

About the third day of Camp, I was hanging out by the front fence, watching a crowd of Filipinos come up Boulevard España, hauling food and clothing and bedding to their friends in the clink. They had to stand outside and shout for the folks they'd brought stuff for. More and more kept coming, until after a while there was a mob out there, crowding up against the wrought-iron fence, yelling out like it was a bazaar, handing stuff over the fence and crying and all, because they were so happy to see us alive but so sad to see us locked up. That got the guards all hot and nervous at once. Hot, because they didn't like seeing these birds they called their "Asian brothers" acting so loyal and friendly toward Americans and the like. Nervous, because they thought they might just have a riot on their hands.

At first it was more funny than serious. See, your Jap official's real high on order. One-two-three, by the numbers. Everybody was supposed to stand out there single-file in a long line and bring packages through the front gate one-by-one to get them inspected by some Jap sitting at a folding table. Well, you know that wasn't going to play. Filipinos aren't much on queuing up for hours in the sun just to please a Jap. A Filipino's plenty easy going. He'll make friends with a total stranger in about half-a-second and invite him home to stay for the next couple of years. But he does like doing things his own way, bristles over being bossed by the enemy. So folks out there in the street just kept flowing around in little groups, washing back and forth like the tide.

That raised Jap hackles. First they tried getting everybody off the fence and across the street, barking orders nobody but them could understand. Then when the crowd didn't move fast enough, they started pushing. That seemed to work at first, but all at once it sprung a leak. The crowd gushed right around them and back up to the fence, laughing and talking like it was holidays. It was hard to take those sentries too serious, the way they clumped around in those big boots and messy-looking uniforms.

But now they started prodding folks in the ribs with bayonets and whacking them pretty good across the head and shoulders with bamboo clubs. I was sure it was going to turn bad real quick, with folks screaming and running and bleeding and dying maybe.

That's when I caught sight of Gregorio and Timotea, the Filipinos who worked at our house out in Pasay. Just a glimpse of old Gregorio first, hauling a mattress over his head and getting swept about like he was riding a crest after a shipwreck. Then there popped up Timotea, skinny as a wet sparrow being swallowed up and dragged back by unseen forces. She was working hard at hanging onto this wicker basket and flapping her way back to Gregorio. Boy, they'd carried that mattress all the way from Pasay. That was miles!

When I saw that mattress, my eyes got about as big as mangos, and I was blind to the rest. It wasn't just any mattress, it was *my* mattress. Maybe I was being selfish, but I'd spent hard nights on the concrete floor, crowded in next to my dad's pal Southy Jack on one thin little mat. I saw Gregorio as my salvation from tight sweaty nights. So I started yelling and waving and jumping up and down, screaming my fool head off. But with all the commotion out there, the chance of my getting noticed was slim to none.

"Gregorio!" I shouted and then, "Timotea!" And I kept it up till I could barely croak. But it was like one of those dreams where you're up on a soapbox announcing the end of the world at the top of your lungs and everybody flat ignores you. Then just when I quit, some old Filipino by the fence took up "Timotea" like a chant, long and thin, in this far off voice. "Ti - mo - te - a," he was wailing, "Ti - mo - te - a!" I've got no idea why he latched onto it, maybe it was his old lady's name or something. But then all around him other Filipinos picked it up too, until everybody was crying it out. It got to be a howling like at a funeral. "Ti - mo - te - a!" rolled back and forth along the boulevard until I think it spooked the Japs. You could tell by the way they kind of scrunched down. The funny thing is I could still make out Timotea and she was wailing it too.

That ruckus brought Mom over. First thing I knew she'd squeezed right up beside me on the fence, breathing hard and looking anxious. "What's happening out here, Johnny?"

"Gregorio's got my mattress," I said, pointing. When Mom saw him, she gave a big wave.

"Kaybígang!" she cried out in this high American lady's voice, and it hushed everything down out there like magic. "Friends!" she yelled. "Amigos!" Everybody looked right at us. "Bring it here, Gregorio," she said. "Come on, Timotea." All at once that crowd just broke like the Red Sea, so Gregorio and Timotea got carried in a kind of current towards us. And before I knew what was happening, they were right against the fence. Gregorio looked Mom right in the eye and threw the mattress up and over the iron spikes, so I could jump up and grab it. Timotea was right there too, but the wicker basket was gone with only a handle left in her hand. Her eyes were wide and scared.

"I have clothes for you, mum, and papaya too," she said. "But they all be gone." She looked like her heart was broke. I felt special about Timotea. We were bonded down in Calamba. When the Jap attack was just breaking in early December, Dad told Gregorio to drive us down there in the Dodge to stay at this big sugarcane plantation until things blew over. He figured maybe that would be safer than the city. All kinds of people were going down to keep out of the war. But pretty soon the Japs hit there too, swooping low and strafing, and we were all running like hell for cover. I was with Timotea, sprinting in the shadows, the roar of engines right over us. But when we got to the first air-raid shelter, they were all Spanish inside and wouldn't let us in because Timotea was mestiza and not *pure*blood like them. Boy, I hollered bloody murder and spit in their faces, but they just slammed the door on us. So we had to run on. But Timotea loved me for that and said, "You my hero, Johnny." I tell you, she was swell.

"God bless, Señora Oldfield," Gregorio said.

"Go away," she whispered cold as a snake. "Now! Quick as you can!" And they were gone. Just melted into the crowd. And before the Japs knew what was up, she'd grabbed me and the mattress just as quick and we were gone too. Up along the fence and behind the darkening trees, moving at a quick walk but not breaking stride, down and across the Plaza and in through that big door to the Main Building, and then straight up those wide stairs two flights and back to my room, where the men slept.

She sent me in to set my mattress down next to Southy Jack's. So I did. But when I came back out she was standing stock-still, looking out into the big patio. She was in a dark mood. Boy, my heart was thumping like a tom-tom, but I wasn't about to say boo. If she was shaking or crying, I'd reached out and touched her. But she was cold as a block of ice. I bet she was thinking about my old man. I bet she was mad because we were left all alone with those Japs. I stood there a minute, but I saw her mood wasn't going away, so I made myself small and slunk off. When my mom was in an icy spell it was best to keep your mouth shut.

When I got back out front again, everything was calmer. The crowd on España had started to thin out. It was toward dusk and even the Filipinos who still had stuff in their arms were turning around to head home. I must've still been keyed up over that near riot, because all at once I could feel myself starting to relax. Sometimes you don't know how close things are until they're over. But gosh, it was something how quick Mom pulled the fuse and changed it all around. I don't know just how. She could do things, that's all. I know it was sure to get bad before she showed.

I was mulling this over when a funny thing happened. A black Buick came rolling up the street, blowing its horn through the crowd right up to the front gate, turned in past the sentries and pulled up just inside. The back door swung open and somebody got shoved out. I heard laughing inside. Nobody else got out. Just this one guy. He was standing there in a white suit, kind of shaky. He leaned up against the Buick for support. That is until it drove off and left him there on his lonesome. Then one of the guards grabbed his arm and pointed him up the line of acacias towards the Main Building.

It's funny how some guys can be tall and good looking as statues and you don't even give them a second glance. Then there are guys you can't take your eyes off. His suit was all wrinkled and dirty, slept in, maybe rolled down the street in, his hair mussed and sweated down, his face stubbly and gaunt. He was squinting like even that half-light hurt his eyes and the trip up the line of trees was looking awful long. Still, I could tell this guy wasn't your everyday, run-of-the-mill harbor rat. There was something about him, even when he was weaving up the road, that made me want to follow. Something jaunty.

He was working hard just then on whistling a verse out of "The Twelve Days of Christmas," the one that goes on about what this lady's getting from her "true love." Only after a couple of bars, his lips got so dry everything petered out into a squeak, and he took up mumbling and humming through the rest. Someone yelled out from the shadows that Christmas was over for this year, thank God! I could hear them all chortling back there in the dark. So he turned real slow and gave them a long stare.

"Don't be such a Scrooge," he said.

"Drunk!" came a voice from the shadows.

"Where's your sense of the mystical? I'm merely celebrating Epiphany. Isn't it on *your* calendar?"

This real haughty sounding woman chimed in with a loud whisper, "Disgrace!" And for just a moment he looked puzzled.

"Virgin Mary?" he asked.

"First it was the whores and the gamblers," she was carrying on. "Now we have to put up with this."

"Madam, fear not. I'll *never* molest you. I swear."

"See here!" this angry guy's voice spoke out.

"I much prefer the company of whores and gamblers to anything long dead."

That's just what he said. It's as near a direct quote as anything here. And he left those birds with their mouths open, I bet. That's the way I pictured them – gaping in the dark.

That was the very first I ever saw of old Harry Barnes. That's how he showed up. Right out of the blue. No bags. Not even a toothbrush. Nothing but the smile on his face, as they say. And definitely no shine on his shoes. But I learned pretty quick that quite a few of our inmates knew of him from one place or another.

CHAPTER 2

When I heard that name, Harry Barnes, it just about knocked me flat. This drunk was *my* very own godfather, the guy my folks picked to stand up for me at baptism. Not that that stuff has much staying power. The name's about all that's left, and maybe the extra card on birthdays. Truth is, I'd never even laid eyes on old Harry. Not since I was peeking out of a crib in China, anyway. But my folks were *always* talking about Harry this and Harry that. And I do recall seeing old snapshots of someone running around with them up in the Western Hills out past Peking, among the temples and the Buddhist monasteries.

We were always getting letters and cards from all around the globe, and I'd hear my mom call out to Dad, upstairs or out in the yard or over the telephone wire to the mines, "Guess where Harry's been! Bangkok!" or "Why do you suppose he's in Istanbul?" And once in a while I'd even get something myself from some crazy place I never heard of, a picture postcard plastered with a bunch of sharp-looking stamps.

He wrote me once from a place in Egypt called Shepheard's Hotel, advising me that since my old man was so keen on mining I should let him know there was treasure galore to dig out of the desert. And the picture on the front was an ancient pharaoh's shiny gold mask. I remember too some guy spinning a prayer wheel in front of queer looking buildings up amongst the clouds in the Himalayas, and a note saying to let my mom know she could rest assured, because there were lamas enough up there in the mountains to keep the world at peace through our lifetimes and several more besides. Crazy stuff to make a kid wonder.

Mom told me he was a writer. When he was fresh out of university, he wrote some play she called "drawing room comedy," said it was the hit of Philadelphia and everybody was praising young Harry as the next George Bernard Shaw. That was something, I guess. But Dad held that play was brittle stuff as far as he could see, and Harry was a whole lot better off with tales he was writing now for *Collier's* and *Saturday Evening Post*. Said there was a lot more blood pumping through them than any drawing room.

I did read one of them once in *Liberty* and it was pumping, sure enough. About some young American who found himself stuck in the Sahara, fresh out of employment, but who got a job with a sheik and fell in love with a concubine in a secret harem and then ended up high-tailing it across the dunes on a wild Arabian stallion. Boy, it was a thriller in three parts. I saw by that he could spin a yarn when he wanted. Anyway, you can see how it was for me trying to square that Harry Barnes with this shaky guy who showed up in a grimy suit.

And Mom didn't make him any dearer to me when she offered up *my* mattress for *him* to sleep on and made me give up my little fling at luxury to perch along the crack between that mattress and Southy Jack's. Specially since Harry was smelling about as rank as bad fish in the sun and snoring off a mean, hard drunk. It was hotter that night than even the night before, with us men packed together like sardines in a can, fifty-some on the concrete classroom floor. The air was close and dead, and big swarms of mosquitoes kept settling down out of the dark to eat us for snacks. I had to battle hard just to get to sleep.

But first I had to ask something. I tried to make out Southy's face in the dark, see if I could catch the glint of his eyes. Southy was a boxer who once worked out of New York and Chicago gyms, a quick lean lefty with a good jab and right hook combination. He fought lightweight at the pro level, and made some good dough at it, Dad told me. A nice little guy, built like a terrier, with a crooked nose and some scar tissue built up around the eyebrows. Mom called him, "Mon Petit Cro-Magnon," but he was sweet as marmalade.

"Southy, you awake?"

"Yeah," he mumbled. "Sure."

"When you figure it's gonna end, Southy?"

"No idea, kid. Go to sleep."

"You figure MacArthur's gonna win it?"

"Odds don't look too good," he whispered. "I wouldn't place any bets." I got closer to him in the dark.

"I wish my old man was here."

"Sure. So do I."

"Where you figure he is?"

"He'll be OK."

"You figure he's off in the mountains some place?"

"No idea."

"Maybe he's hiding out with the Igorots."

"Your old man'll be OK."

"You think he's up on Bataan?"

"No, kid. He's civilian. Too smart for that."

"I hope he gets here soon."

"Your old man's part Injun, right?"

"Yeah."

"He'll know what to do."

"What would an Injun do?"

"Stay out of it," Southy said. He rolled over, giving me his back. But I wouldn't let go of it that easy. I was thinking about who my old man could stay with out there.

"I figure maybe the Japs got about everybody in here already," I said to him.

"There's more out there, kid. Go to sleep." His words were starting to slur.

"Did you know this Mr. Barnes guy before?"

"No."

"What d'you think?"

"He's a friend of your old man's, ain't he?"

"You think he's on the level?"

"A friend ..."

"I sure wish Dad was here?"

"Yeah, then maybe a guy could sleep."

But the next morning, there was the same Harry, fresh-shaved and slicked-up like he was close to civilized, standing nice and straight at roll call. He was still green around the gills, but it was something what a quick wash and a clean set of duds could do. Southy loaned him a shirt and a set of shorts, seeing he was Dad's friend. But that wasn't the worst. Mom hung on Harry like he was a long-lost brother, looking at him and smiling and whispering secrets in his ear. She even spent a good part of the day at the community scrub board, getting his suit as close to white as nature would allow.

She and Southy smoothed everything out for Harry with the Monitors, made sure he got his meal ticket, loaned him a dinner pail, even took him through the chow line so he wouldn't lose out on his rightful share of rice and fish. Treated him no less than royalty. I just kept sniffing around, wondering what Mom had dragged into the family circle.

But the first we heard about how Harry happened to be in Manila came when we were eating out in the dining sheds back of the Main Building. They'd just set up the kitchen and were starting to dish out regular meals. In the mornings we got cracked wheat and some Klim or coffee. It was a job finding a place to sit down in those crowded sheds. There was the constant clatter of spoons against metal buckets, folks concentrating hard on getting something quick into their guts. But we were lucky that morning and got a corner bench. We were just starting to chow down when Harry laid a bundle on the table and unwrapped four beautiful ripe mangos. Just like a rabbit out of a hat.

"My lord, Harry," Mom said.

"Mr. Barnes!" little Mrs. Fitzgibbon said. "How *absolutely* bountiful!" She was the size of a mosquito and had the voice of a frog. But she was very elegant, Mom said.

"Would you kindly share these with me, good people?" Harry asked. Mr. Fitzgibbon, her bald husband from the oil company, gave a good laugh at that.

"You mean, are we too proud to accept a handout? Will we lower ourselves to take charity? Just hand those lovelies right over."

"Where did you get them?" Mom asked.

"Gift horse," Harry said, pointing to his mouth.

"You mean, don't ask?" I asked.

"He means have courtesy and humility," Mr. Fitzgibbon said.

"*How* did you get them?" Mrs. Fitzgibbon demanded. Southy was just wedging himself onto the bench next to me.

"Friend at the gate," Southy said.

"Friend?" Mom asked. "What friend?"

"She wasn't bad," Southy smiled. "Not bad for a guy on just a few days' shore leave."

"Just what have you been up to?" Mrs. Fitzgibbon asked.

"I think it's time you told us just where you've been, Harry," Mom said.

"In general or in particular?" Harry said, peeling and cutting our mangos for us.

"Confess, Harry," Mrs. Fitzgibbon said. "In every particular."

"It's all innocent enough, I assure you." Like butter wouldn't melt in his mouth.

"Oh, yes, we believe you!" everyone said in a chorus and laughed.

"I've come like a lamb to slaughter," he smiled.

"Like a viper to her breast, more likely," Mom said. And that's how they got him to tell. It went something like this.

Turned out he was on his way back to the States from China. A friend had died of some infection to the kidneys, and just before he died he got Harry to swear to take his remains back to his wife and kid in Los Angeles. Barney Jenkins was his name, and along with leaving Harry his body, he'd paid his passage home. Harry said he didn't mind leaving China a bit just then. With the Jap invasion and all, it had gone pretty sour. He had Barney cremated to make him more portable.

Jenkins was this smart reporter who'd taught Harry a lot about China. He'd been covering the Orient up and down since way back before the Shanghai Insurrection, interviewing all the big shots like Sun Yat-sen, Chiang and Mao, even some Russky agent named Borodin. He once took Harry up the Yangtze with him on a flight to a place called Hankow, right in the middle of the big Jap push in thirty-eight. Barney swore it was going to be real important up there, because the Nationalists and the Communists were getting together to fight the Japs for real. It sounded like high times in Hankow, firecrackers in the streets and all, until the Japs showed up and clamped a pincers movement on the town. He said the two of them came within a whisker of getting themselves annihilated.

"Like all of you, Barney and I continue to be blessed with exquisite timing." By which Harry meant his ship had docked in Manila just when the Jap bombers were taking off to blow hell out of our Islands. He figured his ship must be resting somewhere on the muddy bottom of Manila Bay. Harry never much liked Manila. "Too damn many black bugs," he said. "The sweet smell of copra down at the docks and the damn black bugs." Now he was stuck in Manila with black smoke pouring out of Nichols Field and Cavite Naval Depot and Jap Zeros dive-bombing and strafing the harbor and anything they could see along the Pasig River.

He got a room at the Manila Hotel and stayed there off-and-on for a couple of weeks. But it was like a refugee station, people jamming in from all over one day, then scattering off in all directions the next, like so much chaff in the wind. Still, he said, it was OK as long as the bar stayed open. But it was getting on toward Christmas, and he found the idea of the holidays depressing. He couldn't figure out just why, but he kept thinking of Jenkins' wife and kid waiting in LA and him stuck out here with Barney. He tried calling up friends, but the lines were all overloaded, and when he sometimes did get through, nobody was home.

"You *never* called," my mom said.

"You were first. Cross my heart."

"I got other calls."

"I tried, Ruth. Really."

"Continue, Mr. Barnes," Mrs. Fitzgibbon ordered.

He asked about Christmas trees. They told him they usually got fine spruce in from Washington and Oregon, but that was all off since Pearl Harbor. Hell, there wasn't even Baguio pine. He would just have to use his imagination. "Stick around for New Years," this drunk told him. "I got a feeling the fireworks are gonna come through." That's when he grabbed Jenkins and went for a walk. "Spending Christmas in the Manila Hotel was not my idea of the Hallelujah Chorus."

He walked along the Luneta, that green patch by the sea wall on Manila Bay. American troops were still in good spirits, dug in there with sandbags in front of their foxholes and observers scanning the skies with field glasses. But when the Jap planes came, high up and in tight formation, the anti-aircraft fell so far short they didn't even break pattern. It was damn frustrating. The soldiers swore and shook their fists, but the formation moved right on to the south. Harry felt outside it, the way it was in China. He was just standing there in his white suit, the sun shining off the water, the small silver planes high up in the sky. Those soldiers, bustling around on the lawn, making war on far-off unreachable objects, seemed ridiculous in their frustration. "It was like being a spectator at a game."

He walked down Dewey Boulevard along the bay, carrying the urn in against his jacket. When he looked out across the water, the Mariveles Mountains floated pale in the distance, a tropic haze lying over them. When he looked back at the Port Area, there was smoke and the masts of sunken ships jutting out of the water. He knew if he just kept walking south, he would pass through the Malate district and on out of the city. But it was too damn hot for that. He placed the urn against the trunk of a palm tree and sat on the cool grass. He took out a cigar he'd bought the night before. "It was a beauty," he told us. "Long, slim and black." He sniffed it and bit off the end, lit it and tasted the bittersweet smoke. Then he just sat there awhile, thinking about Jenkins and looking out across the bay.

Six Jap Zeros came in high over the mountains to the north, banked above him and went into a dive toward the Port Area. He smoked his cigar and watched the planes playing follow the leader up the Pasig River. Being trapped in this city was like being forced to watch newsreels for the second and third time.

"I felt stupid," he told us. "I had this sudden urgent need to celebrate."

"Sorry we couldn't have snow," Mom said real sarcastic.

"I don't mean Tiny Tim and Jingle Bells. I mean real honest cheer."

"Wassail!" Fitzgibbon offered up.

"Ever feel it might be your last go?" Harry asked. Mom looked really sad all at once.

"Do shut up, Harry," she said.

"No, no," Fitzgibbon insisted. "We asked for the particulars."

"I'm sorry, Ruth."

"Go on," Mom said.

"Last year Barney threw a beauty for us in Shanghai – must have been at least thirty there at this big restaurant called *Sincere*. He had given us plenty to drink but we were still just a little too reserved for his taste. So he got up at the end of the long white table groaning under a huge spread of Peking duck and a slew of local Kiangsu dishes. He looked terribly disappointed. 'You all need to loosen up,' he said.

'If the chopsticks slip and you spill a bit, it won't hurt a bloody thing.' And he raised his soy in a toast. 'Here's to Christmas cheer!' Then leaning over us, he poured a thin black trail down the entire length of that virgin tablecloth. Even the waiters were laughing, and you know what it takes to get a rise out of a Chinese waiter!"

"I'll drink to that," Southy said. His crazy high laugh always tickled my funny bone.

"That black trail," Harry said. "*That* was real."

"Let's break out the champagne!" old Fitzgibbon boomed, and popped the side of his mouth with his forefinger. By then everybody in the dining shed was looking at us cross-eyed for having too good a time and taking up too much space, so we had to leave. You can't blame them. Laughing over a Santo Tomás breakfast was bound to look peculiar.

CHAPTER 3

You know me and my pals were running, all the time, perpetual motion, over wide lawns crowded with people, under dark acacias and hot buzzing skies, up against the shadow of the Main Building and through the loud boom of the tower clock calling the hour, circling the Main Plaza, zigzagging past the Education Building, dodging in and out around the Gym, checking along the tall outer wall. We *were* kids, you know. And just maybe my mom had it right when she said we were running around like a bunch of *wonks*.

Wonks are big yellow dogs we used to see moving in packs when we lived up in North China. Now Mom was working on making wonks sound like the worst kind of curse. Wonks were in no way regular dogs. They specialized in getting themselves filthy dirty, mangy and foaming at the mouth with the hydrophobia. And that's just the civilized ones. Not much good for anything, folks said, except maybe target practice.

Let me translate for her. I was acting like a common ignoramus hanging out with a low crowd of hooligans and would likely come to a nasty end.

But that was just the surface stuff. There was a whole lot more underneath. She didn't pick *wonks* by accident, you can bet on that. She was giving me what I called my "Tyler Whipping." You see, wonks happened to come up big in a story she loved to tell about my brother Tyler, who was older and smarter and a whole lot nicer than me, but who was dead. I remember hearing her tell it to her friends over gin slings under the mango tree in our back garden out in Pasay.

When Little Tyler was maybe four years old, according to Mom, he was already some sort of certified genius. In her story she's out walking with him on this lovely long beach at Peitaiho, up on the

China coast not too far from Chinwangtao. They're strolling along over the sand, conversing in Mandarin most likely. He could chatter on in Chinese like a native – no accent or anything. So there's just Mom and Little Tyler and the waves pushing in off the Po Hai. When all of a sudden comes the pop-pop-pop of rifle fire.

Well, little Tyler knows what that racket means. It has to be Marines – U.S. Marines – from a post just up the shore, guarding who or what I never found out. Gunboat diplomacy, most likely. Tyler's seen those guys march by many a time, strutting their stuff. They're big time favorites of his. Even better than a Chinese funeral. So he stops dead in his tracks and listens real careful, like a little animal sniffing the breeze. And damned if the rifle fire isn't followed close behind by the yelping of dogs. Yipping up a storm, they were. Right off, sharp as a tack, little Tyler says, "Wonks!" Imagine that, just four years old.

You see, wonks were a top military assignment for our China Marines up there. When that wonk population got too big and vicious, they'd start marauding through villages and doing terrible things, tearing up livestock or carrying off a neighborhood tot. That's when local elders stroked their whiskers and called in our troops for support. So the boys broke out the Springfields and headed off on a wonk hunt. It was just the ticket for Chinese-American relations, I'll bet.

Little Tyler listens and listens, eyes getting bright as brass buttons. Then there it is again, carried by the wind cross the sands. The sound of shots and the yelp of dogs. He looks up at Mom and smiles. Everyone in China's sure to be safe now. Those dirty old wonks are being got rid of. Well, after a while, the firing thins out, fades away, and it gets really quiet, with just the gentle waves lapping and the wind sighing. All's right with the world, as Mom and little Tyler, hand in hand, head home. But when they're about to go back into our beach bungalow, what do they hear but more shots, just closer. Only this time no dogs. Not a bark, not a whimper, not a single yip. Just the pop-pop of Springfields.

And it's this part that my mom always loved to tell best.

"That's strange," she says. "I don't hear any wonks."

"Oh, no, Mommy," Tyler says with his bright look. "They're big dogs." And he holds onto it just a second. "Big dogs don't cry," he says.

Well, I guess you can see how hard it was coming second to little Tyler. If you want to know the truth, I don't think Mom'd ever really forgiven me for his dying, even though I was only in diapers at the time, and even though we were thousands of miles and a whole bunch of years away from there now, locked away tight in a prison camp. All she had to do was just say *wonk* and I knew right where I stood. I want you to notice though, she never said I was a wonk, or even that my friends were wonks. She just said we were running around *like* wonks.

But wonk I was and most likely always would be. Thank God Harry was there. I figured he knew a "Tyler Whipping" as good as me.

"It's OK," he said. "It's OK. Let the kid run. Every ragamuffin's got to run it off." And he gave me his wink.

The hooligans I was with were hanging back and squirming around, just waiting on me to get the hell out of there, with this one kid Red even pulling at the tail of my polo shirt. So I broke it off quick and we went dashing away again, out past the classrooms and the kitchen sheds, to this place where the weeds'd grown high and tangled, a kind of little jungle tucked up against the wall at the back corner of Camp.

It was our secret place, away from grownups and Jap guards. Funny thing, this place'd been some kind of dumping ground. Most people didn't even know what was there on account of those weeds. Most likely thought it was too wild and inhospitable. But when you're running around like a bunch of wonks, you'd be surprised what you can come up with.

It was mostly junk like rusted tin cans, broken plates, beer bottles, soggy boots, car axles and school chairs, even sinks and toilet bowls.

But in there among the snakes, toads and rats, there was some good stuff too, if you could find it.

Someone claimed he found a watch there once. Or a compass. Another said he came on some coins. Of course we had to go after it, whatever it was. So pretty soon, without knowing why, we were all digging just like wonks, panting and sniffing and clawing through thick matted grass and dirt, raising big clouds of hopping insects and swarming mosquitoes, each of us rushing to be the first to discover a gold mine or the queen's lost emeralds.

Jerry was the first to try to put some logic to it. Even if she was a girl, she was tough as most guys. In her beat-up shorts and polo shirt, she looked pretty much like a guy anyhow. Skinny, with short hair and scuffed up knees and elbows.

"What're we lookin' for?" she asked. But Red was having none of that.

"You'll know when you find it," he yelled back. He was older and fond of bossing. Just then he was scratching. He was always scratching. All kids scratch, but with Red it was addiction. Scratching his head, scratching his balls, scratching his ass. It was like he had cooties. Maybe he did and thought it was swell. He sure didn't like having girls around. Trouble was, Jerry was first to find *any*thing. She pulled out a bunch of test tubes filled with bloody serum. That was her claim anyway.

"They're straight out of the hospital," she said, holding this pinky-brown specimen up to the sun. "Stuff to track deadly disease. Typhus or rabies or cholera, most likely."

Then Pete dug out a canteen with a rotted canvas cover that said "US" on it, all corroded around the top. It came down from the Spanish-American War, we figured, so it was prime. Pete passed it around with the screw cap off to give us all a whiff of history. It was about as good as nothing, but at least it was something. The best the rest of us were coming up with is a couple of good-sized toads and a skinny black snake that slithered off quick into a dark hole.

But it was Finch who found *it*. He was up on a mound of junk above us, like a balloon against the hot sky, just sweating and shimmering, one foot perched on a toilet bowl like he was ready to lift off. We had to laugh, the way he hollered, shaking something in his fist.

"Hey," he cried. "Hey, hey."

"What's a Finch anyhow?" Red yelled back.

"Some kind of fat little bird?"

"Chirps."

Who'd ever thought *he* could come up with anything. We had this little song. It went to that tune kids sing, "Yah yahyah yahyah yah." He always got red and flustered, he hated it that much, so naturally we sang it all over again.

"Fatty Boom Banana

Had a skinny amah

Amah died

Fatty cried

Fatty Boom Banana."

But this time he got us back.

"Hey," he shouted. "I got marbles!" We stood there blinking up at him, waiting. Then he opened his hand and, just like magic, two little ceramic balls. They did look to be marbles, even clicked like marbles when they came together.

Ordinarily we wouldn't have gone crazy over marbles. We were too old for that. So when the Japs rounded us up and trucked us into Camp, we never figured to bring marbles along. But now with a load of time on our hands, marbles looked pretty good. Most of us probably had a sack full of glassees back home, lying forgotten in a drawer. But what good was that? When you're fresh out of marbles, they can take on unnatural importance.

"Let's see," Pete said, holding out his hand. But Finch pulled back, closing up his fist. It'd dawned on him he might have something really special.

"Where'd you get 'em?" Red asked. Finchy shrugged.

"C'mon," I tried. "How're you ever gonna play if nobody else's got any?" That didn't work either. He just kept looking down at us with a little grin on his face. Asking for it.

"You know what I think?" Red said, scratching his neck. "I think Finchy's looking to get *depantsed*." That froze us all. Probably nothing worse could happen. Maybe getting shot. But even that couldn't be near as embarrassing. If you wanted to put the fear of God into a kid, all you had to do was just mention the word. Right away Finch started looking for escape routes. But we knew how slow he was. All he could do was stand there, his little eyes darting around. And no sooner did we start circling than he started to change his tune.

"I doubt there's any more," he said. "These are probably the last."

"Maybe he wants to get *depantsed* right now," Red said.

"Somewhere round here's where I found 'em," Finch mumbled, pointing at a busted toilet. We were still suspicious but climbed up anyhow. And damned if there wasn't one lying there, half-buried in weeds. Some kind of porcelain stopper, I guess, but it was nothing but a marble to us.

Quick as a wink, we'd all grabbed onto something – big rock or hunk of pipe – and started running around plundering marbles out of toilet bowl tanks in a kind of frenzy. It didn't take long. Half-hour maybe. Just as soon as we'd stuffed our pockets, Red called us down to a little clearing in the weeds, so we could lay our loot on the ground and admire it. Like we'd just tapped into the mother lode.

"We'll call 'em *Clayees*," Red said, picking his nose. "That way we'll know 'em from Glassees." But no one was paying Red much mind. We were too busy taking shots and getting the feel back.

"Nobody's got Glassees anyhow," said Knockers.

"So what? You got to have a name," Red said.

"These are better'n regulation," Finch said.

"Yeah," Pete said. "We came up with 'em ourselves."

"I'm calling this one *Clayee Number One*," Finch said. "First one ever found." But Red just laughed.

"That's till somebody wins it off you."

"I discovered 'em."

"And tried to hog 'em all to yourself," I reminded him.

We got so busy firing off marbles and laughing, we didn't notice Jerry standing frozen, gaping at the wall. Then we all followed her stare. And leering back down at us was this face. Round, with a shaved head, peeking at us through tall weeds. That was all we saw at first – just the face. It was attached to a guard, and it had a grin that made us squirm. Sent shivers up the spine and shut down the blood flow. We all went stiff as boards and quiet as graves, scooped up our Clayees like we were on official business and slipped off without one look back.

We didn't say one word, just walked on until we got back to the bright open field. Then Jerry laughed out loud like she was exorcising ghosts and hollered, "Hey, you guys, we got us some Targets!" And Pete fired back, "Cat's Eyes!" And pretty soon a kid boomed, "Swirlies!" and another, "Clearies!" and then, "Agates!" and, "Rainbows!" and, "Peewees!" and, "Shooters!" and every other crazy name for marbles we could think of. We were all marching along with them clicking in our pockets, making a big display of ourselves and feeling rich as kings, shouting in a kind of chant, "Clayees, Clayees," and then a great big, "We got CLAYEES!" And when I looked around, there was old Finch with a kind of glow on him, all puffed up like he'd just invented the wheel.

You might think it queer, our going nuts for marbles. But it's no different from a lady oohing and aahing over a pair of shoes or a guy over a set of golf clubs. It's just human nature, like diamonds. I can never figure why anyone gets in such a lather over a little sparkly stone. But I've seen it with my own eyes.

Even with Mom. When the Japs came, first thing she sewed into her underwear was her diamond ring, guarding it like it was the key to the American Battle Plan, worrying over it all the time we were in Camp. And you know what she got out of all that? Ended up trading it off for a pound of wormy rice – something you could've picked up cheap at your local bodega in any ordinary year. Even if we were starving at the time, it does tell you something about diamonds.

CHAPTER 4

Southy'd set up a lean-to under a big acacia across the athletic field from the Main Building. It was just a temporary thing – a few poles, some rope and a flap of canvas – but a fine, shady spot away from the crowds. After noon chow, Mom, Southy, Harry and me were just stretching ourselves out on the grass. The sod was still nice and green, with people scattered across it in little groups, looking for a little peace, like us.

But right then the Japanese decided to put the fear of God into us with a live infantry drill. They loved doing stuff like that. Anything to keep us guessing about whether they'd let us live or die. A whole squad came down on us out of the blue, charging across the middle of the field, shaking their rifles and bayonets and hollering "Banzai!" Before we knew what was up, they'd flopped themselves on the ground, their rifles aimed and set to fire.

Right behind them came another crew with a *machine* gun. They set it up quick on a tripod, threaded in a belt of ammo, swung that barrel around and sighted in on a little group of internees under a tree. It did catch our attention. Matter of fact, one lady let out a shriek. People nearby got set to bolt. *Nobody* I know likes having a machine gun zeroing in on his vital parts. Those Japs didn't look to be fooling. I was all braced for the pop-pop, rat-tat-tat and cloud of smoke drifting by. Substantial territory opened up across the lawn. But once wasn't enough for them.

They jumped up hollering again, ran a ways, flopped down and aimed in on a new group. We were all pretty much goggle-eyed by now. But something funny happened. Some little kids who didn't know better put a damper on their show. They'd got so excited watching those shenanigans that they had to jump right in and run along behind, imitating their every move. First the Japs got up and charged, yelling "Banzai!" Then here came the kids doing the same. Japs flopped down and aimed their guns, kids dropped down and yelled "Bang bang!" That cut the fear right out of it. Everybody started chuckling. Couldn't help it. And it shook every last Jap one of them. Pretty soon they'd pulled up shame-faced and quit. It's hard for soldiers not to be taken stone serious.

But when all was said and done, Harry turned out to be the real show that day. No sooner had the Japs pulled out than the Fitzgibbons dropped by with a group of friends to hear more about his arrival in Manila. Word had gotten round and his audience had grown. The Towners were there. And skinny Miss Cornell, this spinster teacher who once worked a one-room schoolhouse all on her lonesome down on the island of Cebu. Plus sundry folks I didn't know so hot.

It got to be something like a séance. Other worldly. The light had grown kind of weird and wet and hazy. A soft breeze off the bay flapped the canvas and sighed in the acacias above. Harry sat there among us cross-legged like Buddha. He did have this theatrical way of talking sometimes, like he'd spent time studying elocution to develop an accent, but was now working overtime covering it up and putting the tough edge on things. He smoked cigarettes, and kept right on talking through the haze. But he could've saved his breath with the tough talk. That culture stuff shows through every time. Still, I've got to admit, I learned something that day.

Everybody was hanging on Harry like he was the feature movie downtown. Maybe they all thought they'd get into one of his stories. He knew his audience and wasn't afraid to work it. He was actor one and two. But the director was old lady Fitzgibbon. She cued him strong on time and place, just so he wouldn't skip over anything.

"All right, now, you left us in the middle the other day. That wasn't nice. There you were, sitting under that palm tree on Dewey Boulevard, smoking your cigar, watching Jap planes dive, thinking about Christmas in Shanghai and holding onto that little urn," she let out in her frog croak. "Now, confess, Harry."

"Yes, a fine Manila cigar," Harry said. "Long and slim and black." He meditated on it a minute, taking a long drag on his cigarette, looking around at us all and blowing some smoke. Then he made it all sound like it was happening right then. "As a matter of fact, that was right when a big Lincoln Zephyr pulled off Dewey Boulevard next to me, and I heard an overdone English voice call out."

"What voice?" Mrs. Towner asked.

"That's a poor spot you picked for a sit-down, fellow," someone said. Harry knew it couldn't be the Filipino chauffeur, so he squinted back into the shadows. A tall thin guy dressed for tennis was sitting there with a bottle of Gordon's Gin on his lap. "He had a long tan face, like a dun mare," Harry told us.

And right here Harry started rattling off some dialogue, going back and forth in two voices, like in a play. Smart stuff, like:

"Hello to *you*, sir," Harry said.

"I say, you're going to get killed out there," this guy said.

"Not likely. They never shoot a man in a white suit. Not *bushido*, you know."

"I've seen a few Filipinos in those suits being chased by Zeros downtown."

"But then, you see, I'm not Filipino."

"Not even from Manila, I take it."

"No, Jenkins and I just got in from Shanghai. Ship's departure's been unfortunately delayed."

"Jenkins?"

"Yes," Harry said. "My good friend." And he held out the urn.

"I see. Well, the least I can do is offer you a ride. I'm on my way to the Polo Club. Why don't you stop over and have a drink." He opened the back door and Harry didn't make him ask twice. One thing I'll say for Harry, just shoot an accent at him, and he could shoot it right back at you.

"This is *damn* generous of you," sounding pretty close to English himself.

"It seemed the right thing when I saw you at sea out there."

"At sea?" Harry said. He was having a time figuring this bird. Didn't seem the type. "I'm afraid I have a hitchhiker's judgment. I'm a little surprised when I got picked up by a Lincoln."

"Shows you what a war can do."

"Just a few bombs make you a Samaritan?"

"So used to the drive, I didn't really look anymore. But now I never know if I'll be back."

"Yes, Manila is going to be different."

"Do you play polo?" the guy asked.

"Do I have to to get in?"

"My son has the ponies up."

"I could play if my drink depended on it."

Then Harry turned to us and said, "You all know the Polo Club, I'm sure. Those long low buildings, nipa palm roofs, broad shade trees. Lovely spot." He saw that pleased old lady Towner a bunch and smiled at her. "Very genteel."

Harry and his new friend were sitting under the trees, sipping their gins, watching the son ride and whack a willow ball around the big smooth field. Everything was so clean there and lush. They were all playing tennis and swimming in the large pool, little kids running and laughing under the trees. He could still see the piling smoke, even closer to the south, but it didn't seem to matter in the shade.

"This beats hell out of the Manila Hotel," Harry said. While the son rode, his Filipino groom held another horse under the trees.

"What do you think of the ponies?" the guy asked.

"Very nice. Why's he out there riding by himself?"

"Got to keep them in shape. And it's good for Roger. Keeps his mind off things." Harry thought what fine cavalry ponies they'd make for the Japanese.

"The sun was so bright on the field," he told us. "And the horse moved so elegantly after the ball. The boy rode well and handled his mallet with fair accuracy. I do love watching polo ponies turn like cats, and that lovely *crack* the ash of the mallet makes against the willow ball, but I've never been able to muster more than a cool enthusiasm for the sport."

"And why not?" Old lady Fitzgibbon asked. A little huffy, I thought. Harry looked at Mom and winked.

"Jodhpurs make me think of hunt clubs and debutante balls back on the Main Line," he said. "All that cool aloofness the right people develop from wearing riding breeches and evening clothes."

"Continue." Mrs. Fitzgibbon squinted at him like she'd just heard something she wasn't sure she liked.

"Would you care to have a *chukker* or two with my boy?" the guy asked.

"Perhaps later."

Harry was just winding up his fourth gin when the wife and daughter came off the tennis courts.

"Hello, Daddy," the girl called. She was gangly and mare-faced like her father. Harry was thinking that she must be hell on the tennis court. And that's when he realized he didn't even know the name of the man he was drinking with. He got up when the women came over, but they barely gave him a glance. He saw no one was going to make any introductions.

"I'm sorry. I'm Harry Barnes," he offered.

"Oh, yes," the guy said. "Haverford here." And that was when Harry's story-telling broke down for a minute.

"I *knew* it," Mrs. Fitzgibbon shrieked like a school kid. "The *Hav*erfords."

"You have them to a tee," Mrs. Towner said.

"Victoria is the dun mare," Mom giggled.

"And she *is* hell on the tennis courts," old Fitzgibbon laughed. "She's whipped me badly."

"They're not *really* English, you know," Miss Cornell said, very sincere.

"I had my suspicions," Harry said

"But working *very* hard at it," Mom said. "Just a hint of American still peeking through the veneer."

"Of course, the women never mentioned names," Harry said, getting back to his story. "I saw they didn't mind my not knowing. But the girl kept eyeing the urn."

"I haven't seen you here before, have I, Mr. *Burns*?" she said.

"No. Mr. Haverford just picked me up on Dewey Boulevard."

"Picked him up, Montgomery?" the wife said.

"What? Oh, yes."

"Picked him up?"

"Told him he was damn lucky he hadn't been shot." The two women kept shooting little glances at Harry, like he shouldn't have been there. He tried to show them he was, after all, civilized.

"I've been admiring your son's riding. He's done a nice job on those ponies."

"Quite. He's very keen on it," the mom said, very stiff.

"Even though the daughter was perspiring full bore," Harry told us, "Mrs. Haverford looked extremely cool. How strange it was to be on the outside. Of course, I've seen this sort of thing lots of times, but never from the outside. Not the slightest attempt to include me. The women are the experts at this, you know. They started chattering on as if I was invisible. Had I really rubbed it off so well it didn't show anymore? She had gotten that crisp English edge down so nicely, I just had to get away."

"I think I'll try the polo," Harry said. "You won't mind my leaving Jenkins here with you."

"Really, Montgomery!"

By now Harry had us all pretty far out of Camp. I guess everybody was just happy to think about those days before all the bad stuff started. Across the field, Jap sentries were still quick marching with their packs along the main road, chanting something. The little kids still trailed behind. But we hardly paid them any mind. Everybody was off with Harry. Mrs. Fitzgibbon got so silly laughing she even slapped him on the leg.

"I'm so glad Haverford didn't offer me his jodhpurs. I'm certain they would have been starched," Harry said. "But when the sun hit me out on the field, I knew I'd been drinking. I loosened my tie, handed my jacket to the groom, picked up a mallet and mounted the pony. I had a *little* trouble getting my foot in the stirrup, but then I hadn't been on horseback since going up to the Great Wall over three years ago." Right here Harry looked right at me and turned on his booming BBC voice. "Here you are, seated nobly atop your steed. Having just dismounted from a long expedition by elephant, you have hurried to the *maidan* to have a few *chukkers* with that ruddy leftenant from His Britannic Majesty's Royal Hussars. Oh, you bloody drunken ass! And only four gins." He nudged the pony into a trot across the field.

"Halloa, Roger!" The Haverford boy reined in to watch Harry come on and wheel the horse in beside him. "Hello. Your father persuaded me to give it a go with you."

"Splendid!"

"I was watching you play. You made a fine picture."

"She's a top-notch pony."

"One *chukker* will do me," Harry said, trying to out-English all of them at once.

"Oh, no. I'm quite sure you won't wish to quit there."

"Let's give it a go, shall we."

"My God, the cane handle of the mallet felt awkward in my hand. I had to give it a couple of rotations to limber up, just get the feel. Then I suddenly saw how I must appear to the Haverford clan, and the whole spectacle took on the lovely appeal of a Charlie Chaplin. But you know, I surprised myself. I rode quite well. It really was a good pony, you see. At first I kept missing the ball, but once I got the range I was whacking away right along with Roger, hearing that solid satisfying wood-on-wood. I was having a swell time, the sweat pouring down my chest and back. When we finally reined in, I was exhausted."

"Have you played much?" the kid asked.

"Not recently."

"You did quite well. Care to go another?"

"Rather!"

"Of course, I toyed with the idea of running young Haverford into the ground in front of his silly parents," Harry told us. "But I felt in such rotten shape all at once, I realized he could probably run *me* into the ground without too much trouble.

"It was shortly after this that I lost my seat and fell trying to whack that ball a good one, staining my trousers nicely on the turf." They were all laughing now, and Harry had this shy smile on his face. "Of course, I remounted at once with casual grace, but the dash had gone out of the game and I was relieved to see it come to an end."

"Thanks awfully."

"Not at all."

Harry strolled back to the Haverfords' table, straightening his tie and putting his jacket on over his soaked shirt. They looked at him like he was an intruder from Mars.

"An enjoyable afternoon," he offered up.

"Sorry you must go," the wife said with her forced smile.

"Yes, must get back. Perhaps I can get picked up again."

He picked up the urn and walked out to the front drive, where he was lucky enough to catch a ride back into the city. They drove in the back way, since the main streets were jamming up with troops.

"Rumor has it they're evacuating Manila," the driver told him. "MacArthur and Quezon have already left to set up headquarters on Corregidor."

"Sort of leaves us floating belly up," Harry said.

"But you know," he told us. "When I got out in front of the Manila Hotel, I realized I just couldn't go in. It's a perfectly nice establishment – handsome entrance, splendid lobby. It must have been all the sandbags piled in front of the windows and everybody jamming downstairs during the air raids. I had this sudden premonition the ceiling would come down on me while I was jammed in next to the likes of Mrs. Haverford. It's hell not to be able to die with some shred of dignity."

Harry'd transported us, like working through a spooky medium. They were all enjoying themselves now like they'd just gathered downtown and were easing back for a long afternoon with tall icy drinks in their hands. That was no small thing in a place chock-full of strangers, surrounded by high walls and guarded by Japs. I looked at Mom laughing away, her eyes flashing. She damn near sparkled. I hadn't seen her so fresh and happy in a long time. I could've hugged her, she looked so nice. Maybe she was thinking of their days together in China, when they were all a whole lot younger and running around like they owned the world. But Harry wouldn't leave it there.

"So I went away," he told us. "Let instinct lead. It took me to the Port Area."

"The Port Area?" Mr. Fitzgibbon asked.

"I don't care for the Port Area," Mrs. Fitzgibbon said. "I don't care for it at all."

Just then, on top of the Main Building, the tower clock boomed four o'clock and went into its Big Ben chimes. Everything seemed to stop and we looked up at the big gray building, the tower and the cross on top, and the tall thunderheads rising even bigger behind. The light out of the west was a thin pale yellow, like somebody just turned down the lights. And it appeared the brightness had gone out of our group too.

"Hurry up, it's time!" Harry called, getting up and brushing himself off for the chow line.

"T. S. Eliot, isn't it?" Miss Cornell asked.

"No," Harry said. "Just London Pub."

"You *are* an anthology," she said.

"But they were bombing the Port Area heavily," Mrs. Fitzgibbon said. "Why would you go there?"

"Can't we go back to the Polo Club?" Mrs. Tower asked, sounding downright pitiful. It was then I caught a look at Southy, who hadn't said a single word that whole time, but who had to smile now at that lady.

"Hold on," Harry said. "We can't just pick and choose, you know. We've got to go where the dance takes us."

"Right now, I think it's taking us to dinner," Mom broke in and took Harry's arm like we were off to a restaurant. But when we'd gone a little way, Mr. Towner called out to us across the field.

"You heard about young Haverford, I suppose."

"No," Harry said.

"Ran off with those damn horses. No one has any idea where he's gone."

CHAPTER 5

If I got to thinking I was big stuff with a pocket full of Clayees, all I had to do was walk into the room where Southy, Harry and me slept. That stripped-down classroom was jammed to the rafters with all kinds. Not just Americans, but English, Aussies, Canadians, French, Dutch, Norwegians, Russkies and Poles, even one Egyptian, all on his lonesome. Must've been at least fifty of us in there and only about three of us kids, one of which could only speak French anyhow. And ours was just one of a whole bunch of rooms they'd squeezed full of people, men in this one, women in the next.

Everybody'd laid claim to a little spot of his own, so we had cots and mattresses and bags piled all over the place, with sheets and bedspreads and mosquito nets hanging off clotheslines to mark off private boundaries. All this lit by the hard glare off bare bulbs dangling overhead. They put cardboard cones behind the bulbs, so the light shot straight down. It got so hot and sweaty and smoky, you could barely breathe. And with everybody talking and playing cards and coughing and complaining in about three different languages at once, privacy was hard to come by.

The room was off the main hall. Somebody took the classroom doors off and put up swinging barroom doors to keep the air flowing. I loved pushing those doors aside like I'd seen cowpokes do in Westerns. But every time I sauntered in like that, Harry greeted me with, "Well, look here, it's Major Mosquito." He probably meant it friendly, but everybody would look up to catch a glimpse of some officer in full uniform and see this short kid standing there instead, so I started sneaking in under the doors, hoping he wouldn't catch me.

"Major's flying low tonight," he said out loud.

"Come over here, kid," Southy waved. He was sitting on a school chair next to his mattress and put his hands up, palms facing me. "Give me a combination, kid." So I squared off and shot out two lefts and a hard right. "Now turn it around and give it to me southpaw." Southy Jack was always working on making me as good from the left as the right, maybe because that was his own claim to fame. He was a lightweight, but for a little guy he had big hands and strong sloping shoulders.

So I turned it around and came in with two rights and a left. Only that always felt awkward. "Not much steam, kid. Keep workin' on the left. Right's good, but the left's lazy." I played along, thinking he must've figured to take up my training while Dad was gone. "Where were you at supper, Johnny? We were all looking for you." He caught me off guard with that one. Maybe he was signing up for substitute mom, too.

"I was there," I mumbled. "Just with the guys."

"Your mom was asking about you."

"I saw her in the hall," I said. She was always worrying about me getting into trouble. "I'll see her again in the morning." Mom slept in this other room that was all ladies. We were segregated from each other. Men could only see women in the daytime. And it was tough on some of the married folks. They were always complaining. But the Commandant didn't want men and women fraternizing. He'd never allow any stuff he called "open show of affection." Even holding hands was bad. And there weren't many places around Camp to be private in the hard light of day.

"Go take a shower quick before lights out," Southy said. "You're looking scruffy."

"Appears he's listing a bit too, over on the port side," Harry said. The man had a sixth sense.

"Yeah, what is that in your pocket?" Southy asked. I didn't want to get into it, to tell the truth. So I shrugged it off.

"Just marbles."

"By the look of things, you had to dig for them," Harry said. I grabbed my stuff quick and took off down the hall to where the showers were.

It was always crowded in the showers no matter when you washed up, and even this late I had to wait around for a spot. It was getting close to lights out and the Monitor'd be by pretty quick for evening roll call, so I stripped off my shirt and shorts, piled them up on my sneakers and got on my wood sandal *bakias*. I wrapped my Clayees up in a washcloth and took them with me under the shower. I had six good ones and just one that had a nick in it, and that'd be plenty to get me into a game. Then I could maybe win some more. So I soaped up my washcloth and lathered the marbles up good and rinsed them so they shined with the clean water on them. Then I wrapped them up careful in the washcloth, put them on the tiles and lathered myself up.

I was just rinsing off when the Monitor stuck his head in and told us to get the hell out. They yelled like that every night, liked to show off and act important, but they were just prisoners like the rest of us. If you stayed in too late, they turned the lights off on you and tried to scare you to death. Then they clapped their hands hard to make it ring off the tiles.

I had my towel wrapped around me and my clothes under my arm, clattering down the hall in my bakias, when I saw four guys out by the door of our room. I couldn't tell who they were right off, but by the way they were bunched together it looked like a fight. The Monitor was yelling at a tall, lanky bird. It was that Mr. Haverford Harry talked about out at the Polo Club. Everybody said he was one of Manila's bigwigs, only he sure wasn't looking so fine at the moment. Then I saw it was Southy and Harry with them.

"I beg yaw pahdon," Haverford was saying, real offended, like he'd just stepped in shit or something. "I beg YAW pahdon." He was none too steady and talking in one of those real loud country club voices.

"I catch you like this again, I'm turning you in," the Monitor said to him. He was hot and wasn't faking it. Southy pushed himself in between them, trying to hold them off each other.

"Take it easy now, Sam," he said to the Monitor.

"Where's your boy Roger?" Harry asked Haverford. For a second it looked like the old fart was going to cry on us. "He should be here taking care of his old man," Harry said.

"Bullocks!" Haverford said. Close up, I could smell the liquor on him. People were gathering to find out what the ruckus was about.

"Be a gentleman now," Harry said, wrapping him up in his arms like a wet sheet. "Show them how nice you can speak."

"Th'idea," the old drunk slurred. "I'm in import, y'know."

"Import?" Harry asked like he was amazed. "Why I had no idea, Southy. A man of import."

"I don't give two hoots what he's in," the Monitor said. "He's gonna end up in the Camp Jail."

"No, no, man's a social icon. A good egg, you know, deserves to be coddled."

"You've no righ'," Haverford said. "Absloolly no righ'." He tried hard to get Harry off him, but was too shaky.

"Mind your diction now," Harry said. "Got to keep a hold on that diction." The funny thing was, even though he was kidding around, I think Harry liked the old guy.

"Somebody should throw you in the shower," the Monitor said.

"Can't you see he's a pillar of the community, Sam? You wouldn't pillory a pillar." But Southy was serious and getting that redness along his neck and ears. It made me nervous, thinking he might pop one of them. He was a hot, little firecracker, Southy.

"This ain't the time," he said in this super calm voice, the one he used on you when you did something *real* stupid. Like he was doing everything he could to keep from blowing. "We're gonna have everybody on the whole floor out here if we don't ease up." Then he just took control. "Get him in the room, Harry. We'll all talk tomorrow. In private." Harry put his arm around Haverford like a buddy, but separated him quick from the Monitor and shoved him nice and firm through the the swinging doors.

"That guy's gonna screw us all," the Monitor said. "It's gonna be our ass right along with his."

"I know, Sam," Southy said. Then he saw me standing out there and signaled me inside. "In the morning, Sam."

They took a quick roll call that night, but it still stayed tense and depressed in the room. I guess it was starting to dawn on everybody that it wasn't going our way in this war, and we were going to be in here a lot longer than anybody'd figured. Everybody was still talking about Bataan and Corregidor, but it was sounding more and more like a funeral dirge. And folks were starting to get on each other's nerves. There'd been some real fistfights. Judging by that, this little scuffle in the hall seemed like nothing. But that Monitor sure seemed worried.

Harry dropped Haverford on his cot, still dressed in his shirt and pants and cussing a storm.

"Bloody nerve," the drunk said over and over. "Absloolly no God'm righ'." Harry tried to calm him down, but it didn't help. He even tried to cool his forehead with a wet washcloth. Finally somebody told him to shut himself up. And that's when he really got riled. "Who're you talkin' to?" he spit. "You know who're talkin' to?"

"Be kind," Harry said. "Poor old fellow's lost his property, lost his station, lost his son – God only knows what else."

"Yeah," somebody snorted, "and I've lost my God damn patience!"

"Serves you righ'," Haverford mumbled, then chuckled to himself. Everybody'd gotten tired of him real fast and sort of shunned him. Southy was right. Your only choice in such a case was to ignore him until he got to sleep or take a hammer and put him out of his misery. Finally, he did doze off, but even then kept mumbling.

When the lights went out, Harry and Southy stripped to their shorts and got in bed. I hung my towel on a clothesline and slipped on some skivvies. Southy was sleeping on the one mattress, and next to him Harry was on the one Gregorio lugged all the way in from Pasay. For *me*. So there was nothing but to sleep on the crack in between, which I hated because the bedbugs always snuck up at night and bit the hell out of me. And it was murder between the two of them. The sweat just oozed off me.

"How you suppose he got it?" Harry whispered over to Southy.

"Somebody's smuggling it. Probably a houseboy." Southy spoke so soft I could barely hear him, and I was right next to him. "They could've done it easy at the bottom of a basket of clothes through the Package Line."

"I guess that's what he meant by 'import,'" Harry said. "Why don't *you* have help like that, Southy?"

"Don't get playful. This could mean some hell to pay."

"Never even invited us to taste his good fortune."

"Fuck him."

"You have to feel a bit sorry for the old boy."

"I'm sure as hell not playing nursemaid to some rich lush."

"Amen," Harry said. Pretty soon I could hear Southy breathing heavy on one side of me and Harry silent as a tomb on the other. But even with the windows wide open I felt like I was suffocating. The heat just sat on me. First I lay on one side and looked at Southy. Then I turned over and looked at Harry. All around me the old birds were hacking and wheezing and farting themselves to sleep. But just when I was ready to doze off, a mosquito started whining in my ear, and I slapped at him so hard I came close to doing *myself* in. I tried to lie dead still on my back, keeping my eyes closed and wishing myself to sleep. But it just wouldn't do.

So I got up and went to the window and stared out at the night. We were on the west side and just high enough to see over the Camp

46

wall past the Seminary and the rooftops of the first houses outside. It was dark enough in the city so the stars were shining bright above us and up to the west and north I thought I saw flashes like lightning against low clouds where the war was going on. If I listened close I could hear far-off booms. That'd be Bataan, I figured, where our army was going at it with the Japs, trying to hold out until reinforcements came. But so many days had gone by, maybe they were never coming. And then where'd we be?

People were always talking about "holding Bataan" and "hanging onto Corregidor," like they were holy places and we could never give them up until everybody fought to the death defending them. Thinking about it, I got a crazy notion. I wondered if maybe generals pick places to fight by the names. I mean, Bataan's a real powerful name. You just say it, see how important it sounds. I bet that was why old MacArthur picked it for his place to fight. Whenever folks said it, they got all choked up, like that place was something special. Most of them had never even been there. And the same for Corregidor. Doesn't Corregidor sound tough? It means the Corrector.

Suppose MacArthur'd picked a place to fight with a dumb name nobody could pronounce. Or one that sounded silly. They've got a lot of those names to pick from in the PI. Would folks be so all-fired ready to fight over a place like that? Mom told me there was a little place outside Manila proper called Singalong. How'd you like to die defending that? "Where'd you say you was killed? Singalong? How'd it happen, bust a vocal chord or a high C just fall on ya?"

I stayed for about an hour looking for flashes against the sky and thinking about those guys fighting out there in the jungle. Then I started thinking about my old man again. I kept wondering where he was. Sometimes I got a real clear picture of him sneaking along like an Indian. Real silent and strong and dangerous. Just a shadow against the sky. Coming up behind a Jap soldier and slitting his throat, maybe. Or taking on three at a time and rocking them with heavy punches.

The city was mostly black now, except for some headlights moving against buildings somewhere out toward the harbor. Then my mind jumped around to when me and Dad were running nice and easy along a tall hibiscus hedge on one of those quiet lanes out in Pasay. We'd just quit skipping rope, the sweat was rolling off us, and all at once Dad says, "C'mon, kid," and we were running smooth as you please, just gliding along. I could hear him breathing deep and steady and see the bright red flowers dancing along the high dark bushes. There was this bend in the lane up ahead with a big mango tree, but I just kept playing the one stretch over and over in my mind, so we never got past the curve where I knew the lane came out on the wide road. It was the best when we were together like that, all alone, moving.

I thought I caught some more flashes off over Bataan. They seemed a million miles away, way out on the edge of the world. I thought about Roger Haverford, riding his polo ponies through the jungle or up some mountain trail, and it seemed kind of ridiculous. How'd he feed them, I was thinking. Where'd they sleep. Then I started thinking about Barney Jenkins, too. All at once I realized I never heard the rest of Harry's story, and I didn't have the least idea where the urn ended up. For all I knew, Jenkins' ghost was out there somewhere, going from place to place, trying to get a drink or find Harry or something. And I started worrying about him. I know it's stupid, but I was thinking he'd probably never even been in Manila before. Maybe he was lost. I got kind of scared, thinking maybe that's how we'd all end up, wandering lost out there in the dark.

Finally I got myself good and sleepy looking out at the night and went back to bed. I took my wet washcloth to bed, the one with my Clayees wrapped up in it. It felt nice and cool pressed against my face and I drifted off pretty quick.

CHAPTER 6

Mom was working what they called "De-bugging de Rice Detail" – a task force of ladies sitting at a table in the hot sun, picking insects out of raw rice. They shook their shallow pans so the bright light could catch the shiny-backed weevils high-stepping through the grains. It took sharp eyes and quick fingers to nab those critters and pinch their little heads off. They picked out little pink worms and gummy wads of cocoon too. Sometimes they missed them and the weevils and worms ended up part of the day's chow. But Mom, she wasn't one to be put off by a few creepy-crawlies. She'd earned her stripes long ago.

After all, Mom was a nurse. And a nurse has got to have a gut of steel, not just washing down dirty patients and emptying out stinky bedpans either. Mom'd worked anesthesia on some pretty ugly operations, from what I'd been told. And traveled from Manila clear down to Mindanao as private nurse to the Datu's daughter. She'd lived in the wilds with the Moros of Davao. The Datu was the muckety-muck. And his daughter was a princess, wrapped in colored robes and dripping jewelry. But she'd been diagnosed as suffering the galloping consumption and given no more than a few months to live. Those Moros took a real shine to Mom. Taught her some words in their lingo, showed her a dance or two, even tried to get her to munch on betel nut and stain her teeth dark as theirs. But in those days they still had skirmishes in the jungle, and when a young warrior came running out of the thicket with this enemy head on his spear, shouting death threats at the Yanks, the U. S. Army sent Mom packing back to Manila for her own safety. "Safety be damned!" she said and threw a fit, chewed the authorities up and down. Then she quit the Islands altogether and sailed off to train Chinese nurses up in old Peking.

When I saw her shaking her pan in the sun, I stopped off to see if I could lend a hand. But that wasn't the kind of assistance she was after. She asked me point-blank and confidential about Harry's Filipino girl.

"You see her?" she asked.

"Yeah."

"Well?"

"She brought him a papaya today, I think."

"What else?" she asked.

"Nothing I could see."

"Was she pretty?"

"Kind of short and dark. Pretty, I guess."

"What was she wearing?" Like I was a dressmaker or something. I thought it over.

"Something in a cream," I said and she curled her lip.

"Why, *John*ny," she said. "Don't you know better than to tease your elders?"

"My elder's acting peculiar."

"What do you mean?"

"I never knew her to play busybody before," I said real sweet.

That's how me and Mom always went at it – thrust and parry and then a big hug, so we could keep track of the other's hands, no doubt. Funny thing is, I think she kind of liked the *wonk* in me. Made her think of Dad.

Typical of us was when I was a whole lot smaller and was acting too big for my britches. I'd just let off a string of nasty cuss words in Chinese. Mom knew the lingo better than me. Since it'd been directed her way, she grabbed me by the scruff of the neck and washed my mouth out with some evil laundry soap. I'd looked up at her just as cheeky and asked, "Does that wash out all the bad words, or just the ones I said?" She stared me up and down, hard and cold all at once. "Why don't you just try some others, dear, and find out?" But straight as she tried to keep her face, I caught a gleam in her eye. That was Mom and me.

But she *was* acting peculiar. She flat refused to go out to the Front Gate to satisfy her own curiosity. Unless I told her Gregorio and Timotea were out there, she was a lot more likely to try to squeeze something out of me or Southy.

"Well, what do *you* think of that little thing visiting Harry at the Front Gate?" she asked Southy. He squinted like he was in some discomfort.

"She's little," he said. "But she appears to show fair-sized loyalty."

"Pretty?" Mom asked.

"As a doll," Southy smiled. "And all dolled up too – red lips, dark eyes, mariposa sleeves and hair as black as night."

Still Mom'd never come at Harry direct about that girl. She'd circle around it, even though we all knew she was dying to find out more. It was after chow one evening out by the lean-to. Mom was knitting some string socks. Or a shirt, maybe. No matter what the materials might be, Mom always had to knit. Her hands flew with those needles, high on nervous energy. And at the end of each row, she pointed them at Harry with a little jerk.

"Why *did* you go up to the Port Area, Harry?" she asked. "It was the very worst hit part of the city."

"So I've heard," Harry said. "Smoke and dust from pulverized concrete hung so thick it shut out the sun."

"Well?"

"It was Christmas Eve and I was looking for *Jesus*." He pronounced the name Spanish like a Filipino.

"Jesus?" Mom asked. She pronounced it English like an American.

"Yes, bartender I met some years back at a little place called La Floridita."

"Oh, that kind of Jesus."

"Floridita's a *turo-turo* place," Southy said.

"That's right, no menu, just look and point. Eat and drink."

"Be merry," Southy added.

"*Jesus* had a nice tenor. Could sing Cole Porter a cappella and shake martinis at the same time."

"And did you find your Jesus?" Mom asked.

"Not quite. Took me long enough just to find La Floridita. Streets were all filled with rubble and glass, streetcars derailed, even a few dead along the way."

"What a place to go!"

"Probably most honest place in town. Never liked wakes without booze."

"Floridita's not far from Pier Seven," Southy said. "They took some nasty hits there."

"Most of the buildings were abandoned. Smoke was drifting down across the Pasig and out of Intramuros. But I found my watering spot all right."

"And Jesus?"

"No. *Jesus* was dead. Ramón was the new kid's name. Nephew. Told me *Jesus* was stabbed a few years back trying to break up a bar fight. I missed his big smile and his 'Night and Day.' Really wanted to spend the holidays with *Jesus*."

"Christmas Eve you had big fires near there," Southy remembered.

"Firefighters had a bad time with water pressure near the docks. Electricity was out. All Ramón could offer was warm San Miguel. Rinsed the dust out of my mouth. Drank a glass of beer to the memory of *Jesus*. Then put the urn up on the bar and we drank one to Barney. Thought maybe we could go the whole twelve days of Christmas. Always wanted to try it nonstop. You know what Ramón said? 'We have big trouble. Pilipinos celebrate many more than twelve.'"

"That's true," Mom says. "With *simbang gabi*, they go from about the sixteenth on. And they don't stop singing till the Black Nazarene."

"I know that one," I said. "When they haul out that statue of Jesus and crowd the streets."

"Told Ramón it might be too late to go for the whole show, but we could still start with Christmas Eve. He was happy to oblige and broke out the scotch. Had some near strikes that night, damn close, but not enough to keep us under the table."

"Someone was putting up flares there to guide Jap bombers in," Southy said.

"That's what Ramón said. Asked him for a light in the bar and he told me I must be crazy. They'd hired thugs out of Tondo to stand guard against looters. Someone down the street got shot just standing in his window with the lamp on. So we went out into the dark with our drinks, sat on a pile of rubble, watched the oil fires over at Pandacan light up the sky."

"What did you eat all that time?" Mom asked.

"Ramón was damn hospitable. Fetched us big armfuls of tinned goods from the abandoned bodega down the street. Had our *turo-turo* right out of the cans. He even fixed me kippers over a little fire in the street one morning. 'I know you like kipper-herring for breakfast,' he said. 'Bery English, but bery good.'"

"Sounds like a kindred spirit," Mom said.

"Even lent me a cot up over the store. Had lots of good company those first few evenings. Troops passing through, merchant marines off sunken ships, stevedores wandering about, even a prostitute or two. Got quite jolly. Ramón's cousin stopped by with duck eggs."

"Where did you meet your young lady?" Mom asked like she just thought of it for the first time.

"You mean *Virgin*?" He pronounced that one Spanish too.

"You don't say." Mom laughed like it was the best joke she'd heard in months.

"Not her true name, of course. Called her that because of the way she held Barney's urn to her breast when we sang 'Silent Night.' Had a white dress, you see."

"And what's her real name?" Mom asked.

"Has a lot of G's in it."

"You don't know her name?"

"Believe her first name's Asunción," Harry said. "Arrived one night just ahead of two stevedores. Afraid it all ended in a bit of a brawl. My mistake really. Shouldn't want to say anything against the other two." The way Harry said it, Southy began chuckling.

"You're determined to die," Mom said.

"Never. All in the spirit of camaraderie. I'd been drinking a good bit with them. There was a big Irish fellow and a Frenchman. Could swear he was Canuck, but the Irish called him 'Frenchy.' Given that, I should have chosen my stories better. But never meant an insult. We were just singing, swapping tales and having a good old time. Got into telling them about the French Concession in Shanghai."

"Your mother never raised you for this," Mom said.

"My mother? My mother never raised me at all. Nannies and schoolmasters, Ruth. Just like you."

"Hanging about with harbor thugs."

"Absolutely harmless. Just a little touchy about that story. Silly, actually. You know the French in Shanghai. Great party people. I just happened to be strolling by their club one day and heard raucous laughter through the hedge. Peeked over and there they were under the trees, dressed to the nines, drinking champagne from crystal and playing at bowls. Very elegant."

"I'm sure your audience was impressed."

"One Frenchman always seemed to be getting the best of the others. Whenever he won, the rest cheered him like the conquering hero – 'Vive le George!' and so on. Hoisted him onto their shoulders and carried him off to a little shed. He always entered with great ceremony while they split their sides laughing. Then after a bit he came out with a sheepish grin and they got back to their game."

"What was going on, Mr. Barnes?" I asked.

"Damn curious myself, but it *was* the French Club, after all. Very exclusive bunch. Diplomatic corps and so forth. So I went on my way. But about an hour or so later, happened back that way and the show was still going on. Only now in long afternoon shadows. They made a lovely picture out there on the green, dressed in their white flannels. Impressionist sort of thing. But when George won again, it was just too much for me. Had to sneak through the hedge to see for myself just what was up in that shed."

"Is this suitable?" Mom asked, nodding at me.

"Wasn't certain. George went in and they all began to laugh again. Uproarious. Couldn't quite believe it when I saw it. Here was this very civilized, elegant affair. And there, tacked up on the back wall of the shed was this calendar, complete with a hand-tinted photograph of an over-ripe nude. Blowsy's the word. And there, with great to-do, our very elegant George was kissing her right on the arse."

"Kissing the photograph?" Southy asked.

"Very wet kiss."

"That's the silliest thing I ever heard," Mom said.

"Exactly. Thought, this is hard enough for me to comprehend. What if I were Chinese?"

"How did Frenchy like the story?" Southy asked.

"Should have noticed his face had stiffened. Smile and camaraderie were gone. Kept looking hard at the mirror behind the bar, smoothing his hair."

"What did he say?" Southy asked with a big grin now.

"'You sayin' French are ass-kissers, buddy?'"

"And what did you say?"

"'I believe our George was nothing shy of the French consul.' Then he popped me. Must say he did it quite well too. Before I knew a thing, I was flat on the floor behind the table and they'd all disappeared. Just Ramón was there, bending over me, offering me a gin. Pretty painless though. Just a bit of an ache, here, under the ear. A little shaky in the legs."

"You're incorrigible," Mom laughed. "And what happened to the femme fatale?"

"Oh, *Virgin* came back all right, after Mass, Not sure if it was me she came back to see or was just on her way home."

"But you came to know her deep devotion."

"Some time after Christmas the mirror behind the bar crashed down and Ramón disappeared. Windows were out too, I believe. *Virgin* found me drinking alone and led me one night across Jones Bridge and up into Tondo."

"Tough neighborhood," Southy said.

"A bit nervy in the dark, going over the Pasig. Could just make out the shadows. Lots of trucks and artillery along the streets, troops on the move. Tondo boys didn't care much for me being there, but she called them off. Took me home and introduced me to family."

"What did you do?" Southy asked. "You pay her?"

"Perhaps it was my calling her *Virgin*. Just the mother and young sisters were there. Father was off fighting in the north. Home was a little nipa shack on stilts. They slept on mats on the floor. Pigs and chickens in the yard. Banana trees. Roosters crowing at the break of dawn. Very bucolic. She hung her white dress up very neatly whenever she was home. A valued piece of professional property. Treated me very posh. Put me up in a hammock."

"There *are* angels in heaven," Mom said.

"Had a merry time till a few days after New Years. Taught them all to sing "The Twelve Days of Christmas" – sounds fine with a Filipino accent. I took her into the city one day and bought her a new dress for thanks. Most of the stores were closed, but we managed."

"Sounds idyllic," Mom said, but not too warm.

"Nice as being under siege can be. Even attended Mass once. Drank tuba palm wine and set off firecrackers. Everybody started getting a bit high-strung though, waiting for the Japs. Finally thanked them all and went back down to the North Harbor. Didn't think it would be too good for them to be caught with me. *Virgin* took me down there to a nice abandoned bar, well-stocked. A little island of civilization hidden in a sea of rubble. I spent my last days there with Barney."

"How did they find you?" Mom asked.

"Wandering by the bay, I think. It's just a bit vague. There was oil slick on the water, shining in the sun. Japanese officer offered me a cigarette from a silver case. Asked him what day it was. 'The sixth day of January,' he told me very formally. Looked concerned when I started laughing. Just so happy I'd made it through all twelve. 'Epiphany,' I said to him. 'Epiphany.' I think he thought I was swearing."

"But where's Mr. Jenkins?" I asked.

"Safe. Quite safe." And he put his hand on my head. "Probably safer than you or I, Johnny. Sitting quietly on a shelf between Mr. Dewar and Mr. Gordon. Given present circumstances, I can't think of a better place to be."

CHAPTER 7

Every morning before chow, they'd roust us out for roll call on the Main Plaza. The monitors'd count us all up, room by room, then add on the folks in the Camp Hospital and the Camp Jail and those out on early morning work detail, and then they'd present that number to the Japs. If it didn't match Jap figures, they'd have to do it all over again, while the Commandant and his crew got nervous and paced back and forth along the line. If luck ran our way, the whole exercise only took maybe twenty minutes. But if there was a slip in addition, we could be out there a couple of hours.

Standing at attention in the same spot got pretty boring. So while they counted us, I counted my Clayees. I couldn't get enough of sticking my hand in my pocket and running my fingers over them. Felt like money in the bank. Time and again I reached in just to make sure they were all still there. Card players in Camp used cigarettes for currency. We had Clayees.

Of course, when other kids learned about them, they started searching the Dump for some of their own. But by the time they got to the toilet tanks, we'd pretty much tapped them out. So that put us right in the spotlight. It was monopoly at work in the marketplace. Just *like* diamonds, you see. Kids we barely knew came up and offered all kinds of things for just one Clayee. Knockers traded a kid one of his worst cracked Clayees for a whole Spam sandwich. He was pretty proud of himself, thinking he'd pulled off the Deal of the Century. But it just got Red mad.

"How could you do such a low thing?" he asked.

"I was hungry," Knockers said. "*Real* hungry." But he was starting to feel guilty, I could tell.

"Might've been his folks' last can of Spam," I put in. But that wasn't the kind of low Red had in mind.

"You leaked a Clayee. That's how it starts. Pretty soon everybody'll have 'em. Then where'll we be?"

That put some fear into Knockers. He smiled at us and let out a little nervous chuckle, but he was scared. Then he rushed off quick to get that kid back in a game. And he had to play him and play him until he won that Clayee back.

Marbles is a funny game. You get a bunch of kids all playing along in the same bumbling way and you can run through awful streaks. For a while I was winning Clayees left and right off just about every kid in sight. Seemed like I couldn't lose. I collected so many I couldn't carry them all with me at one time. I must've had more than twenty. Naturally I started feeling pretty good about myself, thinking all kinds of smart stuff, believing I was special and God must be on my side. Even started crossing myself before the big shots.

But just that quick I got myself into a bad streak and lost and lost till I was way down to maybe five. Then I got to feeling spiteful, wondering why some other kid had to win instead of me. I figured I'd been hexed by sour luck. So I cussed God out for being two-faced. And that's how it went. Those marble streaks can be wicked.

It was during one of these dips in fortune that we got into a game on that flat piece of ground by the Baseball Field. It'd gotten so hard and dry there, we couldn't help kicking up little dust clouds. Before we even got through our warm-up shots, we looked grimy as piglets rolling in a sty. Finch was sweating like a cold pipe in a heat wave, so he got hit the worst. He started changing complexions from beet-red to a kind of mud-yellow, fading into the scenery like a clever chameleon. We all looked at him and grinned.

"Oooh, Finchy," Pete said in a low, scary ghost voice. "Look at you, just fading away. Disappearing into dust."

"Woo-oo-oo," Knockers wailed. "Where's he gone to?"

"Come back, Finchy," Jerry picked up, rolling her eyes. Finch was starting to get a little upset. "Come back or I'm telling on you."

"We're telling your *amah*. We're telling your *yaya*."

"He couldn't play worth a damn anyhow." Red said. "He already lost all his marbles."

"I did not!" Finch shouted, jumping out to show us he was there. He did look awful, little pink rings around his eyes. "I still got Clayee Number One." He held it up for us to see.

"Yeah?" Pete asked. "And what else you got?"

"I got enough," he mumbled, pushing his hands into his pockets so we couldn't see how empty they were.

"Just two," Red said. "He lost all but two." And that really got to Finchy.

"OK, I'll play *all* you guys," he challenged. "Knuckles Down. Right now."

Knuckles Down was *our* game. Sometimes we played others, but nine out of ten, it was Knuckles Down. Not too hard, for one thing, just shooting at holes in the ground. And besides, we were used to it. Everyone knew the rules. So before Finch was done digging the holes, we were all down in the dust together, squinting hard and shooting our way around the course, seeing who could get through all five holes and back first, so he could take free shots at all the losers' Clayees. It was every-man-for-himself. All we cared about was grabbing Clayees off the others.

We were so caught up in it that it was a while before anybody noticed this kid Neddy Nickerson watching us, looking crisp and cool as a cucumber. Skinny white legs sticking out of white shorts, skinny white arms out of a white polo shirt. We only knew him from school. Nobody hung around him much. He was English for one thing, and always looking down his nose at us. At least that was how it seemed. You could never be too sure with Limeys. It might be just the way they acted, even amongst themselves. But finally, his standing there broke Finch's concentration.

"Yeah?" he said. Nickerson had his head cocked to one side with a queer grin on his face, like he was getting set to talk to the servants.

"It is marbles you're playing, isn't it?" he asked.

"Naw, it's football," Finch answered.

"Curious marbles."

"Found 'em ourselves."

"You wanna play?" Knockers asked.

"I prefer Stony-Wop," Neddy said. Then Finch did something *real* stupid. He tried to get sarcastic.

"Stony-Wop?" He made a face like he'd just eaten a big sour lime himself. "Oh, no, we nevah play Stony-Wop." Like the rest of us, he didn't have a clue what Neddy was talking about.

"OK," I said. "What's Stony-Wop?" I figured it might be one we knew by a different name. I sure wasn't set for what followed.

"Well, it's quite like Ringers, if you know that. Not so many marbles though. You shoot for Reels rather than the Regulars, but I should allow you to use *those* just the same." It rolled right out of him. We just stared and nodded our heads. "All the rest – lagging, rounsters, slips -- are just the same as in Ringers."

"You're makin' that up," Finch said. "I bet you're just makin' it up."

"I swear it's cricket."

"Show us," Red said.

"See here," Neddy said. "It's quite simple." He took a stick and drew a near-perfect circle ten feet across. At least, he said it was ten feet. By then, no one was arguing. With all the dust rising, he looked to be a magician standing in a ring of smoke. "After we lag for our place in queue, we put our Ringers three inches apart, in a cross right at the center here. We shoot from over there. And, oh yes, one more thing. Whenever you hit a marble, you must knock that marble out of the circle straightway, or you lose your turn. Is that clear?"

"How old are you?" Jerry asked. "I think he's older." She was good at analyzing things.

"Hell, Red's older too," Knockers said. "What's that prove?"

"Do we need to know all that stuff to play?" I asked. Neddy looked like he thought maybe I was trying to be friendly.

"It's not so difficult. You chaps will see, it's very exciting. It's special to shoot for Ringers."

"You mean Shooters?" I asked.

"Yes, so much at stake. Like a tiger hunt."

"You been to Inja?" asked Jerry.

"Oh, yes," Neddy said, brushing it aside. "Now, do we all have two marbles?" No, Finchy'd already lost one and was down to just his Clayee Number One.

"Aw, Finchy!" we all said, disgusted. But Neddy pulled a marble right out of his own pocket and handed it to him. It was a beautiful red agate! It was like he'd just made Finch king.

"A Glassee! You got Glassees!" Finch said, grabbing it right out of his hand.

"Only a loan, mind," the English kid said. "I've just brought three." He didn't let us see the others right off. First he drew a line in the dirt and waited on us all to shoot at it for position. Then he got down to "lag for place," as he called it. That's when he slipped the first Shooter out of his pocket. It was a clear silver-green dancing in the afternoon light and I couldn't help sucking in my breath. He knuckled down and shot without even preparing. Still his shot beat all ours by a good four inches.

Each of us put a Clayee in the middle of the circle. He showed us where to put them so they formed this big cross, with his green Glassee on the top and Finch's red agate on the bottom. Finch muttered something about wanting to shoot with that one. But the boy was strict with him.

"Just to give us all something to shoot for," he said. He had a queer

62

mouth, kind of buck-toothed and thin-lipped, so he smiled quirky. You couldn't tell whether he was concentrating hard or just chuckling to himself at our expense. It was like he was doing everything in his power just to put up with us. But in the next second he dropped right down on one knee and studied the cross like he was at High Mass on Sunday. And here we were, poor saps, all gaping at him for something to imitate.

Well, if we were impressed by those shenanigans, it was nothing to what we felt when he pulled out his other Shooter. You couldn't take your eyes off it. It's hard to explain. Some marbles are just more special. This one was black, orange and red flames licking at the sunlight. A real dazzler! I'll bet every last one of us was saying private prayers, hoping to get his hands on it.

Only it didn't work out that way. When Neddy finally shot, that marble jumped out in a long spinning blur, chipping not one, but two Clayees right out of the circle. And when his Shooter finally spun to a stop next to our Clayees, it sure made us look shabby, like a Bengal Tiger amongst a pack of yellow jackals.

Neddy crouched in the circle and sighted down the cross at the red agate, but he didn't go for it all at once. He worked his way toward it, one Clayee at a time, chipping them out of his way like little scraps of thrash. The closer he got, the more Finch groaned. Then just when he had that agate lined up at close range and Finchy was chewing his lip double-time, Neddy turned round and went for a much tougher shot up on the arm of the cross. He hit a Clayee there, but not hard enough to knock it out. So he got up, gave us a little twitch of a smile and stepped out of the ring.

"What about your Shooter?" Pete asked. "Ain't you gonna take it out?"

"Oh, no," he said. "This is much more sporting. If we leave our Reels in, we can shoot for position better. You see, if you can touch my Shooter, you get another shot from wherever you land. Just keep track of which is whose." He pushed the Clayees he'd won into a little bunch with his shoe.

That knocked all the confidence out of us, so we shot even worse than usual. I was lucky enough to get a Clayee on my first long shot from outside the ring, but then I messed it up going for the green Glassee. By the time it was Finch's turn, only two more Clayees had been knocked out. He hunkered down and powered Clayee Number One right into Neddy's Shooter.

"Hah!" he shouted. That gave him great position to shoot for a Clayee, but he was having none of that. He sighted in on the green Glassee, too, even though it must've been four feet away. He took a deep breath and fired away, hitting it broadside and spinning it right out of the circle. I got to tell you, we were all amazed. He jumped up triumphant, ran over and scooped it up. "I got it, I got it!" he was yelling to the sky, doing this funny little dance.

"I'm terribly sorry," Neddy said. "But I can't allow that shot." Finch looked like *he*'d been shot, then like he was going to cry. "I'm afraid you *fudged*."

"Buggers!" Finch shrieked. "I never fudged."

"Sorry, but it was a clear fudge." No one said a word. It's like some shame had come over us, and it got dead quiet. Finch was looking around at us for support.

"You're lying," he said, looking at me desperate. "Isn't he lying?" I felt bad about it, but by now I was pretty sure Neddy never lied. "Isn't he, Johnny? Isn't he?" Finch was right on the verge of panic.

"You did fudge, Finchy," I said. But that sounded so stark, I tried to soften it a little. "You've been fudging pretty much right along." But still it seemed too bare, so I added, "Off and on." I couldn't look at him for a while. We all just stood around. Finally he dropped the marble back into the ring. We were all feeling so guilty, we pretty much gave up right there.

When it was all over, Neddy'd taken eight out of twelve marbles, including his own and the one he'd loaned Finchy. But that wasn't enough of a licking for him. He had to do the meanest damn thing of all. He made us take all our marbles back. It was worst for any of us who'd won some ourselves, because of course we had to give ours back too. Then the damn kid just said a quick, "Thank you very much," and walked right off, little dust clouds kicking up at his heels.

Finch tried hard to get us into it again by bragging about how much harder it was to shoot with Clayees. You had to admire the way he could bounce back from a calamity. "We're playing with marbles out of a toilet, you know," he said. But the thrill'd gone out of it for the rest of us. We couldn't even look at Clayees for weeks.

CHAPTER 8

When you're in the clink, there's nothing like that first time hearing somebody just went over the wall.

Day after day, seemed like everybody was just doing what the *Japs* said. Following orders. When to eat, when to sleep, when to line up, when to wear which color armband on what kind of work detail. Sure, sometimes folks acted up. And then got slapped down and stomped on. Sometimes they even got dragged out of Camp and worked over and came back hurt, maybe broken. Or they never came back at all. But the Japs were *always* the ones calling the tune. And it just made you feel low.

Then all of a sudden somebody up and busted out of the joint. And, boy, that put a different color on *every*thing. You felt like jumping. Like spreading your wings.

First I heard a buzzing at morning roll call. The Japs did their count in the Plaza and it didn't come out right. So they stomped back and forth and barked awhile, then counted again real slow and careful, and it was still off. Then they got *real* serious and broke it down to building and floor and room, and one room was coming up short and then another. Then they got real mad and started going through names, and before you knew it they had the whole Internee Committee and Security and Monitors all down in the Commandant's office. Only even then it was all hush-hush, and nobody seemed to know just what was up, except it was bad, dangerous, deadly.

"They went over the wall there, behind the dump," Pete said, nodding his head toward the spot. "I heard some old guys talking."

"How many they say?"

"Three, I think. Two or three."

"I heard it was over there," Harvey said, pointing past the compound where the Spanish priests lived. "Near the Jap Bodega. Over into Calle Dapitan."

"If they did, they're muttonheads," I said.

"What do you mean?"

"Doesn't make sense."

"How come?"

"See the Guard House?"

"So?"

"I guess you don't know *any*thing about breaking out."

See what I mean? We were buzzing. Like getting drunk, maybe. But the first quick surge didn't have staying power. It whirled around and tapped itself out before it got started. There was too little to go on. Who were these guys anyway? Where from? If you couldn't put a face to it, or a name, it was nothing but shadows. Still, not knowing made your heart beat. I was talking so fast about it to Mom back of the Main Building, she gave me her long, hard look. Then she gave me a talking to. She said I'd best be quiet until I knew more. I was all set to take her advice. I was mum. But just then Southy came walking by the Annex and called us away from the crowd.

"It's not just the Monitors that got called down," he said. "It's Harry."

"But why?" Mom asked.

"Harry didn't do anything," I said.

"Remember roll call last night? Harry took the roll."

"What do you mean?"

"Guy's missing from our room."

"Yeah?"

"And Harry took roll, 'cause the Monitor was sick."

"He's in trouble?" Mom asked.

"I don't know. But keep it quiet. Nobody's to know." Southy put his finger to his lips. "Nobody."

You see! *That's* how rumors got off the ground in our Camp.

67

Somebody was buzzing this. Somebody that. If you could just maybe put a face to it. We had to be careful, Mom warned me, or we'd be running on nothing but rumors. "They're no better than hot air, Johnny. Trust rumors and you'll be headed for a fall." She was clever about it too. She checked and double-checked what people were saying and shook facts right out of rumors. "Find out the *true* facts, Johnny," Mom said. "Don't *ever* let yourself get high on rumors." So I held tight and kept quiet until late that morning, when we saw Harry coming out the front door of the Main Building, walking easy as you please across the plaza.

"Thank God, Harry," Mom said.

"It's OK," he said. "Just a mix-up."

"You sure?"

"Takahashi wants to pin something on us, but I don't think it'll stick," he said. Takahashi was a mean young officer in the Jap command.

"How do you mean?"

"They were still here at roll call last night. The Commandant knows we're not crazy enough to cover for them."

"So you're clear."

"Hope so. Monitor's job is over with roll call."

"You *know*, don't you. You know who it is," I said. Harry just put his lips together and shook his head.

"Let's pray they're moving fast," he said.

But later that afternoon we got some hard news. A bunch of us were squatting around down by the Gym. We were always squatting, like it came natural to us, like we were some real Filipinos who had watched their dads and granddads squatting all the way back to before they had a stool to sit on, most likely. We were squatting among the high weeds, scratching the ground with sticks, talking nonsense, when Red and Pete and Jerry came by. Red was hot and busting to tell.

"They got 'em back," he said. "All three of 'em."

"No," Finch said. "Already?"

"Didn't even get five miles."

"Damn."

"Harvey said he saw 'em."

"They're just some guys off a boat," Pete added. "That's what my dad said. Merchant ship. Got torpedoed off the coast back before Christmas, or bombed maybe."

"British," Jerry said, spitting in the dust. "One's Aussie. From your room, Johnny."

"I don't know."

"What difference does it make?" Red said, scratching behind his ear. "They got caught." He was mad about everything, kicking dirt. "My mom says it's stupid, that's all. Didn't even have a damn plan."

"What kind of plan you need?" Knockers said. "What you need's luck."

"Least they tried," I said. It seemed to me it must take guts, going over the wall in the pitch dark and trying to make it out of the city. Three guys trying to sneak out through streets where everybody else was Jap or Filipino or maybe Chinese.

"What'd it get 'em? They just got caught and beat up."

"One guy's hurt bad," Pete said. "He can't barely talk."

"If they just knew the city better, maybe they'd made it," Knockers said. By now, everybody was talking like an expert, but nobody even knew who these guys were.

"They have kids?" Finch asked.

"They're merchant marine, stupid. Off a ship."

"How they gonna have kids on a boat?"

"Well, they could have kids. Someplace."

"At least they tried," I said. "They didn't just sit here, waiting." I knew it was crazy, but right then I was thinking I could go over the wall myself if there was just somebody to go with. Somebody like

Dad. But you didn't want to *ever* let them catch you. You had to sneak around and run like hell and make sure they *never* brought you back. Then all of a sudden it felt scary out there, full of streets I didn't even know.

Mom and I ate with Harry out in the sheds. He didn't look himself. He sat real quiet. Harry wasn't one to look down.

"You OK?" Mom asked.

"Sure," he said, trying to look cheerful. "Takahashi did a lot of bullying today, trying to get all of us to confess to something, but those boys made it clear they escaped after eight."

"Poor devils," Mom said.

"That Jap wants blood," Harry said.

That evening they took the three of them out of Camp. I was near the Plaza when they brought them out of the Jail, but I only caught a quick glimpse. One guy had a beard, but he wasn't anybody I recognized. I couldn't get too close. They hustled them into the back of a car quick and took off. Takahashi was out there strutting around with his samurai. Folks'd heard those poor guys yelling in real pain from the Jail. They said one fellow's face looked like hamburger. They said Takahashi had himself a good time in there with a rubber hose.

That night I tried to get near enough to Harry to ask him something, but he turned away and kept his mouth shut. The Committee'd had a meeting and told everybody concerned to keep a lid on it. That's what I heard. "I can't tell you anything," Harry kept saying. "I just don't know." After lights out he curled up on the mattress with his back to me in the dark. I watched him a long time and knew he wasn't sleeping. I could tell the way he was breathing. I watched him until finally I couldn't keep my eyes open anymore and drifted off.

The next day things took another bad turn. Everybody started talking *execution*. It blossomed right out of thin air. First I heard it from some old guys down at the Gym, then from folks on the chow line, then even from Finch. Worst thing, he said, it was Friday the Thirteenth. Everybody kept saying that, how unlucky it was.

I was trying hard to hang on and use Mom's rumor technique. I shook and I shook for the facts. But I couldn't tell if I was really getting facts or just hot air. Knockers said he heard Takahashi was pushing for a quick execution before anybody outside could put up a stink and stop it. He wanted them killed quick and no interference. That sounded close enough to be fact.

But Pete and Finch said they saw the Commandant, Tomayasu, go out of Camp in his car wearing nothing but a kimono and sandals. That sounded funny. I figured they had to be stretching it. But Harvey told me his dad said the same thing, Tomayasu did go out to plead for the prisoners. Took off his uniform and humbled himself in front of the Jap big shots outside. Did his damnedest to get the guys off. Tears were streaming down his face when he came back in, Harvey said. I don't know how he knew, but he swore to it.

But Southy took a different view. Took the same story and turned it around to look different. He said Tomayasu was just putting on an act. Tears are cheap, he said. He figured Tomayasu snuck off down the street a ways, put his feet up in a bar and had a couple of beers, then came back saying he'd done all he could. Those rumors were as tough as working the pea and shell game. And it went on right through Saturday, enough facts and rumors to make your head spin.

Sunday morning early, they rousted out *all* the guys who were down in the Commandant's office, including Harry. They put them all in the back of a bus before anybody knew what was up and drove them out. The whole Camp was ready to bust. Nobody believed the execution could really happen, but everybody was talking like it would. Beating those guys up was one thing, they were saying, keeping them in a cell with bread and water, even. But how could they *kill* them?

Maybe they were trying to scare us, somebody said, like when they set the machine-gun up on the lawn. Maybe they just wanted to trick us and get us nervous. But then others started to worry about all of the guys who were taken out. Maybe they'd kill *every*body. Maybe they'd cut off their heads with a good sharp samurai. We'd all seen photographs of that stuff. Some'd seen it happen for real. Vicious. You could see the blood gushing. Then what would we do? People went away and tried to forget it. Then they bunched up and started to chatter like crazy. Like scratching bug bites till they bleed.

Finally it got me tight and hot like a fever, so I had to quit. I couldn't even eat noon chow. I sure couldn't stand waiting in a long line. Evil notions kept running through my brain. I tried to get rid of them, but I was thinking all sorts of crazy stuff, like maybe even Harry might not come back. If I could just find a place off in the shade, maybe I could take a breather. Over by the Annex I found a little tree to sit under. I sat by myself and started practicing my meditations, keeping my mind blank. Dad taught me how to do it. He told me to get off by myself, sit real still, breathe deep and slow and concentrate on one thing. It could be anything, like a ring or a ball or a rock. He said if you were good at it, you could make your body cool even when it was real hot. I thought about that circle in the ground Neddy drew. Every time a thought crawled in, I'd kick it out. I was even starting to make some headway. But then Finch came by and sat down next to me.

"Shut up," I said, and started trying to scrub my mind clean of thoughts again. But just then Red and Pete came over. "Don't talk," I told them, but by then more and more thoughts were busting in. Then Jerry joined us. "Not a word." But I knew it was no use. We all just sat there trying to stay mute as mummies. But Finch couldn't stand *that*. He kept mumbling things under his breath and that was worse than if he'd talked out loud.

Finally we saw Knockers coming. We watched him from a long ways off, alongside the shadow by the Main Building. He didn't rush. He took his time. But by the way he was walking we knew what he was going to say.

CHAPTER 9

Knockers didn't beat around. "They executed 'em," he said.

We shook our heads. It wasn't that we weren't ready. But it was like someone'd just let the air out. You wanted to bite your lip so hard it'd draw blood. But there was no pretending. When you looked up, Knockers was still there and he wasn't going away.

"All three," Knockers said.

"They kill anybody else?" Finch asked. We just looked at him. Sometimes it wasn't so good having Finch around.

"Where'd you hear it?" I asked.

"In the Plaza. They're all over there talking about it." So we got right over. But the Plaza was just about deserted, a big open space swimming in light. Only a few old-timers were left hanging out at the edge in the shade under the trees.

"Did they really kill those guys?" Pete asked.

"That's what they say," one said. "Shot 'em dead, just like that."

"Shoveled dirt on 'em while they was still moaning," the other said.

"No ifs, ands or buts."

"Just sat 'em down and shot 'em into their graves," the old guy said. His hair'd gone yellow white. His lower lip looked thin as tissue paper. Big old-people freckles spread over his face and neck and arms. He looked to be Old Man Death himself. "One young fellow just married, too."

"No ceremony, nothing. Just shot 'em dead."

"Nasty business."

"Filthy Japs."

We went all around Camp, picking up what we could from anybody who knew anything. People seemed mad and sad at once. There

73

was a lot of head-shaking. But nobody carried on too much. A couple of ladies were crying, but soft, just brushing away tears. They all spoke low, like maybe they thought someone was listening. Mom wouldn't say anything at all. When I asked about it, she just looked at me like maybe I didn't know better.

"It's over," she said, and then looked down. I knew she meant for me to shut up about it.

But I was getting anxious. I hadn't seen Harry anywhere, and I got a crazy notion that maybe *he* was gone. Maybe it was that stupid thing Finch'd said. It was too crazy a thought to ask about. I just kept looking. I looped back across the Plaza, then out by the Gym and along the wall clear back to the Camp Dump, walking at first, then breaking into a slow trot, checking everywhere. But after the first half-hour not finding him, I started worrying for real.

I went into the Main Building and ran up the dark stairs all the way back to our room. It was empty except for a couple of old guys playing cards. Nobody said a word about Harry, but his being gone was starting to feel like fact. When I broke back out into the sunlight, I had to shade my eyes to look out past the bright plaza, but there were too many people out there scattered in every direction across the lawn, bunched up under the trees.

Finally, I caught something up the drive toward the Main Gate – a couple of figures a long ways off. There was just something about the one. So I ran toward them, ran till I just about ran right into them and then I just stood there panting, staring at them.

"What are you looking at, Johnny?" he asked. He looked real serious, but then he smiled at me. And all the dumb feeling left me like a dream. I felt stupid for worrying.

"Nothing," I said. "Just checking."

They had a Mass in the Spanish Fathers' Garden the next day. I went with Mom and Southy. I always watched Mom so I knew when to genuflect, bow my head and cross myself. A man from the Committee got up and spoke. He said these men'd never be forgotten, that they'd died with dignity and we should be proud of their strength. He talked quite a long time. His voice kind of droned on. He wore glasses and they kept blinking in the dim light under the trees. Then finally everybody said a Hail Mary and Our Father and walked out into the hard sunlight again. Nobody stuck around to talk. Everybody was quiet and went off to be by themselves.

I tried to make some sense of it. Three guys'd just been killed for trying to get out of our Camp, just lined up and shot. They weren't anybody I knew. They weren't soldiers or anything. Just civilians. They weren't even Americans. I never saw them myself, not really. I sure never saw them get shot. Everything about them I learned from somebody else. One guy was from my own room and I couldn't even remember what he looked like.

"Sure you do," Southy said. "Nice looking guy. Real Aussie." Was he the guy with the beard? They could've all fallen down a well just as easy. I swear I could sit sometimes all alone and tell myself maybe it'd never happened, it was just somebody's idea. Like me thinking Harry was gone. I couldn't explain it. But I felt kind of sore and scared. I figured maybe if I could just hear more, but then I figured it'd only be rumors anyhow. What I needed was some true facts from somebody who'd been there. So I waited. Sooner or later Harry would have to give them to us.

All the grownups were working details by then. Mom was doing some nursing, using her training to help out by giving shots over at the infirmary, stuff like that. A Red Cross shipment of needles and vitamin shots got through from overseas, and I kept busy getting every shot I could. It made me feel pretty robust. Most kids hated the old, bent needles, but I didn't mind. Folks said we needed the injections to keep healthy. I figured the more I got the better. So I got right to the back of the line for the same shot two or three times. Then Mom caught me and gave me holy hell.

Southy was working Sanitation, sweeping streets outside the Main Gate, down Boulevard España and out past Calle Noval towards Quiapo. Harry was working Camp Garden Detail. They'd carved a big vegetable patch right out of the old Camp Dump. That was tough work, clearing away car frames, axles and all that other junk, even before they could start spading and turning the soil. They had some tough men working that shift. After Kitchen Detail, it was likely the roughest. Harry and Southy came off those jobs stripped to their shorts, sweat streaming off their hot bodies. We all got together on the lawn at Southy's lean-to.

"You boys are looking ruddy today," Mom said, watching them flop down dead on the lawn.

"Go fetch us water, Gunga Din," Harry drawled and I ran off to fill tin cups at the spigot.

That was our routine. Every day it was just about the same. But this one day I came back with the water and they were already into it, Harry and Southy stretched on their backs, looking up through the tree at the clouds moving by and Harry talking so quiet Mom had to lean close to hear.

"We did all we could to stop it," he was saying. "Contacted everyone we could think of in the city. It wasn't supposed to happen Sunday, you know. They moved it up on us."

"Takahashi," Southy said.

"Probably. Nobody knows for sure. But I'm sure Tomayasu could've delayed it if he'd wanted." I could see Mom getting edgy.

"Tell us," she said. "Please." Harry looked at her like she'd surprised him. I never saw her so fidgety.

"I'm only going to do this once," Harry said. "I'm not for playing town crier to the whole bloody Camp. It's easy to cheapen it."

"Will you *please*," she said. He lay there awhile, thinking.

"The bus took us across the river to a big building. Something official, police station or court. They brought them down the steps with their hands tied behind their backs. I could see they had all been worked-over. But when they saw us, they lit up. They must have thought they were home-free."

"They didn't know," Southy said.

"They thought we had gotten them off, I suppose. Saw us as their saviors. I had trouble looking them in the face. They kept studying us for signs. Every once in a while I glanced at this young blond kid, Day, and he'd give me a wonderful English grin. Very blond. Banged up around the mouth and right eye, badly bruised and red. But he had a wonderful smile. Teeth just a bit crooked. None of them had shaved, of course, and he had a very light boyish stubble."

"How'd they find out?" Southy asked.

"The bus headed north back across the river, but instead of turning right on España and up to the Camp, it stayed on Rizal towards San Lazaro."

"The racetrack?" I asked.

"That direction. Up to the Chinese Cemetery. I think when we didn't turn, they knew something was up. That and the white armbands the soldiers were wearing."

"Blindfolds," Southy said.

"When we got to the cemetery, a work detail was already digging over in a ravine. They lined up the three of them and Tomayasu read the verdict in Japanese. When they translated, Day kept looking right at me, licking his lips as if he couldn't get them moist enough. Father Lindsay stepped over, told them he was a minister of the Church of England and wished to offer them the consolations of religion. The physical life is not the whole life. There is life beyond the death of the body. He assured them they would be remembered. That sort of thing. All very rushed."

"Nightmare," Mom whispered.

"When he told them he hoped to get back to England some day, one chap could only mumble. I couldn't understand him at all. He was pretty badly beaten. But Day reached into his back pocket and pulled out his wallet, then held it in his bound hands for someone to take. A soldier handed it over to Lindsay. Day said he was married just before he left England and might be a father by now. Could that be taken into consideration? When he saw Tomayasu shake his head, he looked away and asked us to please take down his address in London. He looked at me again."

"Poor Harry," Mom said. She put her hand on his shoulder.

"Poor Day," Harry said. One of them asked for cigarettes, and then they all stood there a short while smoking. The grave was finished by then. It was about four by ten. Maybe four feet deep. The soldiers took the blindfolds off their arms. That's when the Australian objected. He said he wished to have his eyes left uncovered, but they put blindfolds on all of them anyway. They made them all sit down together on the mound of freshly dug dirt. Do you mind Johnny hearing this?"

Mom thought a moment. "No. It's our duty. All our duty."

"Johnny can take it OK," Southy said.

"Tomayasu kept telling us how much he regretted it, said he'd done all he could. But the three soldiers *he* had chosen went to the other side of the grave, drew pistols, and fired at their hearts. They used 25-caliber revolvers, so they didn't do the job all at once. The one Brit slumped against the Aussie and the two rolled into the hole. But Day was still sitting there, his blond hair sticking out over his blindfold. They had to shoot again before he fell in. Then they fired down into them from the top of the grave. Takahashi was grinning his head off. There were still moans coming out of the grave. So they fired off a few more rounds.

"Tomayasu said it was too bad they hadn't used the proper equipment. I suppose he would have preferred Takahashi going at it with his samurai. They had to shoot into the grave several more times. Filipino workers came forward to fill in the grave, but the soldiers ordered them back. They insisted on covering the bodies themselves. Pecking order, I suppose. There were still moans coming from the grave."

"They *were* buried alive," I said.

"They kept us from getting close. But I heard moans."

"Bastards," Southy mumbled.

"After the graves were filled in, they planted white stakes with black Japanese characters in the earth. The soldiers tore some bougainvillea blossoms off a vine and put them on the grave. Lindsay, in his cassock and stole, said the service over the graves while the Japs stood at 'carry sabers.' They certainly do enjoy ceremony."

Harry and Southy just lay on their backs, looking straight up, tin cups resting on their stomachs. They lay still as dead men. When I looked at Mom she wasn't crying or anything. But her whole body started shaking. Very slight at first and then harder till finally she came out with a deep sob. Dry, like she was choking. We all jumped when we heard it.

"Oh, Ben," she cried. "My God, where the hell's Ben?" It gave me chills all over. I never heard my old man's name choked out like that.

Harry put his arms around her and held her, while Southy stood up and made sure the Japs couldn't see them together like that. But I saw her face, and it was all twisted for just a minute. And then it went away. It sure churned me up. I don't know which was worse, thinking about that poor bastard Day or watching my mom.

CHAPTER 10

That execution made me look at people different, wondering what they were really thinking. I figured some who were smiling and laughing might be hiding mean sad thoughts. And those acting tough as nails could be soft as mush inside. I knew they likely had no idea what was going on in my head. And what Harry told us about the killing made me imagine.

I had this real clear picture of that Aussie, could conjure him up in a second, standing there strong and tall with a full, dark beard. That way he refused the blindfold gave me something to work on. He was smoking that last cigarette, looking brave and bitter.

The silent one was stocky, maybe, but muscular too. A real merchant seaman. Seemed he had a tattoo. His face looked like they'd been using it for a punching bag the full ten rounds. I'd seen close-ups of a prizefighter like that in *Life* magazine – some Irish mug who led with his head, all puffed up so his eyes were just slits.

But the one called Day was different, always standing out front of the others in my mind, young and blond and shining like one of your Christian martyrs. He had a wise smile on his face, like he'd seen eternity. I could even make out his wife and little kid waiting for him over in London, sitting there on the floor in front of the fireplace. Course I modeled the kid pretty much along the lines of my brother Tyler. And just like my mom, his had been busy knitting a lot of matching sweater and sock sets for the little tike.

"What do you figure it's like, Southy?" I asked.

"What?" We were down in the Gym, where Southy'd found a dusty old punching bag hanging in the back and fixed it up so he could use it to work out on.

"When you're gonna to get executed," I said. He took one rolling startup swipe at the bag and then held it.

"What the hell you talking about?"

"How's it feel?"

"Depends, I guess." And then he considered awhile longer. "Like everything, some guys'll be good, others'll shit their pants."

"But how do I know which one I'll be?" I asked.

"You can't. Not until it happens. Not till you've got it staring you in the face." He started the bag again, rolling slow with it till he got the rhythm, then turning up the tempo till it was like a quick drum roll. Like all pros, he could make that bag sing and dance. Like Gene Krupa, you wanted him in your band. The Gym was a big barn of a place, with maybe six hundred guys sleeping on the floor, and the sound echoed all around.

Some old guys were sitting quiet on their cots, watching him. One yelled at him to knock it off. But when he'd got his rhythm, you couldn't shake him. He just smiled and yelled back. The sweat beaded up on his face and broke free, streaming down his neck and chest and back. He was something to watch. I couldn't get enough. He and Dad made that bag a thing of beauty. The water was flying off him now like spray from a garden hose.

"Couldn't you *get* yourself ready for it?" I asked when he quit. He put his wet hands on my shoulders. Southy had big hands, wide across the knuckles, hard as stones. But they were soft as a lady's when he wanted to be gentle.

"That's a hell of a thing," he said, smiling.

"Couldn't you?"

"Jesus, kid. I never heard such damn ideas. Get ready? Go into training. Work out for the big execution." He let loose that crazy high laugh of his. "That beats all!"

Truth is Southy'd been in training for something right along.

That's what the speed bag was all about. It was his nature. Southy and Dad just naturally seemed to need to put in time keeping their shape.

"What are you keeping in shape for?" Mom'd asked while Dad skipped rope on our terrace.

"What do you mean?" he'd asked back.

"What are you proposing to do with that shape?" You could tell she really liked watching him out there, skipping in the light under the trees.

"Well, it might just come in handy," Dad smiled at her. "Don't you think?"

"I don't think thinking has anything to do with it," Mom said. And she gave him that look over her shoulder.

I don't mean Southy or Dad were Spartans or anything. They drank their cocktails and carried on and all. Ran around and had a good time. Dad took Mom out dancing every chance he'd get. Stayed up late. Went off to the races and the fronton. It's just that him and Southy'd be working and thinking and talking boxing all the time – cutting off the ring, circling with the jab, working the inside moves. They'd take me to the fights with them so I could watch some smart little pro like Razor Tablan do his fancy stuff.

"Watch the hands, kid," Southy'd instruct me. Razor was fighting a guy named Speck from California and had already cut him bad by the fifth. "Watch him in the clinch, how he brings those gloves up at the break, laces first."

"These damn lightweights," Dad said. "All slash and burn." He was always needling Southy like that. See, Dad was a middleweight, maybe even on the heavy side of middle. Not so much dancing with the big guys. But in Manila, you got the small, fast stuff. That was Southy's meat and potatoes.

"Can you see it, Johnny?" Southy said. "Razor's fighting nasty tonight."

"They can swing from the heels, but no one ever goes down," Dad said.

"Mr. Speck's not gonna want to come back here real soon," Southy shouted over the crowd noise. The Filipinos loved seeing their local boy take it to the American.

"You can always tell the little boxer," Dad said. "Every fight's cut right into his face."

"Yeah," said Southy. "And the big palookas stagger around punch-drunk." That's the way they ribbed and poked. They were always good fun together. And you can bet I was picking up plenty of pointers too.

When Southy got through with the bag in the Gym, he moved outside and worked the skip rope on the flat ground. Kids loved watching that, even some of the old-timers. He could spin it so fast you couldn't see it anymore, then slow it down so it slapped hard in the dirt, raising a cloud of dust. Those pros know all the tricks. Then maybe, if he felt like it, he'd shadow-box by and by or jog under the trees. And that's how it was with Southy.

One day he came in from sweeping the streets, bare to the waist except for the red and white armband, and the armband sweated through so the red had gone wet and dark as blood.

"Notice anything different?" he asked real low. We looked at him. Then we looked around the Camp.

"No," Mom said. "What is it?"

"Listen," he whispered.

"It's quiet," Harry said. "But it's siesta." Just then a flock of birds broke out from behind the Main Building and swept up into the sky. It was so quiet you could hear their wings beat.

"It's dead," Southy said. "When I was sweeping the street past Calle Noval, this Filipino walked by real close with his head down and said, 'Bataan is gone.'"

"Jesus," Mom said, drawing in her breath. "Are you sure?" Then we listened again and it *was* real quiet.

83

"He said it so low, I wasn't sure at first."

"Well, it fits," Harry said.

"I watched him down the street and he never looked back. Then I felt how still it was. It wasn't even noon yet and nobody was out. There wasn't a sound in all Manila."

"Don't talk," Mom said. "Just listen." I know she was straining for that distant thunder of artillery, but Southy was right. It was dead as a morgue.

"Well, if it's true, you can bet the Japs will tell us soon enough," Harry said.

That evening it came over the loudspeakers. Bataan had surrendered, they announced. The Battle of Bataan was finished. The Imperial Japanese Army was victorious. And you could hear a deep moan all over. It shouldn't really've been a surprise. Like Harry said, our boys couldn't hold out forever up there, with no food or ammunition. But saying it snatched away folks' last dreams.

Most everybody treated the fall of Bataan like the end of the world. Those who had a husband or a father or a son up there turned pretty near suicidal. It just tore at their hearts. And it got us even more worried about my old man. For months we'd all believed help was on the way. Even after all logic said it couldn't happen, lots of people still went on talking about our boys rolling down off Bataan and busting us out of Santo Tomás. So it was only natural that now they felt betrayed. They bowed their heads in disgrace and gave up all belief in miracles.

But Southy gritted his teeth, gave a tight little smile and went after that bag in earnest. He hit it so hard so often, every once in a while the bladder sprung a leak. He just took it down, laid it across his lap, unlaced the strings, pulled out the bladder and fixed it with a patch and a bicycle pump. All slow and patient and careful. Before you knew it, the bag was up again and he was thumping out a new tune. It wasn't ever a slow sad song with Southy. And never a dirge. It sounded a whole lot more like war drums.

Between the street sweeping and the punching bag, Southy got himself twisted tight as rope. Maybe he was tired of being a lightweight and was dropping down to featherweight. All that was left to wish on now was Corregidor and maybe some bands of guerrillas in the jungles. Sometimes it seemed Southy was trying to keep them all alive single-handed. It took me a bit to catch on to it. But I saw he was using it like one of those Hindu mantras, concentrating everything he had on that small, fast-moving thing. His eyes got a gleam to them, like something was burning inside. And I could bet his mind's eye was staring smack at that Rock sitting out in the middle of Manila Bay. I say this because I could see it too.

That's likely why, when news came about the fall of Corregidor, I got such a queer picture in my head. Corregidor wasn't just bombed and strafed and stormed over by Japs. It *sank*. I could see it clear and real as one of those crippled ships out of the newsreels, still bristling with big guns, but wallowing sideways, flames lapping across its bridge. Then with just the slightest shudder, it slipped down under the waves with a creak and a groan. Finally came that big rush of air, bubbling sudden and violent to the surface from way down in the depths of old Malinta Tunnel. And with it came the bodies of the dead.

"Well," Southy told us one afternoon. "They marched 'em through the city today."

"From Corregidor?" Mom asked. "How did they look?"

"Dried-out," he said, snipping it off so it stood out all by itself. Then he looked right at her and smiled. "Defeated. Demoralized. Disgraced, like us." It made you edgy, he said it so good-natured. And I guess he must've felt guilty about it too. "No," he said. "A whole lot worse than us."

"Anyone we know?" she mumbled.

"Few faces. Nobody I really knew."

"Where were they headed?" Harry asked.

"They'd shipped 'em to Parañaque, I heard, and marched 'em

north." He looked a little distracted all at once. "Did it rain here this morning?" he asked.

"Not here," Mom said.

"Looked like showers over the bay," Harry said.

"Funny. It didn't rain while I was sweeping, either, but the street was wet. Steam rising off the pavement in the sun. When I swept trash into the gutters, there was water lying there."

"Then it must've rained," I said.

"There weren't many Filipinos in the street," Southy said. "But I saw them watching from above the stores all right. I could see their eyes. There was plenty up there in the shadows. Just a little girl was in the doorway across the street. Standing all alone. She was no more than seven or eight. Skinny legs, shabby little dress, big dark eyes. She gave me a smile. I could hear 'em marching before I saw them. Lots of them. Long before they got to the street. It was queer, like a mirage or something. You won't laugh?"

"Why would we laugh?" Mom asked.

"Sometimes when you're alone, you're not too sure it's real."

"We're not laughing," Harry said.

"For a second I was afraid, you see. Just a passing thing, but still. It was the little girl, I guess. When they turned the corner they were three abreast and the Japs marching to the side with their rifles up. The little girl stepped right out in the street and waved to them, gave 'em the 'V for victory' sign. Jesus, I was thinking, they'll kill her. But the first of the prisoners was passing between us, so I couldn't see her anymore. I was busy watching faces go by."

"And you didn't see anybody?" Mom asked.

"Some guys from the Army and Navy Club. A few looked familiar. That Lieutenant Carter, maybe. Then one guy stumbled. He went right down like a sack of rice in the middle of the column. Right in front of me. His legs just went out from under him and he pitched forward onto his face. Almost tripped the guy next to him."

"Gosh, where were *you*, Southy?" I asked.

"Pressed against the wall to make room. The Jap guard next to me swung around quick with his rifle when he heard him go down. But the poor bastard was out like a light. Didn't move. The column was stopped dead and backing up all along the street. Japs were screaming. One of 'em came up the line yelling in English. Get him up or he's dead, he said. Couple of guys got in under his arms, tried getting him to walk, but his legs wouldn't work. They had to drag him along the street and it was slowing the whole column. They couldn't have got far like that."

"And that was it," Harry said.

"Yeah, they went up the street a ways and turned off."

"And you didn't hear anything else?"

"No."

"Then maybe it was all right." Harry put his hand on Southy's shoulder. "I'm sure it was all right."

"It was a hell of a helpless feeling," Southy said.

"I sure hope his legs got working," I said.

"All I could do was watch. Like it was somebody else's war."

"And the girl?" Mom asked.

"What?"

"What about the little girl?"

"I don't know," he said. "She just disappeared. Gone. Like she never existed. When I looked up at the windows, nobody was there either. Street was empty. Just the Jap guard up the street under a tree. It was like I was all alone out there."

CHAPTER 11

The head Jap in our camp was the Commandant, who'd lay down the laws we lived by. Problem was, they kept changing commandants on us, each with his own ideas. Tomayasi was gone, and Tsurumi, and now in our second year, we were onto Kuroda. Harry remembered Kuroda from Shanghai, where he'd been in the scrap-iron business. Now Kuroda was bent on showing us he was as hard as the stuff he'd been dealing. First thing he did was shut down the Package Line and put *sawali* mat up across the front fence to seal off our last view of the world outside.

After that, little news got through except Jap propaganda, which was a very sorry kind of news. We felt the world had given us up and maybe we'd *never* get out of there. People were getting a whole lot skinnier, but nobody was really starving yet. Deaths were incidental, not the rule. It was mostly just the usual dumb orders and occasional beatings. Once in a while someone got yanked out of camp and never came back. Just to keep us off balance, like having one foot to stand on.

That's when I started studying Harry for real. How he did things, said things. He was just different. I came on him sitting alone under a mango tree by the athletic field, carving a chess set out of worn-down *bakia* sandals. It was old, soft wood and he was being slow and careful with it. He barely nicked the wood with the small blade of his pen knife, then blew on it and held it up to the light.

"What's that gonna be when you're done?" I asked.

"King," he said.

"Like Henry the Eighth?"

"No, but Henry might be good for the other side of the board. Of course, I'd have to carve extra queens for Henry."

"Which is it then?"

"Fellow named Asoka, who grew sick of war."

"Funny kind of king."

"Yes, king with a conscience is a rare king. Indian fellow."

"American?"

"No, no. Indian Indian. Very old," he said. And he told me all about this Asoka and how his granddad had kicked out all the Greeks who were left over from Alexander the Great. Seemed the granddad and dad were powerful warriors, but Asoka took up an idea called *ahimsa*, being gentle to all living creatures. Harry said Asoka was into ahimsa long before Mr. Ghandi. Once he'd conquered all his neighbors and showed how tough he could be, he gave up on the whole idea of war. Made him feel bad. Well, that was Harry all right. Ask about anything and he'd answer with some story. "I think ahimsa is damn good policy for a chess king," Harry said.

"He's kind of fat for Inja," I said, squinting at his carving.

"Indian doesn't have to be skinny. Or dark, for that matter." He appeared a little sensitive about my criticism. "Besides, this is a very rich king."

"You sure must like chess to carve a whole set." He looked up at me, giving it serious thought.

"Don't know. Still studying it. I'm onto Capablanca right now. You heard of him?"

"Nope."

"Knows his moves. Nice to think of a world with order. Just not sure it's healthy."

"Seems awful quiet."

"Quiet's not all bad," he said. "Bet you'd like it if you tried."

He sketched a chessboard on the bare ground and started showing me moves. Told me generals played. And poets. And he didn't quit there. He talked chess to me every time he saw me, forever teaching me new moves. Once he'd finished carving his set, he carried it all around Camp in a little cloth sack with a string cinch, seeking out new partners. Way to get to know people, he said. Get them to chat.

He kept luring me into games. He was good at that. Said chess'd go well with my boxing. Showed me how Capablanca opened his games. P-Q4, N-KB3, and so on. He talked about this gambit and that. I caught on quick to starts, was fine right up until about move five. But I seemed to muddle my middles. And I turned downright stupid at the endgame. Couldn't finish anybody off. Chess did have something in common with boxing – how to feel the other guy out, feint and counterpunch, keep up your guard. But you're damned in chess if you go too strong on offense. There's no bluffing a guy across the board with violence the way you can another kid in the ring.

Funny thing was, we'd be playing a game there in the shade, and Harry'd start talking to me like I was another adult. Or maybe he was just talking to himself. I'd just moved B-Q3 and he said, "Maybe we resist too much," in a far-off voice.

"Yeah?" I said, thinking maybe I'd just made the wrong move.

"Have to give ourselves over to it."

"Oh," I said, still staring at the board to see what he was going to do. But he was just looking across the field at the wind in the trees.

"Embrace it. Let it run through you like blood and water." Now I was really at a loss. Like he was meditating. "During that big flood in Tientsin, water climbed over the second floor. We were all punting about in a panic, trying to rescue our possessions from the rising tide. Dumb Westerners with property. Know what the Chinese did?"

"I don't think we were in China then," I said.

"Just stood there, water up to the armpits. One giving the other a haircut. Like any other day." I started laughing at that, I couldn't help it. But Harry was deadpan. "Now that's letting the world run through you," he said. "See what I mean?"

"Sort of," I said, watching him swing his knight over by my king.

"We complicate things every chance we get," he said, like his mind was a million miles away. Then, "By the way, Major, I believe that's checkmate." Damn, the way he played, you couldn't tell where chess ended and palaver began.

One night he got Mr. Haverford into a game. The old guy was looking downright desperate. Southy said it was because of the Japs' shutting down the Package Line. He was sure that'd been the source of Haverford's booze. But Mom said Haverford was going through other bad times as well. It was hard enough having his boy Roger run off. Now there'd been some family row and his wife and daughter were shunning him too. He was edgy as a cat in heat and nasty to every soul in sight. I'd hear him whimpering in his sleep and gnashing his teeth. So I paid special attention when Harry invited him to play. Harry was the only soul left in our room who even tried to be civil to the old guy.

He pushed the chess board across a folding table at Haverford, offering him whites. Harry liked playing blacks, even though it meant going second. Said he wanted Asoka on his side.

"What the bloody hell is this?" Haverford grumbled, holding up the white queen.

"She's Johnny's idea," he said, winking at me. "Anne Boleyn, head tucked underneath her arm. She walks the Bloody Tower."

"Lovely touch," Haverford said. The queen appeared to cheer him up a bit. He looked her over, chuckled, then picked up his king. "And this of course is dear Henry himself. A chap who knew how to treat his women."

"Care to move, Montgomery?"

"Game gives me the jitters."

"Oh no," Harry said in his low soothing voice. "Every piece has a special place, its own little mission in life. So ordered, so comforting."

"Too damned black and white."

"But you've got white, old boy. That's life, that's good. I thought you'd want the whites. It's black that's death and disorder."

91

"Don't be dreary," Haverford mumbled and opened up P-K3.

"Gets us away from personal dilemmas," Harry said and pushed a pawn. They sat there on school chairs with the light from a ceiling bulb blazing straight down on them. Some other guys in the room took notice and gathered to watch. They mostly liked Harry's banter. Haverford appeared to know the game OK, but his hand shook.

"Don't crowd me," he growled at the men standing over him. Harry gave him a sad look.

"I know it's not pleasant having to associate with riffraff, Montgomery. But there are worse places."

"God help me," Haverford groaned. That was when Harry leaned back in his chair and spoke out to the whole room.

"If chess can't break this spell, what about a diplomatic dilemma?" Old Haverford glanced at him, then went back to moving his bishop. "How would you all like to help me solve a problem with the Japanese?" That got a rise out of the room all right. Now everybody was looking at Harry.

"Starvation or execution?" Haverford asked, his eyes still on the board.

"I'll play at your Jap diplomacy," this old guy we called the Colonel spoke out. Harry brought his knight up, then nodded at the Colonel. And while he played chess with Haverford, he started this other game with the rest.

"Here's our puzzle: Chinwangtao, nineteen-thirty-eight," Harry said, setting up the ground rules.

"That's it? That's all you give us?" Haverford complained. "Just a place and a year?"

"Chinwangtao's a Chinese port," Mr. Fitzgibbon answered.

"Very good," Harry said.

"There's marines up there," I put in.

"Very nice, Major. Kid knows his geography. Chinese port, U.S. Marines. Anyone want to try for *thirty-eight*?"

"Has to be about Japs," the Colonel said.

"You are quick, very quick," Harry said and castled. "All right now, situation's this. Jap soldiers and our gyrenes are sharing local bars with the usual merchant men. Japanese are flexing muscles on the international stage, you'll recall, telling everyone they must have their fair share of the China pie."

"My God, Harry, by thirty-eight it had got way beyond that," Fitzgibbon muttered.

"Just setting the scene. Johnny mentioned a Marine Post. China Marines. Very tough band of men. You ought to know Chinwangtao was for R & R."

"Ah, yes, Rest and Recuperation," Fitzgibbon sighed.

"Not a very pretty town for leave," the Colonel said.

"Ports seldom are," Harry said. "It was a small post. Marines' main occupation was attacking the bars and brothels at night. A few got together with some Jap officers one evening, drank them under the table and swiped their samurais for souvenirs."

"Oh, that's bad," the Colonel said and everybody moaned.

"Yes," Harry said. "Poor judgment."

"You can't be serious," Haverford snorted.

"Afraid so," Harry said. "At least, so the Post CO told me. Swell young fellow. And like you, old boy, he knew his chess. Win or lose, he loved the game. Played a good deal together. It went with his belief in order. He'd joined up to put some order in the world, you see. Imagine how upset China must have made him. In fact, we were playing chess when he told me about the samurais. I expressed my concern, but he didn't seem particularly worried. He'd taken steps, he said, ordered them to return those swords immediately, along with sending his formal apologies. I warned him that might not be enough. There had been great loss of face, after all. Watch your flanks, I said."

"Samurais are family heirlooms," Fitzgibbons said.

"Lots of honor at stake," the Colonel added.

"Still, nothing seemed to happen. If anything, Chinwangtao was a bit too quiet just then. Besides, the CO had this other very annoying problem to deal with," Harry said, taking one of Haverford's pawns. "Of the venereal sort."

"He caught the clap!" Southy laughed.

"No, no, his men. Cropped up one short-arm inspection. Particularly nasty strain. Enough to worry even his Medical Officer. Just a couple of cases at first, but he'd never seen anything so virulent. And even though the treatment for it was damn painful, the men were no help at all at tracing its source. Professed complete innocence, said they had been to their usual haunts, had even used the prophylactic station. One had the gall to claim he got it off a toilet seat."

"Well, these things happen," Fitzgibbon said, shaking his head.

"But it was spreading, even with the threat of court-martial. Medical Officer talked possible epidemic, even went so far as to enlist the help of city officials in spot-checking whores. But they all came up empty. Nothing but a few innocuous rashes."

"Well, where did it come from then?" Haverford asked. This was the first real interest the old sourpuss'd showed in anything. It was a wonder Harry bothered with him.

"Drove them crazy," he said. "CO was outraged. Canceled passes into town, confined men to quarters at night. But that didn't help. Next time I saw him, his chess game had gone to hell. Morale at the post was way down and he wasn't a bit closer to a solution."

"What the bloody hell could he do?" Haverford asked.

"Any ideas?" Harry said, throwing it to the crowd.

"Give 'em all mercury shots," Fitzgibbon said.

"Send 'em back home," Southy wisecracked.

"Hell, send 'em to Manila," somebody else offered. "We could sure use 'em!" The whole room was into it now, mumbling and laughing. But just then the Monitor came by and called for lights out. Everybody cursed him for spoiling the fun, but Harry just smiled and pushed his queen two squares on a diagonal.

"I believe that's mate, old boy," he said softly. "Would you check?"

"Fine mess," Haverford moaned and knocked his king over. We all climbed into our racks and the room went black.

"C'mon, Harry," Southy whispered. "Don't make us suffer now."

"Let's hear the rest, Harry," another said.

"Anyone would have to be intrigued," Harry said finally. "Such a good puzzle. And he was a friend. Just did what was logical. Got him to go out mufti one night and take me around to all the bars. Brought a Chinese along to spot any girls who might not be regulars. At the same time the Medical Officer was covering the cathouses."

"I'd volunteer for that right now," somebody said.

"But we hit a brick wall. Every joint was dead. We seemed to be the only ones out in the whole damn town. Even the whores had stayed home."

"Now that is queer," the Colonel said. "Very queer."

"I'd been so damn sure. We hung on in town as late as we could. Met up with the Medical Officer and compared notes. But we never found a single clue."

"Hah, so bloody clever," Haverford snorted. Harry's sour luck seemed to cheer him up.

"Must admit it shook me. All we could do was head back to base, a bit tipsy and so damned disappointed. Absolutely stumped. Went along with our heads down," Harry sighed. Then he stopped a minute. When he spoke again, he sounded a whole lot brighter. "But just then, as we were weaving up the last hill to the post, past this dark thicket in the moonlight, we heard our answer."

"What?" Haverford asked. But nobody answered. "What do you mean, heard it?" Not a word. It got so hushed in the room you could hear the Monitor's footsteps going down the hall outside. Then, out of the dark came this moaning. Not some low sad groan, but something that swelled and washed over you like a wave. It started low and growly and built into a kind of wail, then a pant, like some wild beast in pain. And it was coming right out of Harry's mattress.

"Jesus!" somebody whispered. Then the Monitor shoved his head in the room.

"What the hell's going on in here?" he yelled. But nobody said a thing. It was dead quiet again. After a while he went away.

"That's what we heard," Harry said. "Came from the dark bushes along the road. Stopped us dead in our tracks. Thought it was a banshee. Even scared that Marine CO. But just for a moment. Then we both dove in and searched the bushes. Found her there lying in the moonlight, writhing on the ground."

"Good God, what did you do?" Haverford asked. It seemed maybe Harry finally had him hooked.

"Offered her money, of course. Good honest Yankee dollars and a pint of booze. How could she resist? Followed us like a puppy dog right up the hill. CO ordered the whole post to fall out. Wee small hours. Poor sods had to stand attention in their sleep. He had every damn light in the place turned on. Lit up like day. Then he marched our 'Lady of the Thicket' out for everyone to see."

"I'll bet she was a beauty," Fitzgibbons said.

"She *was* a rare creature in the naked light. Not a true paragon of cleanliness though. Obviously spent too many of her nights on bare ground. Rough as a tree trunk and not improved by age. She flashed the boys a rude smile, minus a couple of teeth. When the CO told them this was what they had been lying with while sloppy drunk, a couple of very ornery-looking guys, big machine-gunner and a mortar man, fainted dead away."

"Beats the hell out of chess!" Southy laughed.

"But don't you see," Harry said. "It *was* chess. Move and counter-move. We had opened with a couple of whiskeys and snatched some samurais. They spotted weakness in our defense and paid the queen to lie in wait. It was tit for tat, a somewhat crude but exotic form of biological warfare."

"God-awful randy," Haverford said.

"But there's a lesson," Harry said.

"Stay out of foreign ports," Fitzgibbons said.

"Foreign parts, you mean," Southy added.

"Never underestimate our opponent's perverse sense of humor," Harry said. "Isn't that so, Montgomery?"

"Spare me," Haverford sneered. "Biological warfare indeed." I think nothing less than a plague and an earthquake could've cheered that grouch.

I was busy laughing out loud with the rest. But I was feeling kind of sorry for that Chinese whore, to tell the truth, being paraded ugly and naked in front of all those men. And that's when the big quiet Norwegian called out from the back corner of the room.

"Pardon me, Mr. Barnes, but would you be so kind as to make us that moaning again."

CHAPTER 12

"Imagine them wanting *me* to teach kids a thing," Southy said. He kept smiling like he had a joke to tell, but he looked nervous too, pacing back and forth, twirling his jump rope and flicking it at the grass.

"You teach me," I said. "You teach me plenty."

"They got two birds to kill, I figure. And they need one dumb stone to take care of it for 'em."

"Oh, you'll be perfect," Harry said. "Natural Pied Piper."

"Bird one, they want Southy the hell out of their Gym. Too many old guys gripin' about the noise."

"Who says?" I said. "Those guys don't count."

"Bird two, they got these young scalawags loose in Camp and need them babysat." And he nodded at me.

"Just work the bag," Harry said. "Give them a drum roll. Little rats'll follow you anywhere."

"I told 'em I'm allergic to kids."

"You'll do a lovely job," Mom said. "In a city of amateurs, you're the only pro we've got."

"Don't you know better than to con a pro?" Southy said.

"You're gonna do it then?" I asked.

"Damn it, kid," he said. "I was born a sap. My old lady always told me so."

And that's how Southy came to take us on. Funny how things turned out. Maybe it *was* two birds, one stone, just like he was saying. I'm just not sure which birds they were. Sure, the old timers were whining, but that was business as usual. On the other hand, the Internee Committee would've been dunces to miss out. You can bet they'd be taking full credit for Southy. Like Harry said, wouldn't every parent just love having a real ringman teach their little man the manly art? And what better way to keep all us hooligans in tow? See how smart it made them look?

Southy had kids mesmerized. All he had to do was start that rope and they gathered in a ring. He did a crossover, and their mouths gaped. He stepped through hoops and they blinked and shook their heads. What Southy had every tough kid wanted bad. Why, it looked to be magic!

Even the Japs bought into it. Maybe it went with that *bushido* stuff they loved to strut. Certain sentries'd been watching right along, on the sly. I saw them. I bet they figured him for magic too. Anyway, they let a detail of our men pick up boxing gloves and a heavy bag from the Manila YMCA. And the Carpentry Detail fashioned Southy a big adjustable stand for the speed bag, so he could work with us out there under the trees. Southy still looked just as good on the bag in the dappled light, but I missed that mighty echo off Gym walls.

A lot of the stuff Southy taught I already knew, so he made me his little demonstration model for a time. And that was a kind of curse with bigger guys. See, Southy was teaching kids from little six-year-olds clear up to lugs nineteen or so. He said, "Let's give 'em a hook, Johnny." So I'd snap one off. "Now let's show 'em how to double up on the jab." It sure felt embarrassing shadow boxing out there in front of guys old enough to be called men. Imagine them looking at this squirt dancing around, flicking punches. "If this kid can box this smooth," Southy told them, "just think what you big fellas can learn to do." And I could feel my ears getting red.

Well, you know there had to be one tough kid named Feeney, eighteen or so, standing with his arms crossed and a little smirk dancing across his face, thinking who is this Southy anyhow that looks small enough to be a kid himself. Course Southy'd seen that look before, so he waved poor Feeney into the ring of kids, had him put on the gloves, and told him to come at him serious to see what damage he could do. "Don't hold back now," Southy said. He looked at me and I had to grin. This sort of thing was always fun to watch.

Nobody who'd ever wandered even two steps into a gym would fall for it. But Feeney bit. And Southy had his partner for the dance. He was a trickster putting on another magic show for kids. Textbook lessons on how you shift and balance and move on the balls of your feet. How you slip some punches and pick off others. How you bob and weave in and out. And how, if you're real good and the other's bad, you can do it all without ever getting hit once. Southy could do it without even breaking a sweat. Till poor Feeney was left out there winded and panting and blushing with shame. Then Southy went over real gentle, reaching a hand up onto his shoulder and whispering soft and husky like a lover in his ear, "You got spunk, kid. You'll do fine." Like a jockey talking to his horse after a quick spin around the track.

But Southy could play a sweet mom to the kids too. Like when some little fella who never even got spanked before got hit hard the first time on the nose and was stunned maybe as much as hurt. Southy squatted there, rubbed the spot a little, and talked soft and calm until he'd dried up that kid's every tear.

Only I don't think he reckoned the next one right. This other kid, about my age, had been watching while the rest of us shadow boxed in a kind of chorus line. Maybe we were a sight. But he just stood there with his hands on his hips while we groaned and sweat. Just a skinny kid, with a scraggly mop and a gap-toothed grin. Swarthy. Then all of a sudden he started laughing. Pretty near hysterical. I was thinking, damn, this kid's got his nerve!

I'd seen him before. He'd come in late to Camp and was living with some old guy down at the Gym. He'd been there watching when Southy worked the bag.

"He's mestizo," Pete told me. But there were damn few of them in Camp.

"You sure?" I said. "Japs don't let Filipinos in here. You got to be American or European to get to be a prisoner in our Camp."

"His old man's American, that's why," Red said. "My dad said he's a *squaw man*."

"Sounds like somethin' out of the old West," Jerry said. She looked skeptical.

"That's what he called him all right," Red said, scratching his belly. Well, the phrase made me prick up my ears. Specially since my old man was part Indian. So I brought it up to Mom.

"You ever heard of a squaw man?" I asked her. She looked right up from what she was doing.

"What a filthy phrase. Who said it?"

"Just heard it someplace," I muttered, a bit ashamed. But the phrase came to mind when I saw him standing there laughing like *we* were the freaks. And that's when Southy saw him too.

"*Mabuhay*," Southy greeted him, which was queer. It's the word Filipinos use to welcome special folks, and this kid was a long ways from that. Maybe that was why Southy had that smile on his face. The mestizo kind of grunted back, then spit in the dust. "Want to join us?" Southy asked. The kid didn't exactly answer, but made a funny little shrug, what folks called *bahalana*. It was about as Filipino a move as squatting on the ground. Meant something between "whatever" and "who cares." Southy took it for a "yes" and asked, "You ever box before?"

"I fight," the kid said, real tough.

"Oh, I'll bet," Southy said. "But can you box?" So the kid gave him another one of those bahalana shrugs. And that's when Southy got his bright idea. "OK, here are some gloves. You can box Johnny."

I was pretty proud of my right, that's a fact. With the big gloves I could hold my own against all the kids my size. Dad and Southy had me sparring at the gym long before the war. I had nothing against a little match. But I sure wasn't expecting what the mestizo offered.

He stood waiting for me with both arms poised down at his side and mayhem darkening his face. As soon as I set up to move in, he started dancing back and forth like he was looking for an opening to shove a knife in my ribs. He had no thought of putting his mitts up, either. His head was tilted forward and real hate lurked there under his eyebrows. He sure wasn't taking this as sport.

The first time he lunged at me, I was lucky enough to turn with him and shove my right hand up hard into his face, but the way he did it kind of unnerved me. It was a lot more mad-dog-get-you-by-the-throat than friendly sparring match. So I squared off again, steady-as-she-goes, and moved in more careful, landing a nice quick jab just as he started sliding off to the side. Then I followed with a combination to his head and body. That felt better. I was starting to settle into some kind of comfort zone.

But all of a sudden he slid off again to the side, and before I could turn to meet him, he rushed in low at me, head down, butting me up under the ribs. I was flat on my back in the dust, the wind knocked right out of me, feeling him pound me with both gloves at once. He was yelling something vicious, and I could hear kids laughing too. But just as quick I felt him lifted off and saw Southy over me holding onto him by the seat of the pants and the scruff of the neck, the kid still dancing full throttle in the air.

Southy was laughing too. He couldn't help it, I guess. But I was burned up and ashamed at once, still gasping for air and chewing dirt. "*No puedes! No puedes!*" Southy was shouting. "No can do!" But the kid just kept thrashing away. It took some time before he'd danced himself out and Southy could put him back on the ground.

The mestizo looked sour. Southy kept hold of the back of his neck and looked right in his eyes. "Only glove, kid. Just punch." He held his fist up in the kid's face. It was a big fist, specially close-up. Southy talked Pidgin English at him, spelling it out real clear. "No kick! No bite! No butt with head!" He did a little pantomime after each one.

"You still with us?" And that's when the mestizo looked up at Southy and gave him his big smile.

"Sure, Southy, I got ya!" He drawled it, like in a Western. Well, you should've seen us, a bunch of open mouths all in a row. The damn kid spoke English as natural as anybody out there. And all his hate had passed like a cloud.

So Southy dragged me out there again to demonstrate, showing the mestizo how to put up his dukes to guard, how to position his feet for balance. But now I was the one who was looking for vengeance. I wanted at that kid again. I couldn't wait for Southy to quit. As soon as we were set, I was firing, throwing shots to his midsection, hooks to his head, you name it. But the kid was just loving it. I gave him my best combinations and he just blinked and smiled and came back for more. I even bloodied his nose. But finally I got too arm-weary, I had to clinch. Damn! You just can't hate a kid like that. You've got to give him a hug. We stood there clinching and panting away, him dripping little drops of blood on my shoulder.

Then Southy hugged us both and yelled, "OK, OK!" I do believe right there me and the mestizo became blood brothers. Later we did the jackknife thing, mingling our blood and looking at it, but I hold you're never closer to any living soul than when you're flailing away at him with everything you've got.

Funny thing is all the other kids kind of ignored me, going right over to the mestizo instead, patting *him* on the back like *he*'d won, and saying, "Swell job, kid," and, "You got heart," and all that sort of thing. They accepted him right into the bosom of our boxing family. And I got absolutely nothing out of being subjected to all that abuse, save delivering his initiation rites.

The kid just naturally loved boxing and threw himself right into it. Everything Southy asked he did double-time. Took to it like a carabao to the wallow. And there was no doubt in his mind Southy was boss. If Southy said, "Skip rope," the mestizo had three revolutions done before the rest of us had even got ours off the ground. He was a devotee. He'd pummel the heavy bag so hard so long, I knew his arms had to be throbbing. He ran extra laps. Sometimes I even caught him off by himself, walking across the Camp, still throwing combinations.

The next afternoon Southy was trying to hang the heavy bag from a big acacia tree. He asked for somebody to climb the tree so he could throw a rope up. Well, before he'd even finished saying it, the mestizo'd scampered up there like a Zamboanga monkey and stood on the branch smiling down at us like Robin Hood.

"Toss it up here, my good fellow," he yelled down real English, puffing out his chest and giving a hearty laugh. He did the Errol Flynn pretty good too. He didn't appear to give two hoots for heights. He just snagged the rope in his hand first try, wrapped it around a branch and came swinging down like one of the merry men.

That's when Southy named him, "Polecat." And it fit so natural, it stuck. There was never really any other. In fact, it was a long time before I ever heard his real name. We all used Polecat from the start and the mestizo loved it. Probably figured like the rest of us that it came from how he'd scampered up the tree. He could shinny up anything in sight, with or without branches. But I should've known enough about Southy to figure there had to be more of a smile to it.

Southy used that very word again later, when we were talking about the old guys who bunked in the Gym near where he worked the light bag.

"Those old guys reeked," Southy was saying. "All around their bunks it smelled. And I mean strong, like a polecat."

"You mean, stunk like a skunk," Harry said. And click! I got the picture. Like a little scene from a movie show reeling through my head.

"Oh, *that* polecat!" I said. Southy looked at me and smiled. He saw that I saw. Something he'd picked out of the air when he first spotted the mestizo. He divined that if *any*body ever threatened this kid, he'd all at once drop down on all fours, stick his little rear end in the air and spray *every*body with a secret killer perfume. You know that had us all laughing.

Southy called it the "Polecat Attitude." And he was dead-on. I can vouch for it. Something that happened a couple of weeks later showed just how it worked. We were playing marbles with Neddy Nickerson behind the Jap Kitchen. More likely, Neddy was giving us another lesson in eating humble pie. Polecat spotted us there and sauntered over, like there was nothing better to do.

"*Mabuhay*," Finch greeted him. He'd heard the boxing story and was likely looking to curry favor. Polecat just grunted but stuck around to watch. Neddy was so deep into the tiger hunt by then, he never noticed the mestizo until he'd finished. It wasn't too good a round for Neddy. He'd only picked up maybe three Clayees. But Polecat went right over to him, real courteous and Filipino, like he was meeting the master.

"I have heard you are champion," Polecat said. Neddy cocked his head and gave him one of those be-polite grins. "Could you teach me how to play?"

"Well, yes," Neddy said. "But have you ever played any sort of marbles before?" I got the feeling Neddy was surprised Polecat could even speak his lingo.

"I have played only with small stones," Polecat said. "Only with Pilipino boys in the barrio." He did it so slick, I wouldn't have known myself if I hadn't just witnessed his Errol Flynn a few days before.

"Oh, yes. Well, I'm sure you could learn. It's quite simple really."

"Yes," Polecat said. "Perhaps I learn from you." So while the rest of us took turns shooting, Neddy explained the basics of Stony-Wop to the poor savage. And when Neddy's turn came up, he went true to form.

"Could we allow this chap a turn in here?" he asked.

"Sure, Polecat can go," Finch said.

"You got marbles?" Red asked.

"Yes, Finch showed me where to find them," Polecat answered. Red gave poor Finchy a hateful look, scratching fierce under his nose.

"Well, then," Neddy said. "You can try your luck right now." Polecat put a cracked Clayee on the ground at the bottom of the cross and stepped outside the circle.

"Is OK from here?" he asked.

"Fine," Neddy answered, ever so patient. Polecat studied the marbles in the ring, chewed his tongue and reached deep in the pockets of his dirty shorts. He brought out a closed fist, spit on it and shook it next to his ear like he was shooting craps. I heard the marbles clicking away like dice in there. Then, real quick, he dropped one into his other hand and put the rest back in his pocket. When he knuckled down, I could just make out the marble gleaming small and silver under his thumb. Then it flashed straight across the circle and hit Neddy's Tiger Shooter with a crack. That orange, yellow and black beauty split right in two.

"Jees!" Finch whispered. For a minute nobody else said a thing. It was just too sudden. Polecat let out one hard laugh. Neddy'd gone pale around the mouth and eyes. Then that queer smile flicked across his lips. "Jees!" Finch said again. "What you got?" Polecat picked up his marble and held it in his open palm. It was small and bright silver.

"You guys got Clayees, he's got Glassees. So I got Steelies."

"Steelies," we echoed.

"But where'd you get 'em?" Finch asked.

"Where you told me." He waved his arm toward where the Dump once was.

"It's a ball-bearing," Neddy said.

"A steel ball-bearing, chap," Polecat said with this real English accent. "From the wheel of a motorcar." Then he bowed. When he came up, he had his big grin. Neddy tried to smile too, but he had to look away. He walked over, picked up his other two Glassees and held them out to Polecat in his open hand.

"Here you are. I shouldn't want you to have to break these too." Then he walked off. He never played with us again.

But from then on, we had to play with Steelies if we wanted to survive. The currency'd changed. Polecat never used the Glassees. He kept them in his pocket, even the split Tiger. He liked the way they clicked when he walked.

CHAPTER 13

Harry carried a little book in his back pocket, written by a Frenchman. Me and Polecat caught him reading it now and again and asked him what it was about. He told us it was an old book, one of those stories with a lesson to it, about this Candide guy who wandered all around the globe, getting beat up by every kind of brute from every race known to man. It was pretty exciting stuff, but all the while this Frenchy kept theorizing and philosophizing on the true meaning of life and finally discovered it by staying home and minding his P's and Q's. "Cultivate your garden," the book said.

"That's the lesson? Farming?" Polecat said. "Sounds *very* boring."

I had to agree. Why is it this kind of story is a whole lot more fun when everybody's running around having high adventures than when they settle down to the happily-ever-after part? If gardening's so great, why do they throw in all that stuff about kidnaps and rape and castration and naked girls getting bit on the ass by monkeys? Well, Harry did have us entertained for a while, so I asked him about this dull ending, and he said we had to try the cultivating business for ourselves to find out. Well, you see what he'd done. He'd suckered us into a work detail. Then, seeing Polecat wasn't buying the whole program, Harry added a bunch of stuff about how boxers like us have to get themselves strong on manual labor. Chopping wood, digging holes and such.

First he volunteered us for the gang that was putting in a banana grove by the Gym. He must've figured it was easier to start kids planting trees than pulling weeds in a vegetable patch. It was tough duty – cutting cogon grass, digging, hoeing and hauling those big buckets of water. By the time we got through, our crew must've laid in more than seven hundred banana shoots. And with what they were feeding us, our energy faded fast. The work did toughen us, true enough, but it appeared Harry overplayed his hand by keeping on too long about how our boxer muscles were growing.

"This not real work for Pilipino," Polecat said, laying on the accent. "This for fun only." He puffed out his chest like he'd been laboring his whole life.

"When was the last time you worked a rice patty?" Harry asked. Polecat stared right back at him a moment.

"Oh, no," he answered with his poker face. "I been cutting sugarcane with my bolo." Harry loved Polecat just for having the brass to pass off such a bald-faced lie. After that he called him "Bolo Man." And when we finally finished our planting, Harry surveyed our grove and heaved a sigh of satisfaction.

"One of these days, boys, we'll sit here under our trees, sharing a ripe banana," Harry said. "And won't it make us proud."

"Yeah, it's not just any old grove," I boasted. "It's ours." Well, maybe it didn't turn out quite like we'd imagined, but the trees did grow and bear some small fruit by and by. Later on me and Polecat'd lie there in the tall grass, watching the lazy banana fronds wave against the sky. But others didn't treat our claims of ownership with much respect. In fact, they swiped the fruit right off the trees before it ever got a chance to ripen. And all kinds of couples kept sneaking down there in the evening to search out places to be private. Of course, we followed them in, low to the ground, and sometimes surprised them in the shadows, wrestling in the weeds.

But it was the Camp Garden that took up most of our time. The really hard work'd already been done by Harry and the others. That's where the Dump'd been, you see – tons of junk piled up over the years, covered with tall, rank weeds. Before anybody could even stick a spade in the ground, they had to drag all that heavy refuse out and pile it nice and neat around the sides, like a stone wall. The great big rusted car chassis and broken axles were tough as tree trunks to pull out of the ground.

Now it was our turn to pitch in and work the ground. And I must admit it made me feel pretty grown-up. This garden was a strange affair, because we were nursing plants anybody would've chucked as weeds in fatter years. Early on they'd tried growing tomatoes, corn and eggplants, but those civilized plants rotted out in rainy season and shriveled up in dry. It took a weed to survive.

These lower-class vegetables had funny names too. *Camotes* were ugly little yams. They grew fine, but we rarely got much chance to eat the underground part. Folks were too eager to trim off the tops for greens. When you're real hungry, it's tough to be patient, and you can cook up camote greens to taste almost passable.

Of course, we liked the taste of spinach better, but had to make do with a poor relation called *talinum*. It sprang up faster and lived longer. Then there was a leafy tropical thing called *kangkong*. It thrived in rainy season and loved swampy places. Southy told us kangkong contained muscle-building minerals, so even though it tasted strong and bitter, we worked hard to get it down for the sake of our strength and our long-standing love for Popeye the Sailorman.

"Say, mate, what's that you're masticatin'?" I asked Polecat.

"King Kong," he mumbled through a mouthful, green pulp covering his teeth. He flexed a muscle in his arm. "Iron," he said. Jerry was sitting with us, mainly because she liked hanging around Polecat. She jumped right in.

"Puts fillings in your teeth," she drawled.

"Tin on your roof."

"Copper in your pipes."

"Lead in your pencil." And we rolled around laughing at ourselves. But no matter how hard we tried, kangkong was hard to get down.

A real engineer'd planned out this Camp Garden. It was a piece of art, with all kinds of special drainage added and water pipe laid for irrigation. Since they'd dragged so much junk out of the ground, the beds were sunk way down and you had to walk above them on earth pathways, like being on a dike.

"You pull this, you keep that," some old guy told us in a big gruff voice. Then he left us on our own. All the rest was dumb numb staying power. We went along hoeing and raking and weeding on our hands and knees through two or three hours of tropic sun a day. In the hot season, we baked out there. After a while we got dizzy in the head and saw little black spots. A couple of guys kept fainting. We started dreaming of just sitting down for a minute in the shade. We couldn't wait to throw down big gulps of water out of tin cups, then slosh the rest over our heads and feel it run cool down our backs. Anything to break the boredom and the heat.

Then in rainy season, we slopped around in muck up to our calves, hoping at least the kangkong and talinum'd survive. We talked nonsense and sang silly songs. Polecat taught me the "Rice Song." According to him, it was the Philippine National Anthem. "Planting rice is no fun, bent from dawn to set of sun," he sang. We pulled this duty after school, day after day for a few months, until Harry turned around one day and Polecat'd disappeared.

"Where's Bolo Man?" he asked.

"He gave it up," I said. "Told me it was sapping his spirit."

"You mean for good?"

"Said he wasn't born to scratch ground."

"What about cultivating your garden?"

"Said you could keep Candide too."

"Well, there you have it," Harry said. His face was red, but he wasn't mad, just trying not to laugh. "I guess Bolo Man doesn't want to travel down the tedious road to civilization."

Harry did try to coax Polecat back, but the mestizo flat refused to involve himself in any more domesticating labor. That was, until it came time for our *greatest* work – the building of our nipa shanty.

All along folks had been setting up little shelters for themselves, mostly collapsible affairs like Southy's lean-to. A few did try to get ambitious, but the Japs'd frowned on anything that looked too permanent. Every once in a while they even ordered everything taken down just to make sure. And they had a strict rule against covering the sides, because they were afraid of hanky-panky going on inside.

Hanky-panky in the shanties caused a furor when the Commandant first learned of some unauthorized pregnancies. He got livid and threw the fathers-to-be in the Camp hoosegow. No excuse for pregnancy, he said. After all, he'd laid down the law: "No makee baby." But as Harry said, if you have even one tree wide enough for two people to go behind, there'll likely be three coming out the other side.

Then we caught a break. With people streaming in from all parts of the Islands, our Camp population'd grown too fast. So the Commandant had to come up with an alternate housing plan. Main Building, Gym, Education Building, Annex had all swelled to bursting. It got just too tight to breathe in there. That's what forced the Jap's hand. He finally had to change his rules and let families build shanties and live together in them full-time.

Before the words were even out of his mouth, the Internee Committee'd drawn up a map and was parceling out lots on a first-come-first-serve basis. It was like the Gold Rush in Santo Tomás, everybody staking claims. Red's folks began setting up in a barrio named Froggy Bottom, Harvey's over in Toonerville, Finch's down in Jungletown, Pete and Jerry's back of the Seminary in Shantytown and Knocker's in a place called Jerkville.

Since Southy's lean-to had always been in the same spot, we got squatter's rights on prime real estate, right at the edge of the big field, where two footpaths met in front of Glamourville. Everybody said we were sitting at the crossroads. "Ringside," Southy corrected. Him and Harry and Mom pooled resources and made plans for a homestead. I don't know exactly how they handled the finances, because they never asked me in, but it had to do with some kind of credit against jobs folks had before the war and their prospects for after the war. Southy sketched a quick blueprint to work from, since he'd done such things for the mining company. Then Mom put in a few little touches of her own, like where we'd sleep, where we'd cook and where we'd sit. It wasn't too complicated, to tell the truth. One room, four walls.

The second break we caught was starting our shanty late. By the time we'd ordered building supplies from outside and put up the bamboo frame, lots of people had already finished their huts and were living in them. And that's when the big Typhoon of '43 hit, reaping havoc and flooding all Manila. What a mighty blow! Knocked out the electricity, fouled the water supply and tore up a whole bunch of brand-new shanties, some with folks still inside. Boy, did it rain! Turned the whole Camp into a swimming pool. Six feet of water sat on top of our Camp Garden and that was too much even for the kangkong. The water was a muddy yellow mixed with sewage that'd backed up out of the pipes. It slimed the first floors of the Main Building and the Education Building, distressed folks down in the Gym and stranded whole families out in the shanties. Men built bamboo rafts and went poling around camp rescuing people from a certain death by drowning.

But me and Polecat had a fine time wading out through deep waters in our shorts, clear across the Plaza and the big field to where the skeleton of our shanty stood. We pushed inside and hung onto the center post, water lapping up against our ribs.

"How do you like our new home?" I asked him.

"*Bahay kubo*," he said.

"Yeah, what's that?"

"Beautiful nipa shanty. You live like Pilipino."

"We'll all live together in an old grass shack," I told him. While we were there talking, I recalled the Chinese guys Harry saw cutting hair in the Tientsin flood. And I meditated a moment on having the world run through me like blood and water. But these particular flood waters had a real ugly look and nasty stench to them, so I gave it up as a bad idea. Good thing, too. As it was, my legs and stomach broke out in boils and open sores that took their sweet time healing. I guess maybe Chinese are just better at standing floods than us Americans.

Over two feet of rain fell in a single month, so we got real used to wading. But as soon as the waters ran off, we were back to work on our shanty with a vengeance. Harry and Southy put in the bamboo floor. Me and Mom tacked up sawali siding and hung nipa shutters. Made so you could prop them wide open for the Japs to see in or shut them down tight to keep a rainstorm out. Polecat tied nipa palm shingles to the roof frame, then swung up to the peak and sat there on the bamboo beam, hauling up the roof, lashing it down tight and whistling at the girls passing by. He called out to them in Tagalog like a street peddler.

Stuff like, "*Magandá dalága!*" and "*Ini-íbig kitá!*" Sometimes they turned around and looked up with silly smiles on their faces. Hardly anybody knew what he was saying, so it was OK till the Methodist missionary's wife came by. Old lady Albright. She'd been big and chesty and always singing contralto in the choir, but had slimmed down in recent months and lost her look of importance.

"Do you know what that boy's yelling at the girls?" she asked my mom with her righteous tone.

"He's just having some fun," Mom said, smiling polite and friendly.

"Lord! Shouting,'Beautiful girl!' and 'I love you so!' Making those dirty clicking noises. Who knows how far this sort of thing will go?" she said. And when Polecat heard her, he let out another loud whistle and rattled off some more Tagalog, all the while swinging from place to place and lashing shingles.

"Poor boy doesn't know better," Harry says. "Can't you see he's got prehensile feet."

"Grew up with headhunters," Southy went on with a forlorn look. "Stolen away from his Christian parents before he'd been baptized." Polecat almost fell off, he was so busy laughing to himself up there.

"Had to play with human bones for toys when he was in knee pants. Only, of course, he never wore pants," Harry picked up. Mrs. Albright got a sour look on her face and left in a huff.

Before we knew it our shanty was standing there finished, and it was a true thing of beauty. It wasn't too big, but it looked pretty much like heaven. A shanty breathes! The breeze off the bay flowed through it and sunlight dappled the floor. You could smell the bamboo and nipa palm mingling with the earth below and leaves above.

It stood on stilts a couple of feet off the ground, wrapped in the shade of a big acacia tree. As a matter of fact, after Southy saw what happened in the flood, he designed this shanty so it was anchored to the tree. One big limb climbed right up through the roof, and the frame was lashed to it, so it wouldn't ever float away. You could sit at the front and look out across the great field to the Main Plaza where we stood roll call in the morning. And above the Plaza, on the Main Building, the big clock boomed the quarter hour. You could stand on the back porch and look down on a little muddy stream, and then up the rise on the other side where the shanties crowded in one on another clear back to the outer wall. Mom spun herself around in the middle of the shanty like the teen queen, her arms stretched out to the whole world.

"My lovely men," she said. "My lovely, lovely men. Thank you for this lovely home." And she got all teary-eyed and smiley at the same time. Then she gave everybody a big hug and a kiss. And even though Harry and Southy still slept in the Main Building at night, it was their shanty too, and they came and spent as much time as they wanted. Meals, siestas or just talk.

It was right before Christmas of our second year, and Christmas that year turned out special. The Japs opened up the Package Line for that one day. We couldn't see our friends at the Front Gate because of the sawali fence, but the Japs did let them leave things. Some two or three thousand Filipinos came by and shouted "Happy Christmas" in the street. Gregorio and Timotea brought us a little fried chicken. That was the first true meat we'd seen in a month. And Harry's friend Virgin left a basket of *calamansi* limes.

At dusk on Christmas Eve, Southy took me up the path to a tall hibiscus hedge and we picked an armful of unopened buds. He set up a stand with a bamboo pole about two feet high and drilled holes for thin bamboo sticks all around it – like branches on a tree – longer at the bottom and short towards the top. And on the end of each one we stuck a hibiscus bud. Then in the morning when the sun came out, all the blossoms opened into a beautiful, flaming red Christmas tree.

We ate fried chicken with rice and okra from the kitchen, and we drank calamansi juice cocktails. You might've thought there was liquor present, we got so silly. When Mom asked Harry if he could go twelve days of Christmas on calamansi, he said he doubted he'd get past one without the gin.

Southy donated the clay stove from his lean-to so Mom could cook a *bibingka* rice cake on the charcoal fire. Everybody swapped stuff and bargained things off just so we could get enough rice flour and sugar and coconut milk. Somebody even came up with a duck egg. Mom said to excuse her because her bibingka lacked cheese and proper shortening. But the way her cake cooked up, wrapped in its own banana leaf and giving off rich smoky aromas all over the shanty, no one was complaining. We knew we were getting the best bibingka ever served.

Harry divided it up real slow and careful into five equal pieces. Mom said the prayer. Then we waited. It seemed an eternity before Mom put the first small bite in her mouth. Until then we just stared at the bibingka, sitting so lovely on its banana leaf. It was hard to explain how it tasted. Smooth and sweet and burnt like caramel, but solid like cake at the same time. The banana leaf gave it a special flavor. Once we got started it was all Mom could do to save a piece for Polecat. He came by late, after spending Christmas with his old man.

Then we all held up a glass of calamansi and Harry toasted my dad. Everybody wished him health and safety and a real long life. Southy came right out and said, "We love you, Ben, you son of a bitch." Like Dad was right there with us. And Harry said it was a good thing we didn't have booze, because we'd just get low and sentimental and that was an unclean thing.

But after they all left and we went to bed, Mom in her cot on one side of the shanty and me on my cot at the back, I got real low and sentimental anyhow. I couldn't help it. The moon was out, and from where I lay I could look out under the eaves at the stars and the silver light edging the small acacia leaves. I kept thinking about my dad and missing him so much it hurt, till all at once I heard far-off voices singing over towards the Camp wall.

I couldn't make out words, but I knew it was Christmas singing. Damn, it sounded like angels. And it rippled and swelled across the night towards me, until more and more voices were singing in all the shanties around us. They were doing "Adeste Fideles" in Latin, so I didn't know if they were getting all the words right, but it was so spooky and beautiful in the dark, like ghosts or something. And that was how I drifted off to sleep.

Only right away I was awake again. I heard somebody crying. The moon was gone, and in the dark it took me a minute just to figure out where I was. Then I got up and went to Mom's cot. She was lying there with her eyes open. I could see the tears shining in the dark.

"Why did the son of a bitch have to leave us, anyway?" she said. "Why didn't he stay?" Well, what could I say? I just knelt there, wiping away her tears and smoothing back her hair. I heard something drop on the floor next to me, and I felt around for it. It was this small comb Dad bought her once up in Baguio. Carved simple and smooth out of ebony. Dad liked simple best. He asked her to wear it so it pulled the hair up off the side of her face and neck. The comb felt cool in my hand. I gave it back to her and she rubbed it against her cheek. "You son of a bitch," she whispered soft to him, so it sounded like a blessing, full of love.

CHAPTER 14

Some things happen and don't even seem that important. When they're going on you can't see them that clear, but later when you look back, they all line up like soldiers on parade. That's how it was with Yoshie's softball game. If we could've seen it clear up front, maybe we could've played it different.

Even the way the game came about got to be a joke in Camp. Yoshie was the new commandant. He introduced himself at roll call in English, said he was a student of America and came on strong about how the Japanese and the prisoners had to work together in harmony. Easy for him to say! After the speech, Yoshie had this meeting with the Internee Committee and kept on with the harmony stuff. So some smart guy answered up, "Sure, you play ball with us, we'll play ball with you."

That was the phrase that set the stage. Turned out Yoshie was a big sports fan too and he jumped at the idea. "Smart idea. American baseball is very good game!" he said. He most likely didn't know first from third, just needed to show every Jap in his ranks he had the inside scoop on the enemy. So quicker'n you could say Hirohito, he'd elected himself captain, manager and pitcher of the Jap team and peopled the field with Jap soldiers. Lucky they had the sense to make it *soft*ball, at least. Somebody could've got hurt.

The Committee wasn't out to make waves, that's for sure. The team they picked was made up mostly of business bigwigs, more diplomats than ballplayers. Soon as Yoshie started pitching the softball overhand, everybody could tell there might just be a problem. They decided to loan him a Yank catcher quick enough to corral the wild pitches. Then they set about making sure they wouldn't lose Yoshie any face. The rule on the American team was, "Strike out if you can, but don't ever hit it too hard or run too fast." Even so, it was tough for the American team to lose. Most of the Japs probably never saw a ball or bat before. Whenever one of them made an error, Yoshie took it personal, like it was a big black mark against the Empire. He barked like crazy in Japanese and threw the ball at that poor soldier as hard as he could.

Yoshie was no spring chicken, so between innings he spread himself on the grass right at the edge of heat prostration, pulled off his boots, wiggled his bare toes and fanned himself with his baseball mitt. They played seven innings, and everybody was nervous about the outcome except Polecat, who couldn't understand why our team was laying down for a bunch of Japs. Me and Polecat sat right on the third base line and he kept crying foul at the top of his lungs. And the one he was yelling at loudest was Southy.

How Southy got to play in Yoshie's game was a mystery to me. He was no business bigwig and he sure didn't qualify for diplomat. Maybe they figured since he'd been teaching kids boxing that at least he was patient. Fact was, Southy was chafing at the bit out there. He was playing shortstop and you could tell he was mad every time he pegged the ball to first. Just about tore old Haverford's glove off.

Harry was there too, but refused to play on the grounds he might upset the social order. His mission was adding some colorful commentary from the sidelines – about this player's fleet-footedness and that one's strength of arm. And he got on Southy every time he came up to bat. "Don't hit it quite so hard this time, old man," he said, even though the last time Southy'd bunted. So Southy had Polecat yelling, "Hit it! Hit it!" and Harry egging, "Not too hard now!" And every time Southy took a soft at bat, you know he must've felt like a traitor to every poor soldier who'd fought on Bataan.

By the time Southy got up in the top of the seventh, the game was tied 3 all, even though the Japs had only got one ball out of the infield. Haverford, who batted in front of Southy, made a terrible mistake and got to first. And even though the Japs were having a hell of a time fielding the ball he'd chopped into the high grass, he looked too nervous to try for second, like his feet were glued to first base and nothing could separate him.

Yoshie was looking fatigued by now. His face'd turned red and his shirt had big dark blotches around the armpits. His pitches kept wandering so far off the plate, the ump was having a terrible job claiming them for strikes. Southy got up lefty, of course, so he was looking right down the third base line at us. And Polecat and Harry gave him no peace.

"Hit it, Southy, hit it!" Polecat hollered.

"Not too hard!" Harry laughed.

Well, what could he do? Maybe he was small, maybe he was starved, but he wasn't that weak. He was still solid as a rock and a damn good athlete. He just *had* to give that ball a ride. Swung from the heels. Went for the fences. I think if the ball hadn't clipped the treetops, it might be going still. It was something just seeing Yoshie corkskrew around to watch it disappear. Jap was impressed!

They never found the ball. And there was nothing Haverford could do but head for home, even though he looked sick about it. If Southy'd tripled, old Mongomery probably could've slowed it down to a double, but this way he just had no choice but to score. Walked home with a scowl on his face.

"Traitor!" Haverford muttered when Southy crossed the plate.

The Committee tried to forfeit, claiming Southy'd lost the ball, but Harry was in charge of equipment, so he rolled out another. And as hard as everybody tried to get in more runs for the Japs, the Imperial Army came up short and lost, 5 to 3. Southy didn't win any bigwig friends that day. Instead of a hero, he ended up the goat. Just me and Polecat were jumping up and down, telling him how great he was.

"God damn Southy Jack! God damn Baby Ruth!" Polecat yelled, but Southy's teammates scowled at him. And it just naturally turned his stomach.

That all sounds friendly enough, doesn't it? But here was the problem. During this same period of brotherly love and cooperation, Jap Military Police'd come into Camp, crashed the shanties and hauled off some of the occupants for interrogation. They gave three poor guys an awful beating. Rubber hose routine, I heard. One of them was a nice guy named Ryan who was a close friend of Southy's. He got worked over so bad he had to spend three weeks in the hospital before he was strong enough to start his jail time. They said his kidneys were bleeding and his face'd been rearranged. We never saw the others until after their three month sentence was done. By then they'd healed up and just looked gaunt and pale. None of them'd talk about it. The crime the Japs accused them of was smuggling. They claimed all three'd confessed to holding illegal cartons of cigarettes. I imagine most folks *would* confess, given the Jap powers of persuasion. And that was the only evidence Japs needed.

Jap inspections were no big surprise. They always came busting in and hunting through our belongings for hidden radios, enemy pamphlets or some such thing. But it irked folks that some guys got so harshly treated while others always got off scot-free. Southy claimed it was favoritism at work in the hierarchy.

The Committee worked hard at having internees police the Camp themselves, and for good reason. They wanted to handle things before the Jap Military Police got involved. They sure didn't want any more disasters like those executions. But it was also true some folks got special treatment. Every time something turned up against those Manila society people, friends on the Committee looked the other way. So while some were getting hauled off and beat up for a pack of cigarettes, others could just about always get their hands on a bottle of booze. That's how it seemed with old man Haverford, and it really riled Southy.

"That drunk shouldn't have more rights than the rest," he growled.

"But we don't have anything on him," Harry said. "Since he left our room he's been living the quiet life in a shanty over in Cottage Park."

"Living it up amongst the bigwigs," Southy said.

"It's in a house divided, I hear," Mom said. "He and his wife don't speak. They put a sawali wall down the middle of the shanty. Montgomery on one side, ladies on the other."

"Montgomery, hell," Southy said. "I smelled the booze on his breath right in the middle of our softball game."

"That won't count with the Committee."

"Son of a bitch," Southy said. "Just cause he's got friends in high places."

"Used to get his liquor through the Package Line," Harry said. "He must have known someone on the Inspection Detail."

"Well, there's no Package Line now," Southy said.

"I know how," Polecat said. He'd been sitting silent on our shanty steps, nobody paying him any mind.

"What do you know?" Harry asked.

"After lights out, there's shadows out there."

"What shadows?"

"Between the Main Building and the shanties ... and the Commandant's Office."

"Whose?"

"Too dark to tell for sure."

"Polecat gets around," I said.

"What about Haverford?" Southy asked.

"I know his shanty, so I know his shadow."

"Where's he go?" Harry asked.

"Over by the garden to the big wall sometimes."

"Has to be," said Southy.

"The Committee should know about that," Mom said.

"Oh, yeah, they'll believe this kid over Haverford," Southy said.

"We'll talk to them," Harry suggested. "Give me a few days." But

Southy was right. The Committee didn't seem too interested in information about Haverford. Certain things got policed, certain things they just let ride. Harry got so mad he went right up to Haverford, but Haverford just got himself *terribly* offended and full of bluster. The charge was *perfectly* absurd. How *dare* anyone accuse him of such a thing?

Things kept simmering until one evening when we were strolling along a back path. It was after chow and not too long before sundown and everybody was getting more and more aggravated about the privileged few.

"Show us," Harry asked Polecat and he led us over to a stretch of wall past the garden. On the other side of this wall was Calle Governor Forbes. "There's not much traffic out on this street," Harry said. "So Japs are pretty lax along the wall here."

"What time's Haverford come out?" Southy asked.

"About one hour past lights out, maybe," Polecat said. He nodded back toward some shanties that were better made and bigger than most. "He lives back there."

"Does he always pick this same place?" Harry asked.

"Don't know," Polecat said. "I'll check."

The next day, we knew for sure something was up when Polecat showed for Garden Detail. He grabbed a hoe like he loved it and led us up along the wall to a place by some kangkong beds, right near where a detail had just put in a drainage ditch. There was a big tree that cut off the view from the shanties and the other buildings.

"If you rake right here, you'll see footprints in the morning," Polecat said.

"Sure, Jap sentries come by here," Harry said.

"Maybe Japs, but Haverford for sure." So we raked all around there like we were busy working the garden. We weeded the kangkong beds and hoed around some talinum that was just coming back after the flood. We worked the whole area over real nice. Up behind the tree and all the way to the wall.

The next morning after roll call, we got right back. Southy came too. We checked behind the tree and over by the wall. We saw clear where the Jap sentry had come by. But it was the other set of prints we were really interested in. They came up in a straight line from the tree to the wall and stopped. Then they led off again to the side and back down the path to the shanties. Right at this spot along the wall, a vine had grown up. And from the street you could've probably just seen it peeking over the top of the wall.

Me and Polecat stood in line at the Kitchen for breakfast – cracked wheat and carabao milk – and then took it back for everybody at the shanty. While we were eating, Southy busied himself sketching in a pad, making a careful drawing, like the blueprint he drew for our shanty. Then he put in straight lines with the distances measured out from the vegetable garden and the shanties and the big tree and the wall. And every one of those lines ran to the same place – where we'd just seen the footprints.

Then he started sketching ropes, knots, nooses, things like that. While he was doing it, he kept asking questions.

"Tell me, Barnes, just what's it gonna take to persuade that damn Committee?"

"Evidence. Hard. Clear. Fool-proof."

"Got to catch him with the goods," Southy said.

"Maybe we can get the Committee to go over at night," I suggested.

"Yeah," Polecat put in. "See for themselves."

"They don't want to know, boys," Harry said. "They need their noses shoved in it." It was a dilemma all right. But Harry he liked puzzles just fine and Southy he just kept sketching.

"What's that?" Polecat asked him, pointing at what looked like a rope on a stick.

"Snare," Southy said.

"How'd you learn it?" I asked.

"Your old man," Southy said.

"No kidding?"

"When we were down on Mindoro looking into gold mines," Southy said. "Native told us about a little wild water buffalo running along the forest trails."

"That's a *tamaraw*," Polecat said. "My papa told me about 'em."

"Ben bet me he could catch one alive," Southy said.

"Boy," I said. "What'd he use?"

"This one right here." Southy pointed to a drawing of a rope attached to a bent tree limb. "Hauls your prey up in the air. Worked like a charm. Cost me a month's pay."

"What about the tamaraw?" Polecat asked.

"Little bull. Mad as hell, limped a bit, but took right off soon as we set him loose."

"Afraid snares are out, boys," Harry said. "How'd you like to hang a Jap sentry by mistake?"

"Too bad Ben's not here," Mom put in. "He'd say never use a snare when a noose will do."

"Simple." Southy slapped the side of his head. "Simple's best."

It made sense you could control a noose better than a snare. But it wasn't all that simple working our trap out in the dark. We had to sneak out after curfew. Mom didn't like the idea of me going at all, but Harry and Southy swore they'd take care of me. Polecat came by after dusk and we slipped quiet along the crowded shanties in Glamourville, then across the dark road through Toonerville and into Cottage Park. Harry and Southy met us near a fork in the path. Soon as we got there, they popped out of the shadows in front of us. Nobody said anything. It'd all been planned before, right to the tee. Southy and Polecat climbed the tree with the rope. Harry grabbed me and we hid in some bushes nearby. He had a blanket under his arm.

Then we hunkered down and waited. It was real dark now. A little light from the sky in the open areas but solid black against the wall and in among the shanties. All we could hear was the soft hum of voices rising out of Cottage Park. After maybe a quarter hour, the Jap sentry came by like clockwork, heavy footsteps up along the side wall and down past the Camp Garden, then left at the corner and going away along the back wall. He passed by so close I could here the swish of his pant-legs rubbing together. Harry whispered that he was the last Jap for an hour or so.

Pretty soon somebody else came up the path behind us and headed for the tree. He was long and lanky and muttered to himself. When he got to the tree, he lingered a minute in the shadows, then walked straight to the wall. He whistled real low, three short notes, like a bird. There was this faint muffled sound – a kind of dull thunk. Then a clink, like two bottles make when they knock together. And that long and lanky shadow was reaching for a dark bundle coming down over the wall.

Harry took off just when Haverford was pulling the two bottles out of the sack. The blanket was over his head before he could cry out, the noose settled down out of the tree and over him before he could move, cinched in around his middle and yanked up tight so he was left standing up on his tiptoes. It was all done so perfect, without any more sound than someone slipping into bed.

Harry turned on his heel and headed right off to get someone from the Committee, leaving me to keep lookout for Japs. Next Southy dropped down out of the tree to take charge. There was a low moan from under the blanket. Two arms came out holding bottles, like he was offering them up.

"Shut up or I'll rap those over your head," Southy growled, and the blanket got very still and quiet. I heard Polecat cackling like a chicken up in the tree. He yanked that noose even tighter.

When Harry came back, he had our old Monitor from the Main Building with him, as well as Mr. Michelson from the Committee.

That was when Polecat dropped the rope out of the tree and uncovered our prey. Haverford just stood there, blinking. He never said a word. He never even relaxed his hold on the bottles.

"I'm terribly sorry about this, Montgomery," Michelson said. "This is a sad day for Manila."

"Manila, my ass," Southy said.

"I knew that son of a bitch was trouble," the Monitor said. "Damn lush'd sell his mother for a drink." Just then Southy yanked a bottle out of Haverford's hand, twisted off the top and took a slug. He smiled at Haverford and handed the bottle over to Harry.

"I guess one bottle's evidence enough," the Monitor said to Michelson and took a swig himself.

Some think the Committee went a little overboard on Haverford's punishment. Southy said it was because he'd disgraced his class. They gave him a week in the Camp Jail. But that wasn't the worst. They made him parade across the Camp wearing a sign with "Camp Drunk" painted across it in big block letters. That left a bad taste in everybody's mouth. I know it made Harry feel guilty. In spite of everything, he'd always had a soft spot for old Montgomery. Mom said she couldn't look Mrs. Haverford in the face anymore. But Southy said that snob got off easy, since they never even brought up the smuggling charge. They claimed they were afraid the Jap Military Police might hear about it. Then there'd have been even more hell to pay.

CHAPTER 15

Not long after Mr. Haverford's disgrace, Harry switched work details. Even with more of us digging in the gardens, food kept getting scarcer. Harry figured he could do more by working with the crew buying food out on the Manila market. At least, that's what he said.

Santo Tomás had to feed itself. The Japs kept us prisoners, but they didn't include board along with the room. It was left for the Committee to make sure some three to four thousand of us didn't starve. Work crews went out scrounging for food anywhere they could find it. They wore armbands and rode out on a truck early each morning. By afternoon they came back, hauling big drums of *sap-sap* or *dilis* fish, rice, camotes, kangkong, mongo beans or anything else they could work a deal for.

Mom swore Harry changed to the new detail to meet up with Virgin out there. He hadn't seen her since the Package Line'd closed down. Well, if he ever laid eyes on the Filipina, he never said so. They always had a Jap guard with them anyway. I found Mom's logic peculiar. But every once in a while, Harry did pick up some bits of news, like which ships were at the docks or how Filipinos were faring or what was happening in the war.

One day I was playing him at chess and like always losing bad. We were at the table in the front of the shanty. He'd learned some way of marching his pawns down the board that had me back on my heels. I was just sitting there, moaning over my fate, when all at once he said something that made me and Mom just about drop our pants.

"I heard something from up north," he said off-hand. "About a tall guerrilla with long black hair."

"Really?" Mom asked with a catch in her breath. "Where?"

"Somewhere past Baguio. Banaue, I think. He's been causing havoc with explosives." I caught Mom's eye. By now my heart was pecking away like a runaway typewriter.

"Didn't they say who he was?" she asked.

"Just a code name," he said. "Geronimo."

"The Apache?" She went to the back of the shanty and looked across the muddy stream.

"Everyone in the army yells it when they jump out of aeroplanes," Harry said. "Could be just about anyone."

"You remember when you first brought Ben around?" Mom asked.

"In China? When you were nurse at Union Medical. Ben was advisor over at the Tangshan Coal Mines."

"You brought him riding with us in the Western Hills."

"He was a good horseman."

"Remember what you told me?" she said.

"You fell the moment you saw him on a horse."

"Something about his hair."

"I said it was the wind in his black hair."

"That's just what you said," she whispered. "He did look lovely riding."

"It could be coincidence," Harry said.

"Yes" She touched his arm. "That's why you told us."

"Let's be quiet about it," Harry said. "Absolutely quiet, Johnny. Imagine if the Japs learned it was Ben."

"It is him," I said. The hell with coincidence. Dad used to tell me Geronimo stories, how he hid out in the desert mountains in Arizona and Mexico, how he gave old General Crook the slip time and time again. Geronimo was a master guerrilla, my old man said.

"Don't ever tell," Harry said. "Not a word. Not a soul. Swear." So I crossed my heart and swore on my mother's grave, which she sure appreciated.

That set me thinking like crazy all over again about my dad. I slipped in under our shanty and lay on the cool ground all alone during siesta. I lay so quiet nobody even knew I was there. I looked up at the light sifting down into the shadows through the split bamboo floor and listened to people's voices in the shanty above. I smelled the earth and lay quiet as the grave. But all the time I kept thinking about the Benguet mines and the steep mountain passes and the narrow roads that run high up above the rivers. That's savage country up there among the Igorots. Villages with wild men who cut your head off and eat your heart. All this time we hadn't known whether he'd been captured or killed or what. It got so I didn't want to say his name, because it hurt. But that name Geronimo was a clincher. That guerrilla was Dad if he was anybody.

My old man once took me and Mom up near Banaue to where the Ifugao tribes live. Near those rice terraces that reach to the sky. He took us to one of those native *cañao* get-togethers. Like a pow-wow. We had a couple of friends from the Army along with us. Lieutenant Stokely of the cavalry and some sergeant from Camp John Hay. Ifugaos are small dusky folks, like the Igorots. Men wore g-strings, with bolos on their hips. Women had bright striped skirts, but their tits were bare. Boy, my eyes just about popped out of my head seeing young girls dancing with their tits naked and free. They were beating brass cymbals and singing up a storm. It was like *National Geographic* come to life. But their tits moving like that gave me an odd feeling, even though I was pretty young at the time. I couldn't ever let on with Mom sitting next to me. So I never said boo. I never even twitched a muscle. Just kept my eyes glued.

It appeared Dad knew the people up there pretty well and was even friends with the chief. It was hardrock mining in the Benguet Mountains and even further north – gold and silver mainly. Dad liked hardrock better than coal. Said it was tougher, but cleaner. And there was copper too, up at Lepanto. Dad knew the region, that was sure. If you're a guerrilla and want to survive, he used to say, you better know the people as well as the lay of the land.

I asked Southy about that country since he was a miner too, but he had little to say. It was before boxing practice and he was setting up, hanging the light bag, unpacking the jump ropes and gloves, stuff like that. But he played dumb about it, claimed the mines he worked were all down in South Luzon.

"But you did go up to see Dad in Baguio, didn't you?" I asked. He looked at me funny.

"Maybe, couple of times," he said. "But it was a trek up there. Train to Dagupan, bus to Baguio. Too much time to lay aside." He didn't want to get into it. Hell, I knew he'd been there plenty. I'd heard him talk about it with Dad. But if he didn't want to let on, there must've been a reason. So I asked Polecat what he knew about the Benguet.

"Mountain people," and that's all he'd say. But later, after boxing, he took me into the Main Building. Around back and up on a landing, off the first floor, was the University Museum. The doors were heavy, dark wood with frosted glass windows. I'd tried opening those doors about a year before with Pete, but they were latched. Polecat looked around to make sure nobody was there, then held his finger up to his lips and eased the door open. Inside it was shadowy and crowded with cases and cabinets, stuff piled all over, some covered with drop cloths. The air was heavy and close and smelled bad. Not just museum smell either. It smelled sweet. On one side of the room was a big double bed.

"That's where the crazy ones sleep," Polecat whispered.

"You mean the old people with accents?"

"They smell funny," Polecat said. Mr. Fitzgibbon said they were Slavs, but Mom said that was just rumor. You can always tell a White Russian, Mrs. Fitzgibbon argued, by the perfume and the henna hair dye.

I knew the old couple all right. They were the only ones in Camp that never slept apart. Refused to be separated. Some folks said they got away with it because everybody thought they were nuts, even the Japs. Japs get spooked by crazies. Others said it was because they didn't wash and nobody wanted them in their rooms. They'd been sleeping in the same bed long before other husbands and wives got into shanties. The old guy said they'd been together too many years to be separated now. And it stuck. At first they had the bed out in the hall. But that embarrassed the Committee too much, so they moved them into the museum.

The old guy was tiny as a gnat. He slicked his hair with some sweet-smelling oil and wore an old loose vest and greasy tie. He had baggy pants and big feet that splayed out to the sides when he walked. The old lady was a mountain and hissed when she talked. You couldn't understand a word – all Z's and S's. She wore a load of lipstick, rouge and beads, and perfumed herself like a gypsy. Her hair was gray to red and bushed out all over. She always had a trumpet up to her better ear, trying to hear. But it did her no good that I could see. Kids shouted down the trumpet as loud as they could and she never even blinked. Like all big women, she'd shriveled up on our diet, but she wore so many layers of clothes you could hardly tell. "Ruskie peasants," folks said.

People called it "The Honeymoon Suite." When my eyes got used to the light, I could make out a huge taxidermied python that ran all along one side of the wall from front to back. It looked like it could swallow you up just for a teatime snack. On the other side was a big stuffed man-eater shark. There were lots of other neat things up there too – nasty spears, axes and shields, birds, reptiles, wild animal heads and a whole monkey hanging by its hind feet. There were no windows to the outside, so the air was dead. It was creepy in there, light dust all over, but Polecat showed me a back corner where they had these miniature villages laid out on tables – thatched huts and tiny people carved out of dark wood. Some were farming the fields, planting rice and corn and squash. Some were fishing in the river. Kids were playing near the huts, while old folks sat around cooking or looking off into space. This gang of warriors was down in a gulch, laying ambush for another gang. They were hiding in the tall grass, their long spears and axes at the ready. I studied them real close, all the while thinking about my old man living there. Polecat told me these were Bontocs, but that maybe I'd missed something inside.

He took some tiny *sawali* siding off one of the tiny huts and showed me something I never could've picked out on my own. The huts were on high stilts and I guess it must've been siesta time, because there were people lying around nude on *petates* spread out across the bamboo floor. Everything was carved to the last detail. Polecat picked up a little mahogany woman and little mahogany man. They were about the size of my finger.

"What you see?" he said.

"Two little people," I said. "Taking a nap."

Then he put them together. They fit so perfect, they made a click.

"*Kantot,*" he said. He pulled them apart. "*Matulog.*" He put them together with a click. "Fuck." He pulled them apart and put them back on their *petate.* "Sleep."

"You think the padres know about them?" I asked. Polecat just smirked.

"Some of them sure like this stuff."

There was this old dusty map back there, half-hidden under the stuffed monkey, right next to a wild pig. The map showed what they called "Tribes of Non-Christian Peoples." I studied that part of North Luzon, all around Benguet and the Mountain Province. The tribes there are called Kalingas, Apayaos, Ibaloys, Bontocs and Ifugaos. I could follow the main valley up from Baguio way up to Bontoc, then another from Bontoc clear down to Bagabag. Those looked like big valleys, but there were lots of smaller side ones too, and plenty of places to hide. And there was lots of space without towns further north. It was what they call a topographic map and you could see just how steep the mountains ran down to the rivers.

While we were studying the map, the old folks came into the room. She was talking in that high hissing way and I could hear him answer in a low singsong. It struck me how little guys sometimes have the real deep voices, like in a Negro spiritual. They were busy with themselves, so we ducked down low and slipped out of there without them noticing.

I stood in the chow line with Polecat for about a half-hour just to get some rice and kangkong. Then we took the dinner pails over to the Gym. It smelled rank in there too. Then it hit me how I'd been spoiled by sleeping in the shanty with nothing but a mosquito net between me and the outdoors.

I'd never met Polecat's dad. He was sitting on his cot, all kind of gray and yellow. He had on loose white clothes that had yellowed too. And a scraggly yellow-white beard. Boy, he looked ancient, and it surprised me. I'd never seen him up close before. He looked too old to be Polecat's dad.

Polecat had me hold his chow bucket while he helped his old man up and led him outside. The old guy was stiff as a board. Looked like he'd break if he fell. We sat on a bench in the sun. And Polecat introduced us real formal.

"Papa, this is Johnny Oldfield. And this is my father, Señor Manny Gallegos." The old man gave me the once over, squinting into the sun.

"So, you're Benito Oldfield's boy."

"Ben," I corrected. "Ben Oldfield."

"He's Southwest Territory," the old guy said. Even the whites of his eyes had gone yellow. "Miner fellow."

"Yes, sir," I said, a little hesitant.

"Oh, don't be surprised. Everybody knows everybody in these Islands, and I've been here since near the start. Been here since the Insurrection."

"Then, sir, you know the Benguet Mountains."

"Oh, sure, I been there all right. Not recent, but I been there. Chased Aguinaldo and his bunch. Damn renegade! He hid out up there and over on the East coast too. Stole the bells right out of the church in Sablán, dragged 'em up in the hills and melted 'em down for ammo."

"You were a soldier?"

"Soldier, hell. I was a fightin' man. Been to Mindanao with Pershing. Fought the Moros with a forty-five. Wildmen, those Moros, wild as any Injun. Found one of our men in the jungle, strung up by the feet and gutted so the intestines hung in his face while he died."

"Tell him the part about Pershing, Papa," Polecat said, real respectful.

"Oh, yeah, Ignacio," the old guy said, patting Polecat's hand. "My little Ignacio." Polecat snuck a look to make sure I wasn't smiling. He looked like he'd eat my liver if I ever told. "Nobody ever beat the Moro, boy, before us. We pounded them jungles, but he kept sneaking into the bushes and losing us. We'd catch his warriors and interrogate 'em, but they'd never talk. Until old Black Jack Pershing had him an idea. You know how he done it, boy?"

"No, sir," I said.

"Pig blood. He got him a Mindanao pig and slit his throat, right in front of a tough Moro warrior. He filled a bucket with blood. Them Muslims were fearless, boy, fearless. But they got the superstition about pigs. Black Jack said, talk or I'll slosh this blood over your infidel head. And that Moro sure talked, my, didn't he talk. A blue streak. Drew him a map, so Black Jack could ride. And he did. Rode alone on a white stallion through the jungle, right up to the Datu's door. And that's how peace come to the Islands."

It appeared all this excitement relived had tuckered the old guy out. He did talk on, but he got vague and wandered all over from place to place. He told how it rained four feet in two days up in Baguio back in '11. "Four feet, you know what that is, boy? Some *people* ain't four feet. Imagine what got washed downstream up in them mountains." He told how they'd captured Aguinaldo with a clever ruse at Palana. And how he loved Filipina women because they had tiny, skillful hands, perfect for embroidery. That was his business, stitching and macramé. Tiny virgin hands, trained by nuns and quicker than the Irish. Two wives he'd had, good Filipina women, but the first died of consumption and she was the best. He had good boys all through the Islands and people still called him squaw man because they were ignorant.

And all the time I answered him, "Yes, sir," and let him talk, until it was time for his siesta and Polecat led him off to his cot. I could tell the way Polecat handled him, he was more than just fond of the old guy. It was like Polecat was his slave. Just when he was leaving, old Manny turned around and looked me over.

"I was a corporal, boy, two stripes," he said, stretching two long fingers across his sleeve. "And you can tell your Benito Oldfield his old man was a squaw man too." Old Manny Gallegos had himself a good laugh over that.

CHAPTER 16

I can't think of one thing without the other. One half's cheering and shouting and crazy happy, and the other's so sad I can hardly tell it straight. They drift and mix together like Harry and Southy running pass patterns through shadow and light across the great field.

The two of them were practicing for the East-West Touch Football Game. Harry'd played some quarterback in prep school, Mom said, and maybe a year or two at university. He could still throw a ball far enough to dazzle me and Polecat. And Southy had the quickness to cut and spin and chase down most any long spiral Harry could launch, man and ball racing like clouds out and together in the late afternoon light. Then there were the others, like Max Murcheson, Stu Walters, Crow Shroeder – big bruisers in their twenties and thirties. A bunch of bully boys who could block and run. That was the sort that made up our East team.

The game was part of Colonel Yoshie's plan to keep us exercising so we'd forget our hunger. But the guys who drew up the rules for the game knew the truth, so they shaved the quarters back to just seven and a half minutes and padded each team with a couple of extra players. To make it more sporting, teams had to make twenty yards in four downs, but the whole field was just eighty, so scoring was high. Me and Polecat played waterboys to the East, chasing out with a bucket and tin cups during time-outs.

Still, it was Harry and Southy that made it fun. They were the old-time tricksters of the game, running the "Statue of Liberty" and the "Double Reverse" – all kinds of nonsense to mix up the West and get everybody laughing. My favorite was what they called the "Sleeper Play."

Southy collided hard with a defender on a crossing pattern and went down in a heap. He lay there about a minute stretched out on the turf with Harry whispering in his ear. Boy, did he have us worried. Finally, he got himself up real slow and with Harry's help limped off to the sidelines. Everybody clapped because he was such a gamer, but it appeared he was so shook up he just had to lie down again. He had us all fooled, including the West. You see, Southy never really stepped out of bounds. He was the *sleeper*, lying in the grass. The only one who paid Southy much mind was Yoshie. He kept studying him with a quizzical look on his face. I was wondering if it had anything to do with that homer Southy'd spanked off him.

Harry took the snap and drifted to his right like he was going end-around. The West defenders swallowed the bait and collapsed in to cover that side. Meantime Southy, the forgotten man, was up and off like a greyhound, sprinting deep up the other side past the whole lot. Now all that was left for Harry to do was wind up and lay one out there on a long high arc, floating it so light and airy Southy could reach out and pluck it as he crossed the goal line. You should've heard everybody laughing and cheering. Yoshie was clapping like a madman, and the bunch of Japs behind him were all busy nodding heads, even though I doubt any one of them knew what for. But the whole West team sure knew. They'd just been suckered like a bunch of rubes.

Only already I was hearing the rumor. Me and Polecat were kneeling there, watching the game, and all the time it was moving along the sidelines, stirring the crowd and setting folks on edge. I couldn't catch just what it was at first. All I could make out was some whispered words like "military" and "deserter" and somebody "ratting to the Japs."

Jerry came over and knelt down next to us, touching Polecat's arm.

"They're saying there are soldiers in here," she said.

"What do you mean?" I asked. "There've always been soldiers."

"American," she said.

"Who?" Polecat asked.

"I just heard some people talking in the crowd," she said. "They say there's army in here." At first we figured it was just the usual hot air. I mean, anybody could see what she was saying couldn't pass a real fact test. How could American army guys get into our Camp? Why would they want to? But it made me uneasy anyhow. And it put a damper on the rest of the game. That was the nasty thing about rumors, whether they were true or not. There was still plenty of funny business going on out on the field, but I'd lost the spirit for it. I kept looking at Yoshie and trying to figure what was going on in his head.

After the game everybody stood around joking and laughing like nothing'd happened, but that evening Harry dropped some hard truth right in the middle of our supper. Chow was rice, mongo beans and pigweed, with a light flavoring of sap-sap fish.

"You hear about Shaw?" Harry asked Southy.

"Yeah," Southy said. "Heard the Japs were grillin' him."

"He told them he was army," Harry said. Southy sat real quiet, like he was waiting for the other shoe to drop. He and Harry kept looking each other over.

"Why would he say that?" Mom asked.

"Don't know," Harry said. "I guess they had him to rights and he wanted to offer something back. He told them there were others in here."

"Oh, Jesus," Mom said. "The rat."

"Guess he was scared," Harry said. "Nobody seems to know who they are. Just a few names floating around." Southy kept looking at him.

"You think it's true?" Mom asked.

"You know how confused everything was when we first came in," Harry said. "Southy?" Southy didn't answer. He just kept looking at him. "You know Shaw?"

"Just seen him around," Southy muttered.

"What do they do to a soldier who isn't in uniform?" Mom asked.

"They might shoot him, I guess," Southy said.

"I have to tell you, Southy, they've been saying your name," Harry said.

"That's crazy," I said.

"He's a miner, like Ben," Mom said.

"Can you guess why?" Harry asked.

"Shaw doesn't know me from Adam," Southy said to himself.

"Something's fishy," Harry said. Then all at once Southy leaned forward and whispered to us real confidential. It was so soft we couldn't quite hear, so he said it again.

"Maybe they got a list."

"What?"

"Names," Southy said. "From files at headquarters. MacArthur's list, Wainwright's, who knows?"

"What are you saying, Southy?" Mom asked.

"No one could know otherwise," Southy said.

"You want to tell us?" Harry asked.

"Hell, I guess I got to tell somebody," Southy said. "Then maybe we can all keep a lookout. See, MacArthur was asking for help. And Ben and me know explosives, right? So the Old Man figured maybe the time might come when he could use us. Might want to blow a bridge or a depot or a mountain pass, who knew?"

"What do you mean, you and Ben?" Mom asked.

"Gave him our names and addresses, that's all. Told him he could count on us."

"How could you?" Mom said. "Ben never said a thing about it."

"Damn, Mrs. Oldfield, we never thought it'd amount to anything."

"Did he give you rank?" Harry asked.

"Reserve, I think. Lieutenant or captain, I don't even remember," Southy said. "I sure don't have any papers."

"Stupid," Mom said. "So damn stupid."

"Did you blow up anything?" Harry asked.

"That's the damn shame of it," Southy said. "I never got a chance to blow up nothin'. They never even called me up."

"All right, it might just be rumor," Harry said. "Perhaps it'll blow over. But something's fishy. How the hell could they have gotten your name? I'll try to poke around. But remember, nobody's to know."

Mom wasn't feeling any too kindly toward Southy just then. She was into one of her icy spells. If I'd looked up, I bet I'd have seen frost on the eaves. Southy felt it too and didn't stay long. He slunk off early that evening.

But I was so damned scared, I stuck to Southy like a shadow. Even though there was no boxing class the next day, I still hung out with him and watched him work the bag. He was concentrating hard on it again, controlling his feelings. But the way I kept gawking at him spooked him after a while.

"Jesus, kid, don't make it a wake," he said.

"What's gonna happen?"

"Look, these are all I got," he said, holding up his fists. "What the Japs are gonna do, they'll do."

"Damn, Southy." I was feeling so scared.

"Listen, kid. You ain't just a squirt anymore. And this ain't the end of the world."

"Sure."

"You're tough enough. You gotta be tough, like your old man. He was trapper boy in the mines before he was near your age. Breaker boy too, picking slate."

"I know."

"Apprentice to his old man, working a mile under by the time he was twelve."

"OK."

"Listen, it's not just you. I owe him too. He picked me up off the deck. I wasn't doing too damn much when he first came to the

Islands, you know. I sure didn't know much mining. He got me my first job as a shifter. Taught me the ropes. Don't think I didn't appreciate it. He's the one who first showed me how to plant a squib so I wouldn't blow myself to kingdom come. Made me a demolition man. Takes some know-how and time on the job. Your old man knows his mining, Johnny, and lots of other things."

"How come you told me you didn't know the Benguet?" I asked.

"Keep quiet about Ben and the mines," he said. "We got no idea what he's up to. If he's a guerrilla, you don't want Japs knowing you're his kid." I knew I wasn't supposed to say anything to Southy about Geronimo. I almost told him, but I decided it was too risky. Harry'd said so.

"I just wanted to find out more about that country," I said. "And my old man."

"Sure," he said. "Well I'll tell you about your old man. I owe him plenty. No one knows how it feels when you're deep in that hole and hear the mountain move over you the first time. Like thunder. Like the roof's coming down. He taught me how to tell when it's *really* gonna cave."

"Sounds scary," I said.

"Mining ain't easy, but your old man's a tough bird." All of a sudden he let loose one of his crazy high laughs. "He was made tough, I guess."

"What's so funny?" I asked.

"Just thinking what he told me once about his mom, your grandma. Little flea of a woman. Ten kids. Most of 'em big strapping boys, but she wouldn't take guff off any of 'em. That's where he got his Injun, Ben said, from his mom. If any of 'em ever acted up, she wouldn't show 'em anger. She'd just yank 'em by the earlobe down to her size, look 'em in the eye and say, 'Sonny, Wednesday, three o'clock.' And Wednesday might be a whole week off. Whoa! That's a sentence! That could chill any kid to the bone. Ben said waitin' was the worst.

143

Waitin' and not knowin' what kind of lickin' it would be. Any kid'd suffer agonies waitin' for his execution hour." Southy was bent over laughing. "Ain't that sure remedy! And she never forgot, wherever they were – on a picnic, doing chores, even right in the middle of a grocery store. Wednesday, three o'clock, she'd pull down their pants and give 'em their due."

"You sure Dad was the one told you that?" I was a little jealous maybe he'd told Southy and not me. But mainly I was thinking about that execution hour.

"Did he tell you different?"

"He never told me nothing about it at all. And he never used it on me either," I said. Truth is, he never had to. "He just looked me real hard and steady once, told me he liked me fine when I was a smart kid, but he couldn't stand me when I was a smart-ass kid." Then Southy was laughing for real.

"Oh, Ben. What a cockeyed wonder! And I'll bet that worked just fine. I like a smart kid, but I can't stand a smart-ass kid. Didn't it, Johnny, didn't it work just fine."

But I guess he could see I was still worried sick, because he grabbed me by both arms, looked me straight in the face and said, "Don't you worry, kid, Southy ain't gonna be one of those that shits his pants." He said it hard and defiant, like it was the tenth round and he was hanging on. But nothing he said could help me out. It was like I was deep in that hole and the roof was caving in. And there wasn't a damned thing any of us could do about it.

The Japs made the announcement at morning roll call. They said they'd learned through investigations that persons connected with the U.S. Military were living in Santo Tomás. And they ordered them all to report to the Commandant by evening roll call or face severe punishment.

"You hear anything?" Southy asked Harry.

"You sure you didn't tell anyone?" Harry asked.

"Sure, I'm sure. Why in hell would I tell anybody?"

"The Committee told me Yoshie asked them about you in particular," Harry said. "But nobody knew where he got your name."

"Then I got to sign up," Southy said, just like that. Like he was signing up for another work detail.

At boxing practice, he told us all to keep after our lessons. He said we were doing fine and was sure they'd have another boxing coach working with us. He said he'd heard they were even going to let us have real matches by and by. This one little kid had big tears rolling down his cheeks looking up at Southy, and I just about joined right in with him. After practice, me and Polecat went with Southy to the shanty, and he pulled out a duffel bag he kept under my bunk. Inside was a little leather box. He took out two medals. He got them boxing somewhere in the States, he said. And he gave one to each of us.

"Even your old man couldn't give you one of these," he said to me. "Those other kids are OK, but you boys are my best. I want you to go out and hit that bag regular. And think of Southy when you're doing it. Nothing but Southy." He messed our hair and talked to us about helping my mom and keeping strong, and we just sat there like we'd been struck dumb. "Now cheer the hell up," he said.

Next day thirty-some men lined up out on the Plaza, most of them big young guys like the ones from our football team. The Japs made them line up in two groups – Army and Navy. Some of them'd brought bags, but the Japs made them leave everything behind. Some of them were married with little kids. There was a big crowd out there, and everybody was crying. They loaded them all standing in the back of an old truck that belched a load of smoke when it started up. They had a couple of Jap guards up there in back with pistols. Southy looked like a little kid among those big guys. Like a skinny little kid. He gave us a smile, but he didn't wave.

Someone threw a pack of cigarettes up to the guys. Then the truck took off up the road to the Main Gate, Polecat running after it, yelling out, "Southy," loud as he could, but he got too close to the truck and a Jap knocked him down.

Later me and Polecat went down to the banana grove and he told me they took his mom and uncles away like that to Fort Santiago and executed them for being suspected spies. He told it soft like a dream, like it happened to somebody else in another time, but I could hear the choking creeping into his voice. And we lay there on the grass under the banana fronds and cried ourselves sick.

CHAPTER 17

You can cry all you want. You can ache and feel empty inside. But that's just chewing on sorrow, Harry said. It sounded hard, but I knew it was true. We had this big ugly hole in our lives. And we just had to go about filling it the best we could.

So me and Polecat went back to boxing, bound to keep ourselves fit. But boxing wasn't the same anymore either. The new guy teaching us, Mr. Nordlich, had been an amateur at college someplace, so his whole style was different. He liked to fight straight-up like John L. Sullivan, and he tried to change us over from crouching down and bobbing and weaving the way Southy'd taught us. Polecat got disgusted quick.

"Where's he get off trying to change us? Southy'd make a monkey out of him."

"Southy ain't here," I said.

After a while we lost our dedication. We kept going, but boxing wasn't our burning passion anymore. There was nothing there to dazzle us. We did keep pounding the bag and jumping rope though, the way Southy'd told us. Trying to fill up the hole. And all the time I whispered mantras to myself. "Southy." And then, "Ben."

Southy was never too talkative, but not having him at the shanty left a big hole there too. I know Mom was feeling low and guilty about how she'd treated him at the last. It wasn't just that he was Dad's good friend, he'd helped us out a lot. He was family. And at the end she froze him out. Naturally, that made her feel mean. Even Harry appeared adrift. He used the shanty more and more during the day. He came over as soon as he got off his work detail. And Harry and Mom invited others too. Trying to fill up the place.

So pretty soon the whole Camp seemed to be drifting by and hanging around.

And you know what they talked about? Food. That was another hole we were trying hard to fill. But it was no regular food they fantasized over. Nothing like a plain steak. It needed special gravies and sauces, wines and mushrooms, cherries and peaches. Mrs. Fitzgibbon got into truffles and soufflés and all varieties of rich chocolates. Mom kept dreaming over brandied dates. This Scottish guy started salivating over his dear dead mither's shortbread, whimpering over all the butter and the sugar. Then Mr. Towner added a double-decker mocha cream pie, and Miss Cornell got onto roast duck with a candied orange glaze.

It was something to listen to them, all wasted down to mere shadows now, hallucinating over food that'd make them sick in a fat year. I don't just mean names, either, but whole recipes. Why, this one grand old gent – who dropped by with a Panama hat, walking stick, and worn-out, two-tone, wing-tip shoes – he could recite entire menus out of his head from his favorite restaurants all around the world, including wines and after-dinner cordials. He roasted this, and flambéed that, served it up piping or chilled, smothered it in onions or wrapped it in coconut, until we were all near delirious. One thing I did notice about this crowd though, they never ever dreamt about a salad. Nothing with leaves.

After they'd dragged us through a seven-course banquet, Mom and Mrs. Fitzgibbon started teasing Harry about old girlfriends, trying to make him tell about the dark little Russian who danced in her bare feet in Shanghai, or the Eurasian he showed up with at some cabaret in Tientsin, or that Aussie blonde whose father traded horses in Hong Kong. But Harry's lips were sealed. Every woman has her right to privacy, he said.

"Confess, Harry," Mrs. Fitzgibbon ordered in her best frog croak, but he was having none of it.

One afternoon I came by the shanty when Harry was telling a crowd a tale about the Shanghai British Concession. The Nickersons, Neddy's folks, had drifted in with the crowd. They lived up the path behind us a little ways into Glamourville. The old man was a big bag of hot wind as far as I could make out. He'd been engineer with the waterworks or some such thing. Always huffing and puffing about the Raj and the King and the Wogs and all that "sun never sets" malarkey. That was most likely why Harry picked this particular little incident to tell.

Him and my old man are just a couple of young bachelors out for a spin in a Renault coupé with the top down on one of those golden Fall days in Shanghai, when a Chinese coolie staggers into the road with a load of stuff on his back – bundle of firewood, pots and pans, even live chickens tied by their feet – probably every damn thing the poor guy owns in the world. Soon as he sees the car, he panics and freezes, then fakes left, but goes right and runs right into the car. Coolie and all his life's savings go flying in the air. Well, Harry and Dad, thinking they might've killed him, jump out of the car to help, but before they can get to him, he's back on his feet, right as rain, just a little dazed maybe, picking up his things, bowing and smiling and apologizing like crazy.

Now, it's the British Concession, remember, so out of nowhere a big turbaned Sikh policeman comes down on that coolie like a clap of thunder, beating him silly and cussing him up, down and sideways for getting in the way of European traffic. That's when my dad starts the brouhaha. He's now ready to take on the Sikh and his whole platoon in defense of the poor coolie. Harry's doing everything he can just to keep him from popping the big guy and causing an international incident. "Jesus, Ben, this is China," Harry's hollering in his ear. "They'll throw us in the bloody hoosegow."

Well, it was both pretty awful and pretty funny at once, the way Harry told it, so we were all chuckling away, except for Mr. Nickerson who got his back up over the idea that my old man could possibly dare to interfere with the British Empire and its Crown Colonies.

"Mucking with justice," he called it.

"Right," Harry said. "We can't have that. Damn American just couldn't seem to understand colonial justice."

"Somebody has to keep the order out here," Nickerson puffed. "Sikhs are bloody fine on the line."

"That's precisely the point," Harry said. "This Oldfield fellow was a disruptive force. An obstruction to the order of things. Terrible, too, how he got your Sikh to soften his stance. Big fellow lost the punitive edge and eased right up on that coolie's punishment. Practically let the Chinaman off scot-free. Didn't wallop him nearly as hard as he deserved."

The Nickersons didn't stay too long after that. The old man saw pretty clear he was amongst renegades and turncoats, so he headed home first chance he got.

"Let's be off, Mathilda," he said. Mrs. Nickerson never said too much, just nodded and smiled at us when she left.

"He's right, you know," Harry said. "Ben's always been a terrible influence. Damn men of action will be the death of us." You could tell by the way he talked he felt a lot for Dad, just in his own way. He missed him like the rest of us and was filling the hole the best he could. Said it was criminal how Dad knew just what to do by instinct and never had to think about it.

"Not like you and me, Ruth, who were ruined at birth when they dressed us in our first little straight jackets."

Then Mom got caught up in the storytelling too. "You remember that Chinese hamlet where you almost got us killed?" she asked, giggling like a kid skipping school.

"Over a silly pack of cigarettes. That's what I mean. Ben wasn't even there and he still had a bad influence."

"Served us right, wandering through out-of-the-way places."

"Nonsense. We were always hiking out that way."

"You should have seen dear Harry playing he-man."

"I *was* your escort, after all," Harry said.

"What happened?" Mrs. Fitzgibbon asked.

"We were up a little cul-de-sac – squalid little place – just trying to get some directions from the locals. No one understood a word we said." Mom started laughing so she could barely talk. It was real happy, but it sounded a little too bright, if you know what I mean. "They spoke some strange dialect. All jabbering at us, like we were the oddities."

"And we were, Ruth," Harry said. "About as foreign as they had ever seen. All decked out in hiking clothes."

"Then suddenly there was that monstrous coolie," Mom said, making her voice deep and mysterious. "Gargantuan. He must have been at least seven feet tall. Horrible, filthy creature. Like something out of a murky myth."

"At least we could make out what he was saying. He only spoke one word."

"Yes," Mom laughed, clapping her hands.

"He knew 'smoke.' Said it with a grunt. So, of course, I brought one out for him."

"Then he wanted the whole pack. And while you were thinking what to do about it, he decided he really also wanted your jacket, and then your hat and your trousers and your boots."

"Limited vocabulary," Harry smiled. "But he could point. I saw myself standing out there in nothing but my underwear. Why did it take us so long, dear girl, to understand we were dealing with the village idiot?"

"We were surrounded by a howling crowd of yokels who thought it was the funniest sight they had *ever* seen. And that's when dear Harry had to show what sort of hero he was."

"Blame it on Ben, not me. Ordinarily, a cooler head would prevail. But I was all at once your sole protector, your knight. The bloody spirit of Ben had inhabited my body."

"Silly picked up a rock," Mom said.

"Only weapon in sight."

"He actually tried to threaten a mastodon."

"Just holding him at bay so Ruth could get herself out of town. I ask you, wasn't that the right and manly thing?" He looked at me. "Johnny, wasn't it?" I could just smile.

"But our village idiot was not at all impressed," Mom said. "He just grinned, bent over and picked up a rock of his own – *twice* the size of yours."

"Talk about a dead-end game."

"I know it was terrible, but I couldn't stop laughing. When I looked back, you were still standing there, looking up at him, with an even larger rock in your arms. That's when the giant picked up the *boulder.*"

"It took that to bring me to my senses," Harry said. "Leaned over, slowly put my rock back on the ground and held up my pack of cigarettes. Carefully opened the top, took out the cigarettes, then threw them all in the air and ran like hell. The whole town was howling by then. Crazy Harry on the run. When I looked back, they were all on the ground fighting over my butts, all except the idiot. Poor Atlas was still standing there, the world on his shoulder."

"It was exquisite!" Tears were running down Mom's face. The old man with the Panama was thumping his walking stick on the floor.

"And all the while I was cursing. Cursing Ben, you, the chivalric code, the Star Spangled Banner, the whole crazy thing," Harry said. "What the hell had I gotten myself into?"

"But, Harry, you know you have to get in to get out." Mom said, in this sweet voice. "And you do so love the getting out!"

But as much fun as all the talk was, it ended up making me miss Dad all the more when it was done. It didn't fill up anything. There was still the big empty hole. Maybe it was the diet, but I got so damn weary and fidgety and sad.

A couple of days later, I was lying all alone on the cool ground under our shanty. It was during siesta, and I was just watching the afternoon light move across and seep down through the bamboo floor, listening to the murmur of voices over me and letting my mind wander. I was remembering a cockfight Dad took me to in a little barrio with the heavy sweet smell of sweat and tuba palm wine and the men so drunk and cheering and betting with their hands to the bookmaker *cristo*. When the cockfight ended, the guy who owned the dead cock took him up in his hands and was kissing his bloody head and crying over him like it was his wife or kid that was killed. He was real drunk and had probably bet the hacienda on that fighting cock, but still. It's funny where folks put their feelings. I mean, he was kissing that dumb bird's bloody head and just wailing.

While I was thinking about this I could hear my mom's voice, far-away from above. Then I heard the name, Tyler, so I listened so hard I barely breathed. She was saying that when she was a nurse in Peking they'd brought in a little Chinese boy who had a car run over his head. She sounded real sad now, telling how his little head went down into a hole so the wheel didn't crush it but just banged it up a little and gave him a concussion. She was crying that it was a miracle to see that baby whole and healthy and why oh why hadn't they had such a miracle with little Tyler. All he'd had was a burst appendix, she was sobbing, such a silly thing for a little boy to have, but he'd died anyway from peritonitis. Why did he have to be the one? Harry was trying to comfort her, but you could tell he was getting annoyed too. I was pretty near in shock, because you see, my mom was such a strong person usually.

"Jesus, Ruth," he said. "Tyler's been dead over ten years."

"He was so clever, don't you see, so special. We were so close. He was just like my brother. You have no idea how close Tyler was to me."

"You've got Johnny, Ruth. Just thank God *he's* got a lot of Ben."

My eyes were dry as the desert, but my heart was sure beating. I was wondering if she'd be saying that if my old man was there. And if she'd be crying like that if it was me who was dead.

CHAPTER 18

There was something else lurking in the shadows waiting to mess up my life. It kept reaching out to touch me in ways I couldn't quite figure. But sooner or later I'd have to face it. Like Harry's Chinese whore up in Chinwangtao, it was bound to get dragged into the harsh light.

Me and Polecat were walking along this path between shanties during siesta hour when we heard it. A deep moaning sound something like Harry'd made in the dark when he was telling about saving the China Marines. It stopped us dead in our tracks.

"*Kantot*," Polecat said.

"What?" I asked, but the way he looked at me made me feel ignorant.

"Fucking."

Once in a while we caught a glimpse of a couple clutching at each other in a dark shanty or wrestling in the grass down among the banana trees. Nothing too clear, just a little snapshot. It got me interested all right, but I didn't ask any more questions, because Polecat seemed to be up on it already and I didn't want to look dumb again. I figured maybe it would just up and show itself to me by and by.

One day when we were down in the banana grove, Jerry told me and Polecat right out of the blue that we could kiss her. We kind of smiled at each other and thought it over. Then I kept lookout while she touched lips with him and he kept lookout while she and I went at it. But she seemed to be mostly interested in Polecat, to tell the truth, and that was OK with me. I didn't like the way she tasted much anyhow. And she was so skinny, it was like hugging a guy. So after the first couple of times I just kept lookout for them. It got so they kissed a good long time and hung on each other.

After that, Polecat and Jerry went around by themselves for a bit, walking to classes up on the roof of the Main Building, eating chow off together, but it didn't last long. Her old man found out and forbid her to spend time alone with him anymore, because he was mestizo. He told her she was just making a spectacle of herself and ruining the family reputation. That surprised me, since I never heard anybody talk about her family much, one way or the other.

But Red was the one who really ran into a serious situation. We all had a good laugh at his expense. You see, the Plumbing and Carpentry Details got together and built this outdoor shower for women who lived in the shanties. It had a nipa roof and sawali siding and sat up on bamboo stilts, just like a shanty. Only they gave it duckboard flooring so the shower water'd run down through it. It was that duckboard that got Red in a mess.

Red got an itch he didn't know how to scratch. He spent his time lying on the ground under the duckboards, staring up at ladies showering in the all-together. One of them happened to see his eye at the crack and screamed. So they rushed out and nabbed him in the act, with a muddy backside and all, and paraded him along by the scruff of his neck, all the way back to his own shanty down in Froggy Bottom. They made him confess to his folks in front of a crowd of neighbors. And his folks screamed and yelled at him so loud, all Froggy Bottom learned the details.

Red lost whatever standing among us he had accumulated through his advanced age. We called him "Red Eye" and "Muddy Bottom" and asked him if he'd ever heard that Peeping Toms are likely to go blind. But the funny thing was, for all Red's new reputation, I bet Jerry's old man would've let her hang out with him anyways and never said a word against it.

But my real education in these matters came from something me and Polecat discovered up in the University Museum. We were sneaking in there pretty regular after siesta, whenever the old couple was out. Finally we checked out the Honeymoon Suite too, around the big double bed. And that's how we found the little black book. It was called "Advice to a Young Couple on their Honeymoon" and it was by a medical doctor. The first surprise was it was in English. The second was that a couple as old as them would be reading sexy stuff like this. But it appeared to have been thumbed over a good bit through the years and pretty recent too, by the smell of it.

That little volume made a real impression on me. It got hard to even think about sex without remembering those little yellow pages and the strong perfume. We pored over it, laughing and whispering at the way the doctor said things. It was by no means a recent book, probably from before the turn of the century, so it said things stiff and peculiar. Talked about "bundling before marriage" and stuff like that. But it was highly instructive, it really was.

Told us about the penis when it's at rest and in its state of erection and preached against circumcision. Said the foreskin's job was covering up the head of the penis so it'd be more sensitive during intercourse. Told us how to make love if we were tall guys and our women were small. Talked about how the bride should hold the groom's penis in her hand, give it a name and talk to it like it was a person. It went into minute detail about the parts of the vagina like the vulva and the clitoris and all. Boy, we memorized that.

But the best two parts as far as I was concerned were the one where he talked about opening the labias of the vagina like a flower, petal by petal, so as not to bruise a single one, and this other where he spoke about the pubic hairs. Even though he couldn't prove it scientifically, the doctor was convinced that during "the ecstasy of true love" the pubic hairs carried a current, like electricity, and made sexual intercourse more of a "charged experience." Polecat really laughed over that. The book said pubic hair was very important, especially for women, and it came in all varieties – wavy, kinky, straight, short and long, some bushy, some lank.

This doctor claimed he had consulted with women whose pubic

hair grew clear down to their knees. I guess they were pretty proud of it and took great care to keep it clean and perfumed. But Polecat told me he didn't think it was true. He said, if that was the case, they'd have to wear real long dresses all the time. He'd seen quite a few naked women and never once noticed any hair hanging down like that.

Regardless, this book gave us many a wild afternoon, and each time we finished with it, we put it back careful where we'd found it. That was almost always a different place, which proved to us these folks were reading it plenty too. Then we snuck out of there and went down to the banana grove to discuss it further.

This one day we were lying around in the tall grass discussing labia majorum and labia minorum. And out of the blue, Polecat said it.

"That's where I saw your mom and Harry."

"Where?"

"Right over there, under that tree," he said, pointing and smiling at me. "Right there's where he was kissing her."

"What?"

"For real," he said.

And that's when I hit him. It wasn't something I planned. I just threw a big stupid roundhouse and hit him high on the cheekbone. I hit him again and kind of jumped over on top of him when he fell back. It's not too clear, really. I went kind of crazy. I don't know how many times I hit him or he hit me. All I know is I wanted to kill him. And all the while, I was screaming, "Shut up, you God damn son of a bitch Filipino!"

It sure surprised Polecat. He didn't even know what he'd done. Luckily, he squirmed loose and popped me a couple back. Then I saw I'd split his lip and given him a bloody nose. And I just turned away. I couldn't even look at him, I was so ashamed. I lay down with my face in the grass. I didn't want him to see me. I couldn't help it. It was like I'd been looking at what'd been going on all the time, and his saying it just made me see.

"Jesus Christ, Johnny! What's wrong with you?" he yelled.

"Just leave me alone," I said. "Get the hell out."

I lay there about two lifetimes, feeling miserable and sorry for myself, cursing Polecat and Harry and my mom, even little Tyler. After a while I went over and lay down where Polecat said he'd seen them. I swear I chose to lie there just to make myself more miserable. I stayed there right through four o'clock chow, even though it was no time to miss a meal. I kept thinking about that poor Chinese whore they paraded out under the lights in front of all those Marines and it scared the hell out of me.

Finally, I thought of Southy and how mad he'd get if he saw me moping around. So I tried to pull myself together. And I was just getting somewhere with it, when I looked down and saw my mom's ebony comb lying in the grass. Boy, that just made me feel rotten all over again. I sat there about another two hours, right through sunset, running my fingers over the smooth hard wood, contemplating double murder and suicide. But by the time I left there, I'd come up with some kind of plan.

When I got back to the shanty, the light'd faded so I could just make out their shadows at the table up front. They were talking and laughing, but when they saw me they quit.

"Hello, Major," Harry said, but I didn't say anything. I just went to the back and lay down on my cot.

"Where've you been? I've been worried about you," Mom said. I didn't answer her either. "Come here and let me look at you." After a while, I went over and stood by her. She put her hand up and felt very lightly along my right eyebrow and then along my cheekbone where it'd puffed. "Why, this is nasty. Who did it?" But I backed away from her.

"I had a fight, that's all," I said. "With Polecat."

"Why would you mess with Bolo Man?" Harry asked. But I didn't answer that either.

"Did you eat?" Mom asked.

"I'm OK," I said. I sat at the end of the table away from them. Everybody was real quiet, and after a while Mom picked up her knitting.

"We were just talking about your dad," Harry said. "I was telling your mom how I first met him up in Durango, Colorado, in a speakeasy. He was working at a mine near there. We hit it right off."

"Harry knew your father long before I did," Mom said.

"Did you know your dad was the only one in his whole family to go to college?" he asked. "The original self-made man. Taught himself to box in mining camp. Got himself through school on sheer wit and drive."

"Normal School at Las Vegas, New Mexico," I mumbled.

"So you know," he said.

"I know some things," I said. Mom was real quiet, knitting up a storm. Knit one, purl two. "What are you knitting?" I asked.

"Socks. String socks."

"Who for?"

"Depends," she says. "If they turn out smallish, they'll be yours. If they run big, they'll be Harry's." And that's when I saw my opening.

"We were just talking about a lady who took up knitting while her husband was away at war," I lied. "In school."

"Oh?"

"Yeah. She had all these suitors who kept after her because her husband was gone so long, but she stayed faithful to him, said she couldn't marry anybody until she'd finished her knitting. Every night she ripped it out and started over, so she'd never finish. Her name was Penelope."

"I believe she was weaving," Harry said in this far-away voice. "At the loom."

"Oh yeah, I guess that's right. Our teacher said the husband was away for twenty years and those suitors never got near Penelope that whole time. In the end him and his son killed them all. Shot them full of arrows." Boy, I was on a roll, just talking right along and everything real hushed around me. "Twenty years sounds like an awful long time, doesn't it?"

"Legendary," Harry said. Nobody said anything after that and pretty soon he left. He gave Mom a little peck on the cheek and then he put his hand on my shoulder. "Take care of that eye, Major. And make sure you make up with Bolo Man. Good friends are hard to come by." I watched him walk away into the dark, just a thin, light figure, melting.

Me and Mom sat there a good long time and neither one said a thing. Then I took the comb out and put it on the table in front of her. God, I was so shaky I barely got it out of my pocket. It felt like just before a fight. Like not knowing what would happen. But she let it sit there on the table and kept knitting.

"Well, now let me tell *you* a little story," she said after what seemed about a week. It took her a while to say the next, like she was getting herself straightened up. "Do you know why my father named me Ruth? He told me loyalty and faithfulness were the most important traits a woman could possess. Those were his words: 'a *woman* could possess.' He said Ruth was the most faithful creature in creation. From the Bible: 'whither thou goest, I shall go,' and 'where thou diest, I will die, and there will I be buried.' He engraved it in my memory, did dear Daddy, the great Judge Tyler. You are Ruth, ever the loyal young woman." I noticed her voice'd gone up a notch, and she attacked this next part pretty fierce. "Then, when I told my parents I was becoming a nurse, my mother feigned a heart attack because nursing was just this side of prostitution on the Philadelphia Social Register, and the dear Judge told me I might kill that fine lady. When I told him I was off to the Far East, he said it was no place for a young lady of my standing to go. And when I cabled him that I was marrying a wonderful exotic creature who was part Indian, I never heard from him again." She was really steaming along, working herself into the wind-up. "The name Ruth and a nickel, dear Johnny, will get you downtown and no further." She felt so far away all of a sudden, her face just a smudge. "I hope you haven't inherited the judgmental side of the Tylers." But I wouldn't give in either.

"I wonder where Geronimo is tonight," I said.

"Wherever he is, I hope he knows how much I love him," she said. "Your father's a very loving man."

By the time I went to bed, I was feeling none too steady, but I chalked it up to missing afternoon chow. I wished I felt better about what I'd done. But it was kind of damned if you did or you didn't, I figured. I lay there real quiet, listening. But there wasn't a sound from her bed, like she wasn't even there.

Harry didn't come by the shanty the next day, or the day after. Then it got to be a week. I saw him at roll call, at a distance, sometimes talking to Mom, but then he was off on the truck, and I didn't see him anymore the rest of the day. I was glad in some ways. I figured I did the Ulysses business pretty slick, sort of out-Harry'd Harry, if you know what I mean. But I missed having him around, to tell the truth.

Mom froze up too for a pretty long time. She didn't talk much. It was like she was thinking all the time. Then one day she just up and volunteered for nursing duty at the Children's Clinic. Later she moved on to Santa Catalina Hospital, where the older people were sick and dying. She said it was important, she had to keep herself busy. It was what she'd been trained for and she wanted to make herself useful.

But what I'd done was small potatoes next to what was going on all over Manila. The Jap Military Police, what they called the Kempeitai, were on the move, picking up Filipinos left and right, hauling them off to Fort Santiago for interrogation and execution. Before the week was out, they made visits into Santo Tomás too and hauled off a few of our internees. One of them was Harry. I never saw it happen and we couldn't even find out what it was about.

Mom asked around, but she couldn't get anything pinned down. Even the Internee Committee didn't have a clear idea. Polecat heard that the Japs suspected some people in Camp of working with the Filipino underground.

"Virgin," Mom said in a flat voice.

Maybe that was it. But it all stayed shadowy and mysterious. I got damned worried about Harry, the sudden way he'd disappeared. He even left his chessmen all set up on the front table, like he'd figured to stop by for a game with me. I kept staring at Anne Boleyn, with her head tucked underneath her arm. It made me miserable. Somehow, in some crazy kind of way, I guess I felt responsible.

CHAPTER 19

Terror's like a toothache. You can't stop tonguing it. As much as you try to stay away, you just end up rubbing and worrying where it's bothering you. And it turned out that tonguing business is what got me and Polecat together again.

We couldn't stay out of each other's way too long. We both had to get back to the speed bag to do our Southy mantras. While I was waiting on Polecat to get off the bag, I noticed how concentrated he was going at it. And I could tell by that just what he was thinking.

"Where you figure Southy is, anyways?" I asked. He turned around and looked at me like it was already clear in his mind. My question just broke the dam.

"Cabanatuan or O'Donnell. Some say Bilibid. But that don't make sense." He talked excited with his hands, jabbing at my chest. "They took 'em because they're military, right?" He put his arm on my shoulder and started leading me away where we could talk in private. "Sooner or later, he's got to go to a military camp."

"North of Clark Field, right?"

"Where they marched that first bunch off Bataan. Before I came in here, I heard things. Guys dying like flies all along the way. Some they stuffed in railroad cars. Most they made march the whole way in the hot sun. No food, no water."

"Jesus, how many you figure died?"

"Who knows? Thousands of 'em. Starving, with malaria, dysentery, you name it. Crazy with the heat. Passing out all over the place. If you fall down, they bayonet you or shoot you in the back of the head. You'd still be marching after dark, hearing shots, seeing flashes. They caught a guy with some Jap money, poor son of a bitch! Pushed him right down on his knees, no questions, and chopped off his head with a samurai. Head rolled down along the line of guys. Blood spurting all over."

"Shit!"

"If they didn't kill Southy, it's still gonna be more hell."

"Well," I said, feeling more miserable than ever. "Southy's tough. You know he's tough."

"I hear they stacked Americans and Pilipinos like firewood along that road."

"Maybe he'll escape."

"Yeah, he could escape."

"What about Harry?" I asked, trying to move off Southy while we were thinking more positive. "I guess they took Harry to Fort Santiago."

"You figure he did something?"

"Or maybe they think he knows something."

"Sounds like they're gonna torture him," Polecat said. "That's what they do in Santiago. Torture and execution."

We sat in the sun and discussed torture and execution quite a while. We went through everything we'd heard the Japs did. We pretty well tongued it to death. We talked about how they stuck bamboo slivers under your fingernails and beat you silly with a rubber hose. Kicked you in the balls. Tied your hands behind you and strung you up like a side of beef. Polecat knew a lot about Jap torture. He'd picked up a lot from other Filipinos, and Filipinos knew by experience.

They used two kinds of water torture. One where they made you hold a bowl of water in front of you and look at it for days at a time, but if you raised it up to drink, they whipped you with bamboo across the backs of your legs, or across your face. You'd be dying of thirst, cracked lips and mouth so dry you got no spit, but you could never drink a drop. The other was even worse. They shoved a hose up your ass and pumped you full of water, then jumped on your stomach. Broke you up inside.

But the one that was the scariest for us was this special cell the Spaniards'd built. It had no windows, just a grate on top, and when the tide moved up the Pasig River, that cell filled with water, inch by inch, until you drowned. We talked about that one a whole lot. We figured you could get pretty desperate in there, trying to get to that last gulp of air. Fort Santiago's part of the old walled city, called Intramuros. It has a special gate called San Carlos, Polecat told me. When you went through that gate, chances were you were headed for the dungeons. And, boy, chances were even better you weren't ever coming out.

"Well, Harry knows how to get by pretty well," I said.

Mom told me folks did return from Fort Santiago sometimes. She'd seen them at Santa Catalina Hospital. They were in sad shape, but still alive, just skin and bones with big hollow eyes, legs swelled with the beriberi and bodies covered with open runny sores from the wet dirty cells. When she heard this one guy'd come back from Santiago, she tried to get him to tell her about it. But he was afraid. He latched onto her arm. His eyes got wild and panicky.

"Don't say a word," he whispered, real close to her ear. "Somebody could be listening. This place's got eyes and ears, I tell you. You never know who's listening."

When Southy and Harry were still around, we'd built a little garden out back of the shanty – couple of banana trees, talinum, pigweed, some camotes. I still went there regular and watered it down with buckets of water out of the stream. I'd get down on my knees, weed and dig around with a fork to loosen the soil. Being there made me feel close to them. I even started chuckling to myself sometimes. I remembered Harry telling about Candide off in the jungles of South America, trying to save the little naked girls from their lover monkeys, and I had to laugh out loud. It could be dangerous when you were all alone. Polecat happened on me once when I was like that and thought I'd gone around the bend.

But mostly I just got lonely and restless and started roaming about. That's how I happened to wander down the path along that tall hibiscus hedge where me and Southy'd gathered buds for our Christmas tree. Tucked away back of those bushes was the Nickerson's shanty. It sure was trim. Everything about the place was lined up straight as an arrow. Mr. Nickerson'd been trying his hand at what he called "a spot of gardening." English are mostly fond of puttering in the ground, I know, but the Nickerson's vegetable patch looked like it'd been measured out with a ruler, like if any plant dared grow crooked he'd punish it.

It seemed quieter around their shanty, even though it was built off the same stream as ours, with the same rise on the other side, crowded with shanties. Just a thin screen of smoke from their charcoal stove settled in the hollow. Bright red canna lilies lit up the shade near the stream. Morning glories climbed along their nipa palm roof.

It was right after siesta. Mr. Nickerson was sitting under the eaves, fanning himself with a palm fan, sipping some tea and cussing the heat. Even though he was thin enough to see ribs, he was still a big-boned bird with wide shoulders and a heavy red face. He cut his sandy hair short, in the military style. "Terrible stuffed shirt," Harry'd said. Something of a bully, too. His wife was humming to herself inside the shanty when I came along, and dancing around a little. Nothing wild, just bending back and forth real slow, all by herself. I could just make her out moving in the shadows. Sort of sweet and girlish. The old man muttered to her to keep it down, and she froze like she'd been slapped. Their little girl, Sissy, stood in the yard gawking at me with her mouth open. I think she had the adenoids. They always put her in little white dresses, like she was off to church or a party. But as soon as she saw me she ran up the steps into the shanty to hide behind her mom's skirts.

At the back of my mind were rumors that made me feel funny about the Nickersons. I heard them from Mom or Harry or Polecat, I forget. Something about them being too well-off and having more food than others. Seemed somewhere in their shanty or buried in the bushes, they had tins of Red Cross food they got black market and were hoarding. I was never sure if it was true, but it made me edgy to think about.

Neddy was down by the stream, scooping wet clay onto the bank. He was mining some raw material for a new batch of what he called his "lorries." Since he'd quit marbles, lorries had become his obsession. He knocked out those trucks pretty near all day long. Had himself a little assembly line that would've made Henry Ford proud.

"Very proficient," his father said. "The boy will make a fine engineer in future."

Neddy never changed the look of his lorries that I could see, just kept repeating the one model over and over again. It was no more than maybe eight inches long and built real squat. Kind of an ugly little snub-nosed thing. Square front, square cab and a square bed with a rounded canvas cover on top. Then he just slapped on four wheels and that was it.

"What's the difference between an engineer and a mechanic, anyhow?" I asked. The old man looked at me like I was a troublemaker.

"Mechanic merely repairs things. Tools parts. Engineer has to be a designer. You can see what an efficient piece the lad's come up with."

"You mean an engineer works with his head, whereas a mechanic just works with his hands?" I asked. But I could see I was bordering on what my dad called smart-ass, so I let it go.

Neddy never played with his lorries that I could see. He was very serious about it, like it was his job in life. He never put them into any battles or even maneuvers. He just kept building them steady as he could and lining them up in this long convoy across the yard. He must have had two hundred or more out there, all along the side of the shanty and around by the hedge, spaced out regular as gravestones in a cemetery.

"What're they all for?" I asked him.

"To carry personnel."

"How come you don't make tanks or cannons?"

"I prefer lorries."

"Don't pester the lad," the old man said. "Can't you see he's occupied."

"I don't mind," Neddy said. His dad didn't much care for intruders, that was pretty clear, but since he fancied himself such an expert on everything, I put a question to him anyhow.

"How much longer you think we'll be in here, Mr. Nickerson?"

"No idea."

"Well, how long you figure?"

"It really depends just how long it takes Viscount Montgomery to defeat those Nazis."

"Single-handed?"

"Don't be cheeky," he said. I could see he had a very low opinion of contrary views.

"You mean they won't even get to us until they finish over in Europe?"

"Our Royal Forces can only accomplish so much at a time."

"What about Yanks?"

"Oh, I imagine they will be along with our forces, whenever Sir Winston feels the time is right." It was clear he didn't just feel the world was a better place for having England. Without them, it would just be no place at all. I imagine Harry could've worked some fun out of the conversation, but I got my fill real quick and headed home.

Besides, Neddy'd given me an idea and I had to get to it. I started as soon as I got back to my shanty. Scooping away the mud, getting down to the clay. Pulling handfuls up onto the bank, patting the water out, firming it up so I could work it into the picture I was holding in my head.

Of course, it wasn't that simple. Neddy'd had a lot of practice on lorries and just made it look easy. At first I tried a full-length figure, but that didn't work out. The clay wouldn't firm up enough, so the legs kept collapsing and the arms falling off. Finally, I settled on just doing a head. I worked pretty feverish at it, all alone in back of the shanty in the shade of the acacia tree. I had all kinds of things to work out. The right shape of the head, the way it joined the strong neck. I didn't want it stiff, that was sure. It had to feel alive. But it was sure hard. Whenever I was through for the day, I wet down a towel like I'd seen Neddy do, and wrapped the head to keep the clay fresh. Then each day, soon as Mom went off to the hospital, I got back to it again.

I worked the broad forehead pretty well, and the straight thin eyebrows. The nose was strong, but just a little bent to one side. And the nostrils flared a bit. The mouth was wide with a full lower lip and a little curl at the corners. Not smiling really, just friendly. The jaw was real determined. The hardest part was the eyes. At first I tried keeping them shut, but that made it look dead. I went around studying the look of other people until I got the open eyes right. Now they looked out at you nice and honest.

All this took me a long time, but I kept so concentrated, whole days passed before I even knew it, then a couple of weeks. I kept thinking about it even when I couldn't get to it, studying everyone who came my way to make sure I'd got the features right – the way the sides of the face rose from the jaw to the high cheek bones, that nice groove that came down from the nose to the upper lip. I forgot the ears at first, so they went on late. Finally I worked the long hair so it hung out over the ears a bit and down the back of the neck. I even added a wide headband across the forehead to hold the hair in.

Every once in a while, I got dizzy working at it. Then I wrapped it careful in the wet towel, put it under the shanty and walked away. I went over to boxing, jumped rope or hit the light bag and concentrated hard until I saw the face clear again. Then I headed straight back and monkeyed around with some tiny detail. It was a good long time before I brought it out for anyone to see. It was my secret until I'd finished. I let it dry out a couple of days and just tinted the band around his head a light red with some paint I got from school. Finally I put him up on the shelf next to the clay stove so he'd look down on us.

Mom came home from the hospital late at night and went straight to bed. Next morning, after roll call, I had to stand in the chow line for our breakfast – a couple of ladles of mush, teaspoon of sugar, some coconut milk and coffee. When I got back to the shanty, she was standing there looking up at it, all misty-eyed.

"You like it?" I asked. She came over and took my face in her cool hands.

"You're a son of a bitch," she whispered. "Just like your dad."

CHAPTER 20

Polecat thought my clay head was pretty sharp.

"Looks like a chief," he said.

"I made up the headband," I said. "He doesn't wear a headband."

"Who is it then?"

"My dad," I said.

"Looks like a guerrilla." Boy, that scared me.

"Shut up about that stuff," I ssid.

Jerry, Pete and Finchy thought it was OK too. But Knockers was a little more critical. He said the eyes didn't appear to be the same size. Red never said anything at all, just looked at it once and scratched himself.

But I couldn't take my eyes off it. It looked pretty unbeatable up there on the shelf. Strong and sure. That was, until the weather got hot and dry and the ears fell off, one by one, and broke on the shelf. He was never the same after that, and when the face opened in a long jagged crack, it got sad to look at. Now it was just plain ugly.

One day I couldn't stand looking at it anymore. So I took it down and laid it in the stream. Real gentle. The dark water clouded up gray around it. The next day the nose was gone and the eyes were just shallow holes. In a week the whole thing'd gone back to mud.

I thought about scooping the clay from the stream and working it with my hands. How it felt making something special out of dirt. Maybe the idea'd come from watching Neddy, but not the thing I'd made. That was different. That was mine. Now all those little trucks lined up in the Nickerson's yard left me feeling mean.

I was out front of our shanty, doing one of my chores. I was slicing canna lily root real thin, then laying it out on a mat to dry in the hot sun. When it was dry, I'd grind it for flour. Me and my friends were squatting out there, watching it dry and chatting about this and that. Finchy happened to mention something about Neddy and his marbles, wondering what he was doing without them.

"He's making trucks," I said.

"Trucks? What kinda trucks?"

"Just little square trucks," I said. "One after the other."

"Sounds like he's gone funny," Jerry said.

"Whole family's funny," I said. And then I told how Neddy stamped out one dumb truck after another and then just left them sitting in the sun, how his old man blew like a bag of wind under the eaves, how the mom hid up in the shadows of the shanty, little Sissy gawking out from behind her skirts, and how the whole bunch just couldn't help thinking they were the swellest people on earth. Then I capped it off by telling them how the English were going to win the war and save us all by themselves.

Sometimes it's like you get pulled along by the tide. Maybe you wouldn't choose the same direction all on your own, but things carry you there. While I was talking, getting more and more descriptive, I could see Polecat's eyes lighting up, so I did what I could to fan the fire. Pretty soon he got up and started pacing back and forth. He looked around for signs, checked the tower clock for time, followed birds swirling up over the Plaza, glanced at the squad of sentries down by the Main Gate.

"I think I'd like to visit," he said.

"Visit?" Knockers said. "Visit who?"

"I think I'd like to visit with the Neddy." He clicked the Glassees together in his pocket.

"When?"

"Now."

So we went down the path to the Nickerson's. Not all of us. We didn't want to overdo it. Just four went. Like envoys to a foreign land.

When we came into their yard, it looked just like I'd left it. It'd been almost a month, but I swear time'd stood still. Maybe there was another brigade of lorries on the ground, but I didn't think anything else had moved an inch. This time Sissy bolted early to her mom in a streak of white dress. Mr. Nickerson was so surprised, he failed to jump up to welcome us.

"Hi," I called out. "How're you, Mr. Nickerson."

"Pleased to meet you," Polecat said and gave a little nod toward the shadow in the shanty.

"This is my friend, Polecat," I said. "Youngest son of Señor Gallegos. You know Jerry here, I'm sure."

"Hello, Neddy," Jerry called out, giving him a little wave. He was sitting on the ground reading, but he did look up and blink.

"And this here's Finch."

"Mabuhay," Finchy said, real cheerful. But it stayed pretty strained out there.

"I was telling my pals what Neddy's been doing," I said. "They just had to come and see the Lorry Brigade. I couldn't keep 'em away." I'd been smiling like a diplomat but I was stopped dead by the old man's look.

It was a foul look. A look you might expect if he'd just caught two mongrels fucking, turned around and locked end-to-end, stuck solid and yelping like they were being electrocuted, right there in the middle of his yard.

"What's that you're reading, Neddy?" Polecat asked.

"Kipling." Neddy did not look up.

"Oh, Fuzzy Wuzzy," Polecat said. "Mandalay. Danny Deever." He was spitting out names like a broke ticker-tape machine.

"Oh, you know Kipling?" Neddy's mother asked.

"Gungha Din, Mowgli." At first I thought he'd really read all of them. But then he stepped out-of-bounds. "Sabu." Neddy just smiled, but his old man went for it big.

"Fine man of letters, Kipling," Mr. Nickerson said.

"And Walter Scott?"

"What about him?"

"Also a very good English writer."

"Oh, yes, I dare say Scott is fine too."

"Ivanhoe's tops, don't you think?" Polecat went on like he was crazed. We'd been reading Ivanhoe in school and I knew for a fact Polecat thought it was a bunch of hogwash. It was hard to keep a straight face.

"My, you *have* been reading," Mrs. Nickerson said.

"Oh, yes," Polecat smiled bald-faced at her. "All about knights and ... and knightliness." Right there he knew he'd tripped, but he righted himself before Neddy's folks noticed. "Good breeding, you know."

"Breeding is important," Mr. Nickerson agreed.

"Blue blood," Polecat added. Mr. Nickerson gave him a funny look, but Mrs. Nickerson followed right on.

"Neddy comes from very good stock," she said. "Just like those knights of old." And she actually went into explaining how he'd descended from an earl or duke or some such folderol. Pretty soon breeding was the whole topic of conversation.

"My aunt says we're from somebody who came over on the Mayflower," Finch confessed.

"Came over to where?" Mr. Nickerson boomed out.

"The States, I guess."

"Damned Puritans," the old man said. "Nothing but a lot of heretic snivelers."

"They was the first in the States," Finch muttered in defeat. But Polecat was damned if he was going down so easy.

"I myself am descended from the Pope," he announced.

"What?" Mrs. Nickerson gasped.

"That's right. Papa told me so."

"Nonsense," her husband said.

"You know *apostolic succession*?"

"Of course."

"You know *mestizo?*"

"Yes."

"Who makes mestizo?" Polecat asked.

"Why, it's when Spaniards mix with the natives."

"And the Spanish who mix most with natives are called *padres.*" Well, the old man got even redder in the face than usual and began to sputter and laugh. But Mrs. Nickerson's mouth had dropped open.

"Why, that's out-and-out sacrilege."

"The Pope makes the bishop, the bishop makes the padre, and the padre makes the mestizo," Polecat smiled, clapping his hands. "So, I am descended from the Pope. That is apostolic succession!"

"That is religion," the old man growled. "It has not anything to do with breeding." He was hot now and not too happy with any of us. He looked over at Jerry and then back at Polecat. "Breeding is keeping the pure-bred bitch away from the mongrel." And that was his last word on it. He got himself up off his chair under the eaves and went into the shanty. All he needed was a door to slam.

You can just imagine how bowled over we were by Polecat's performance. But he wasn't even started. Soon as we got back to my shanty he asked for a piece of paper, and started sketching the Nickerson layout down on a piece of paper. I felt like I was watching Southy at work. He even drew lines between the points and approximated the distances. I learned quick that like every good envoy he was also a good spy. Now he sat at our table like a general formulating battle plans. He measured the stream and the hill from the shanty, put in the hedge and vegetable patch, even drew Neddy's line of lorries.

Next day we met secretly at lunch. Six of us – me and Polecat, Jerry, Knockers, Pete and Finchy. The only one who didn't show was Red. We knew he was scared. He didn't want anybody parading him back to Froggy Bottom for more crimes. We didn't need him anyhow. Six was just perfect, Polecat said. He showed us the map and gave us assignments. Four of us would handle the frontal assault. Pete and Knockers were posted up on the rise across the stream for a flanking movement, and maybe diversion. We'd meet where the two paths crossed in front of my shanty at seven that evening.

Just then I had to ask, "Did any of you ever hear of old man Nickerson dealing black market?"

"Sure," Polecat said. "Nickerson's been in it right along. Just like old Haverford."

"Really, Mr. Haverford too. How's it work?"

"Simple. Say somebody's flat broke but dyin' for a butt. He's just gotta have a smoke. So they say, OK, old buddy, but how do we know you'll pay us back? We need some proof. What can you give us for guarantee? Stuff like that."

"And?"

"Maybe the guy says, Jeez, but I'm flat. And they say, well, what about that Red Cross kit you got last month? What's left in it? And he says, some crackers, some chocolate, maybe. Or how 'bout your wife's earrings. Then, cause the guy can never pay them back, they keep the loot and deal it for more."

"So the guys with the goods get even more goods from the guy who's flat."

"That's how it goes," Polecat said.

"And Nickerson's one for sure?" I ask.

"Nickerson and Haverford. That's what they say."

Now of course that's not why I joined in. Not really. It was really about this anger that'd been building from the start of Camp. About seeing people who figured they deserved to have it cozier, who figured they were better than the rest. But when you feel yourself drifting along toward something like that, it's nice to know you're on the side of justice, too. I felt like I was where Southy would've been, and Harry. And specially Geronimo.

At seven the sky was still bright enough, but the shadows were thick under the trees and along the paths. Polecat's first order was for everybody to go to their posts while it was still light enough to see. Not to stop, just to walk by and check positions, so we'd feel better when it got darker. Knockers and Pete headed up the rise behind my shanty and cut across. The rest of us went down the path.

We peeked in over the hibiscus hedge. Neddy was putting away his unused clay, wrapping it in a wet towel. Sissy was standing there watching him. The last glow lit up her straw-colored hair and her little white dress. In the shadows under the eaves, the mom and dad were sitting back and having a smoke. Hibiscus flowers were closing up for the night. They quivered in the light like they were about to dance. Everything seemed so peaceful.

Then, in a shanty across the stream, a baby started to cry. Maybe it was hungry. It sounded like a pretty small baby. Old Nickerson moved around in his chair. He didn't say anything at first, just rumbled real low. But the crying got louder. He crossed and uncrossed his arms, like he was pumping up for an explosion. I glanced over at Polecat, and he gave me that wild grin. Finally the old man burst into this great eruption of curses. Me, Jerry and Finch were laughing ourselves silly. But Polecat clicked his tongue twice and we took off for my shanty to meet the others.

By the time we were kneeling by the stream, scooping clay up onto the bank, the shadows had grown thick. We patted the clay solid with our hands, turning and dropping it on the ground to shake out the water. Then each of us made a few big balls of clay. We carried them in our shirts like women carry things in their aprons. When we got back to the hedge, the baby was still crying and Nickerson was howling.

"Shut that bloody thing up. This is quiet hour." But it sounded like that baby had the hysterics. The good thing was it called everybody's attention away from us. We waited for Polecat to give the signal. Over by the stream, Neddy was getting swallowed in darkness, but it seemed to me he was looking our way. Then Polecat clicked his tongue, we all raised our arms together, he gave us his big savage grin, and all at once the sky and yard were a shower of mud. Big hunks streaked down on the Nickersons. I threw my first mudball at the old man and the next at Neddy. One kicked a group of black trucks into the air. We were all firing so fast, I couldn't tell which shots were mine. One hit Neddy, squatting in the dark, and knocked him over backwards. I caught a glimpse of Sissy blinking her eyes and beginning to cry, her dress streaked dark gray. Mr. Nickerson roared into the open and bellowed at the hedge. Polecat danced and whistled and shouted curses in Tagalog.

"SIP-SIP-BUTO!" he cried. The rest of us fired off our last volleys and ran.

"PU-TANG-INA-MU!" Polecat challenged the man who pawed the ground like a mad bull across the hedge. Then the man charged. Finch, who was late coming down the hedge, almost got caught, but Polecat saved him. He danced between them like a bullfighter and took the attack with him, scampering back into the Nickerson's yard. As the man ran after him, he fired his last volley square into him. Then he danced behind Sissy, whistled loud at her dad, dodged around her and down toward the stream, pulling Nickerson into the flanking attack from the hill. Two more balls of clay hit the man as he stood there panting and confused. And Neddy was laughing, I mean, really laughing this loud happy laugh.

But Polecat wanted more. He ran back in front of Nickerson again to start another charge. This time we almost lost him. With the man moving forward and Polecat cutting across, Nickerson caught hold of the kid's dirty yellow shirt. Luckily the shirt was old and rotten and Polecat was moving fast. There was a loud rip and they spun to a standstill. The yellow shirt was a rag in Nickerson's hand, and all that was left of Polecat was a dark shadow.

Then they were off again, sprinting around the yard, the big man gaining in the stretch. All of a sudden, Polecat stopped. But before

Nickerson got to him, he looped back like a fox losing its scent, circled around Neddy, jerked sideways and jumped across the stream. Nickerson tried to cut after him, but slipped on a line of new lorries and sprawled headfirst into the water. We could just make out the wiry little figure dancing a victory dance on the hill and the mud-soaked man rising up from the black stream. He was still clutching Polecat's shirt in his fist. It was almost too dark to see. In a moment we'd all disappeared.

Of course, we all figured there'd be some hell to pay. We waited a whole week. But everything stayed quiet. Maybe old Nickerson was just too ashamed to complain. Or maybe the committee kept it quiet, afraid they might get the Japs involved.

CHAPTER 21

People go crazy for fireworks. Just shoot a few lights into the sky, a couple of good booms, you can get a crowd oohing and aahing in a shot. But not me. I hold out for memory. If I could just bring back a few months out of this last year, I bet I'd have you oohing and aahing big time too.

It wasn't just one thing like a light show. It was everything, fireworks outside and in all at once. It's not all that easy to tell just what it felt like. The closest I can come up with is for you to lie down on the railroad track and listen to a big diesel coming, first a long ways off, then closer and closer, just building and building, bigger and bigger, until all at once it's shaking your eyeteeth right out of your head. You want to yell at the top of your lungs, it's so big, so loud, so much to take. But you're too busy just holding your breath and praying. Then, just like that, while you're all in a sweat, it stops. You don't know if you've been hit clean out of this world or it all just went away. You shake all over and cry like a baby. And you know why? Because you're weak. Those sons of bitches made you weak. Kept cutting the rations and cutting the rations, until you were limp as a dishrag, and an old rotted-out, mildewed dishrag at that.

Me and Polecat figured we had it beat. We were young. We could run and dodge. We weren't like those poor old fogies with purple veins running down their skinny legs and beriberi creeping up from the ankles to the knees like poison, like slow floodwaters easing up toward their hearts. Beriberi was a killer you could watch, level by level, puffing up the joints. And even if me and Polecat were lean as cur dogs at the garbage dump, no beriberi was ever going to get a shot at us.

You'd see old guys down at the Gymnasium, skinny and yellow with the jaundice, so tired they could barely get themselves to roll out of the rack in the morning, taking long loud-snoring siestas in the afternoon, then easing quiet as shadows back into their dark racks at night. They played a lot of chess, those old birds, slow chess, sitting long and quiet under the acacia trees, looking deep into each other's hollow eyes to see if they could see old man Death lurking there in their neighbor.

It got so you could count on two or three or even four a day going out in plain wood boxes. And you know, not a whole lot of surprise or ceremony got shown by the rest of the Camp. I guess it's what we'd come to expect. They mentioned which names to cross off at roll call and even said a few words at chapel, but all and all, those boxes passed out of Camp with about as much of a ripple as a burial at sea. Just a few little kids scattered along the path to the front gate singing, "Didja ever think as the hearse went by that you might be the next one to die?" Only there wasn't a single hearse anywhere in sight. Not even a horse-drawn carromata. They'd just wheel them out on these little handcarts. The kids always sang nice and cheerful, putting a sweet little emphasis on the part where "the worms play pinochle on your snout."

Mom, who was working nurse at the Santa Catalina Hospital, told me most of the old ones died pretty quiet, just got weaker and weaker, with the diarrhea usually, and then sort of slipped off. But one geezer yelled and cursed all night in his sleep for three nights running, came up with wild word combinations Mom never heard before. When he finally croaked, the rest of the patients were pretty happy about it. Relieved. Seemed like peace and quiet had got to be more important for some than staying alive.

You cut somebody's daily ration down to a dipper or two of thin rice gruel – lugao, they called it – and you will definitely cut down on that person's energy. Some of those old birds would've blown over in a light breeze. Some of them couldn't even wait long enough to get to the hospital. Too impatient. Died right in their beds, right in their chairs. One old lady was so quiet about going, she sat most of a day in her shanty before anybody noticed she was a bit too still. Her jaw drooped a bit was all and she'd quit snoring.

Now here's the funny part. Every time the Japs cut the rations, this old guy we called the Colonel would say in this real loud voice, "You got to take the bad with the good." That would send Polecat rolling on the ground. We loved that old coconut plantation philosopher.

What do you mean by the good, Colonel?" I asked him. He was no army man, but once grew coconuts for Peter Paul, those chocolaty candy bars. And after the Japs'd taken my old man's pals, Harry and Southy, out of Camp, we started going to the Colonel for our answers. He'd just scratch his head and smile at us.

"Why would a Jap want to starve a poor Yank?" he asked real solemn and mysterious, like it was the last question in some holy test for monks.

"I asked first," I said.

"Cause we're beating the piss out of him, sonny. We've looked at him hard and long. We've stared him to a standstill. Now at last we've unleashed the dogs of war." Polecat really loved that.

"Unleashed the dogs of war!" Polecat repeated, smiling like he just had breakfast.

"It don't feel like we're winning," I said. "What's telling you we got the upper hand?"

"Don't you hear the news," he scolded.

"You mean all those names of battles we're supposed to remember? All those downed planes and sunk ships? How many got killed? It's nothing but our rumors against Jap propaganda."

"The tide's turned, boy," he scoffed at me like I was too dense to fill up his time. "When you hear 'Guadalcanal' and they take away your meat, that's victory. When you hear 'Midway' and your last shred of chicken disappears, that's glory. Now you just heard 'Leyte' and you're slurpin' gruel, Johnny. What's that tell you?"

"We winning big!" Polecat shouted. But I just couldn't put a good face on it.

"Couldn't we cash in one little battle for a bunch of bananas?" I asked.

"No, you stonehead," the Colonel said. "You got to give to get." But I shook my head. If this was victory, I could wait a long time for peace.

But I'd discovered my own secret formula for staying alive. Sticking with Polecat. He was the best hater I'd ever come across. And I was damned if I was going to let him out-hate or out-last me. Hate is strong medicine. People talk a lot about "Love thy neighbor as thyself," but for staying alive in a prison camp, hating is the best. Keeps your mind sharp. Gives you resolve. Anytime I had any notion of letting down my guard, I'd just take a good look at Polecat flashing his gap-toothed grin and it gave me a backbone of pure steel.

Every place me and Polecat went, he'd want to race. Sure, he knew damn well he could run circles around me with those wiry legs of his. We'd be off and dashing along under the trees, me straining and puffing to stay close. And every time, just when I felt like I was going to bust a lung, he'd look back over his shoulder, smile at me wicked and taunt me, "*Sige na!* Hurry up!" Every time I'd run I knew I'd lose. But I knew I had to keep on running until I dropped. Polecat was my cross against the vampires. My silver bullet. And if we died, which we never held likely, he was damn sure going to die first.

Thank God my old man taught me boxing. That was one I'd always have on Polecat. He was quicker, tougher, maybe braver. But boxing was one place I brought superior education to bear. My old man learned the skills and passed them on to me. As long as a ref was standing in, making sure everybody lived up to the Marquis of Queensbury, I had him licked. And as luck and the Commandant of Santo Tomás Internment Camp would have it, those were the conditions we battled under.

Just when everybody was getting so low on energy he thought every step would be his last, we got us a Commandant who believed in the Olympic Athletic Ideal. Maybe you never heard of the Olympics of 1944. Somebody told me they canceled them all around the world. But they were held, sure enough, in Santo Tomás Internment Camp.

"Your problem is not diet," Commandant Yoshie announced to us with a happy smile. "Your problem is lack of exercise." Well, you can bet your last Mickey Mouse Jap Peso he got a good groaner from the crowd on that one. You take a man who's been using his last ounce of energy concentrating on just keeping his heart beating and tell him it's now high time to skip rope, and you're bound to break that man's concentration.

It was mid-afternoon. We were in direct tropic sun. Around three and a half thousand starved internees had been kept standing attention for two hours waiting for Yoshie to come and greet us. Seven souls'd already fainted dead away in the Main Plaza. And he'd no sooner taken his first look at us than he recognized just what it was that was killing us. We were under-exercised.

It was tough enough just to think about exercise in that third year of our incarceration. It'd been a few months since anybody had even so much as suggested tossing a softball or swinging a bat, so we were a little slow to catch on at first. But folks did give it a try. And, as you probably figured, the tossing and the swinging were the least of our problems. They weren't near as tough as running to first after you got a hit or running down a ball lofted over your head into centerfield. I noticed the innings in those World Championship Games kept getting shorter and shorter. And, in just a little time, everybody got so skilled at playing that they could figure out who won in just three innings and quit right there, instead of waiting the full nine.

But our Commandant didn't stop there. He had the true Olympics in mind, with all kinds of races and acrobatics and exhibitions of skill and endurance. Well, the highlight for us young guys was the pugilist's art. And that was my game. They built a real ring – four wood posts, three strands of rope. They handed out the ten-ounce gloves. And they divided us up by age and weight. Me and Polecat were in the division called "Flyspeck." Every day we had a different match, three rounds of what Hollywood calls "slow motion." It was amazing how graceful we all looked. You could've made a film at regular speed and people would think you'd monkeyed with it and made it look soft and lazy like some genius of the cinema.

Me and Polecat dragged ourselves through three such matches into the finals. He got there on street guile. But I still had a lot more hours practicing under my old man's eye. Polecat knew I had the foot-work and the jab, the old left-right-left combination. So he tried to trick me. He came up with this little dance. Sort of a rumba or a samba, I think. He came at me kind of off-center, with a big grin on his face and a little hitch in his rear that got everybody laughing. I could hear them chuckling and snorting all around me outside the ring. He was moving so many parts to the rhythm, I could almost hear the drumbeat. Somebody was saying, "I do believe it's Fred and Ginger!" But I was Spartan as my old man always taught me to be. I stuck to my business.

About three-quarters through the first round, just when Polecat looked like he wanted me to Charleston, I caught him a pretty good one flush on the side of the head. It stunned him, caught him off balance and put him on his rear for a second or two. He lost all his sense of humor real quick. That put an end to butt twitching. And once he quit laughing and dancing, he lost his rhythm. He kind of lunged and stumbled through the rest of it.

Now I wouldn't be the one to challenge Polecat in a dark alley, but with ten-ounce gloves in the light of day, I could keep jabbing and moving pretty good. At least, good enough. Yeah, he gave me a red cheek and a runny nose, but I knocked him down twice and drew some real blood. A couple of good shots right on the button did it.

Got his respect, I could see it. And if I never won another thing, at least I took those three rounds off Polecat. Even though he said the decision "stunk like a rice paddy" and swore everybody from the ref on up to God must be blind, I got the bamboo cup.

It was a beauty, carved from a section of bamboo pole, my name and all the details of my heroic exploit etched and colored on the side. "Flyspeck Champion of Santo Tomás." I know Dad would've been proud. Polecat glanced at it sideways and licked his lips. He'd have killed for it. Pure envy narrowed his eyes.

But if he was worried, he didn't have to sit around long waiting for my glory to fade. I'd no sooner put my cup on the shelf in our shanty than I saw the first dust start falling. That hunk of bamboo had bak-bak and I had to watch it just sit there and crumble. That guy, old Ozymandius, from a poem they made us recite in school, thought he had it bad. "Look on my works ye mighty and despair," he said. At least he got a couple of thousand years to admire what he'd done. No one ever got to despair over my works. Not even Polecat. Sure, Ozymandius might've had some drifting sands to curse, but he never had to put up with the bak-bak. I barely saw my cup whole once. But as the Colonel said, "You got to give to get." When just a little pile of those termite shavings were left, Polecat's feelings started to mellow towards me again.

CHAPTER 22

You're asking where are those fireworks? Well, just be patient. You know you got to start with the little rockets first and build. I've got to set the stage. I've got to tell you more about this hate business of Polecat's. When I first met him, he spread it all around like grass seed. Wherever it landed, it sprouted and grew pretty good. He hated all us colonials pretty much as good as the Japs. So he spent a lot of energy practicing on folks who were supposed to be his allies. But along about the second year of Camp, he started shifting it all over onto Jap sentries and the Commandant. Finally, by that third year, with all that valuable practice behind him, he got so he could really concentrate and narrow it to just one person. And that was a Jap named Abiko.

Abiko was head of the Guard and about as mean as you're likely to run across. First off, he looked nasty, with a long sour face, a shiny shaved head and high polished boots, strutting by and looking around like he was searching for someone he could swat for being insolent. There were sure plenty of reasons to hold a grudge with that villain. I saw him haul off and sock a lady just because she didn't give him enough of a bow. You see, he was the one who stood us all out in the hot sun for about three hours, keeping us at attention while he taught us, all three and a half thousand, individually, the high art of the Japanese bow. Just so from then on, twice a day at roll call, we could bow correct to all those Japs.

But there's something funny about the American body. It just won't bend right in the middle. Even with starvation, it did seem awful hard for us to get down the real deep respectful Jap bow. Most folks didn't mind a little head nod once in a while, but they'd been shying away from that folded-at-the-belt variety. Old Abiko marched up and down the ranks dealing harshly with our obstinate breed. He grabbed people right out of line and gave them private lessons until they got it right. He pushed down and rapped them on their heads and shoulders to help them fold themselves in ways they never dreamed possible.

Then he laid down strict orders. From then on we had to bow to every solitary member of the Imperial Japanese Military, even your run-of-the-mill sentry. It didn't make any difference if you said you didn't see him or not. You had to bow or else. That lady sure didn't get it right that time with Abiko. She didn't bend the way he'd taught us. In fact, I'd say her bow was a whole lot more like a twitch. Abiko didn't offer her a private lesson. It was too late for that. He hauled off and punched her silly. Matter of fact, he broke her jaw. And that's what set Polecat off.

Abiko's bowing class got him mad enough. But you wouldn't catch Polecat bowing if he didn't have to. He'd almost always see a sentry coming far enough off to slip behind a shanty or start walking off in the other direction, yelling out to some imaginary buddy across the field. But when he heard about Abiko breaking that lady's jaw, he started pawing the ground. He wasn't even there when it happened and it drove him nuts. He swore his vengeance. From then on Abiko was Polecat's private vendetta.

The Colonel tried to talk sense into him, but Polecat didn't seem to be buying any. We were sitting on the bamboo floor at the entrance to the Colonel's nipa shanty, looking out across the great open field where Abiko was training raw recruits. They'd come into Camp, dragging these old wood wagons by hand, straight out of some rice paddy, most likely. Things were getting thin in Japan, I bet. The field was big and yellow now under the hot sun, and old Abiko was sweating his tunic through.

"What you think makes that Jap so ornery?" the Colonel asked us. Abiko was barking orders at the recruits, but they were awful green.

Even I could tell. All left feet and not a thumb in the crowd. Abiko was getting close to the end of his leash.

"Who cares?" Polecat said. "*Putangina*." He blew a cloud of blue smoke into the shadowy air. We were smoking what we called the War Pipe. The Colonel had this long showy corncob pipe, kind of like old General MacArthur's. We'd go around picking up any butts we could find lying on the ground all around camp, bring them to the Colonel's shanty and shake out all the tobacco into a little pile. Then we'd fill her up and have us a War Pipe. I took a slow drag and started coughing.

"Maybe he don't like bein' a Jap," I offered.

"You boys know about *shinto* and *bushido*?" the Colonel asked. He looked grand when he smoked. It was his old yellow mustache and the way the smoke curled up through it and then around his eyes.

"I think I heard of 'em," I said. "But just can't remember."

"Monkey talk," Polecat said, by which he meant Japanese. But the Colonel set us straight. He said this shinto stuff was like a religion where the Japanese islands and mountains and woods and such were the gods and the Emperor came straight down from the sun in the family tree and was a god himself. They weren't even supposed to look at him, he was so special. So they went around bowing all the time, afraid they might look up and see this god and be blinded or burnt to a crisp or something. It was pretty strange stuff, I can tell you that. Bushido made a Jap want to die for the Emperor more than just go on living day to day.

"So why does that make him mad at us?" I asked. "We don't care about his dumb islands."

"Hell, boy, he's not mad at us for wantin' his islands. He's mad because we're even living this close. Because we're not his Asian brothers. Because we walk around like big shots from America and don't believe in his gods."

"We make him very happy," Polecat said. "Give him a big bushido and kill him for the Emperor." He had his pocketknife out, clicking the blade in and out. Just then Abiko hauled off and kicked one of those recruits in the ribs and sent him squirming and whimpering in the dust. He had those young Japs crawling back and forth across the field all afternoon, just trying to keep their rifles off the ground. But they sure looked like they'd never seen a rifle before. And never wanted to see another one again.

"He's mad because they're losing the war and they got nothing left but a bunch of dumb farm boys who stand around grinning," the Colonel said. "He's probably the only real soldier out of the whole bunch in here. Heard he was in the China campaign and took a bullet in the gut. So he got this sorry prison camp detail. Maybe he's mad because he's not out at the front someplace."

"Looks like he's sure mad at those young Japs," I said. The Colonel took a long drag off the corncob and held the smoke inside awhile. He was thinking. Then he blew the smoke down through his nostrils like little darts. It made his eyes light up and get teary. He looked awful wise.

"He's embarrassed," the Colonel said. "And there's nothing makes a Jap madder than being ashamed." But Abiko persevered in his kicking and hollering. And it was pretty amazing. By the time the long shadows reached out across that dusty field, those recruits were keeping their rear ends down and crawling pretty good. Kind of like alligators and crocodiles. I guess if you're halfway good at what you do and keep at it, you can make something halfway fanciful out of a sow's ear. Why if he'd had another year, old Abiko probably could've even got those birds to march in step.

Polecat loved to call Japs "monkeys." He'd do his imitation of Abiko every time we were with the gang. It came from a speech the Jap gave us at roll call when they couldn't account for some poor sap on the roster who'd just been transferred from the Camp Jail for being drunk and disorderly to the Hospital for being sick and dying.

Anybody with half a brain should've figured out he couldn't have been there even if he would've. But after about a half-hour of this frustration, Abiko went stone-faced and started yelling in Japanese, because his men couldn't get their numbers straight. Then he started pacing back and forth and speaking to us in this real low stone voice. He mispronounced his English something terrible.

So after that, Polecat lined us all up – Red and Jerry, Pete and Knockers, the whole gang – and started his mimicking, with big, stiff steps, like he was carrying a long samurai sword. He could do it real good.

"You American say Japanese are monkeymen. But we are supermen. We all supermen!" And we'd all pull in our breath and bow to him – that big, deep bow we'd never do for the real Japs.

"Ohhh!" we'd say all together. "Velly collect, rootenant!"

But then things happened that really stirred Polecat up, made his face get stiff and got him buzzing inside like a soldier bee when you mess with the queen. When Abiko punched that lady, Polecat sure went bananas, but she repaired herself by and by. Maybe she had a toothache and found it hard to talk straight right off, but when the swelling reduced, she looked pretty much the way she always had. But the next two things that happened bang-bang hard on each other, they could never be made right.

First, we heard sentries caught two Filipinos during the night. We never did hear clear what went on, but Polecat said they were hoisting food over the wall to Americans and it was some kind of smuggling where they got caught red-handed with the booty. Well, maybe so, but if they'd been heaving stuff over the wall, how come they got caught and not the Americans who were supposed to be on our side to catch it?

Pete Bailey said there was a whole gang of Filipinos that beat up on a Jap guard or two, and they all got away save these two who couldn't run too fast. Well, that sounded a whole lot closer to logic, so

I leaned to that story. But you can see what we had. We were just like a horse with blinders running at the racetrack. He can run and run, but when it's all over, he's got to ask some other horse to find out who won. There we were in the heart of Manila, but with that big masonry wall all around Santo Tomás, we couldn't tell what was happening in the street right outside unless we had a good rumor to believe in.

They dragged those two poor Filipinos into the front section of Camp, up by the Main Gate, where Abiko had early on made a work crew put up a sawali fence. That made it tough to see. Sawali's woven together like a mat, so unless you find yourself a hole, you can't see through. But me and Polecat and Pete crowded up there with some others and found us a peephole in the fence where we could see them tie those poor boys to posts and beat on them with big bamboo clubs. And you could hear them cry out and groan in pain just as plain as if you were right there beside them. It made us sick to watch it, but we stuck it out, first Polecat looking through the hole, then me, then Pete, until their bodies sagged down unconscious. Then we went away, feeling low and vengeful but stupid, because we couldn't do a thing. I heard one died and the other was thrown in a cell in old Fort Santiago, where his broken bones all knit wrong and he was crippled. That's what I heard. I don't know if it's the whole truth. And that whole time I only heard Polecat say one thing.

"Fucking funny monkeys."

But something like that's most always catching. I guess everybody concerned was plenty edgy. The Japs were putting a lot more time in on practicing their martial arts and such. You'd see them out on the big field, early in the morning, dressed in just those fundoshi g-string things, doing their exercises, getting ready. Then you'd see them all duded up in bamboo suits of armor, whacking on each other fast and furious with bamboo poles. Polecat said they thought they were Ivanhoe or something, which was a book we had to read in our Camp School. But those old knights used metal swords and armor, so there was more of a clang-clang sound. This was more of a thwack-thwack. Polecat guessed maybe they got confused about which war they were supposed to be fighting.

"Next week, they ride horses and joust," he said. We got us a good laugh over that craziness.

But there was nothing funny about what happened the next day behind the Jap Commandant's Kitchen. Polecat got me over there to scout the joint for something. He was cooking some plan, I knew that, but he wouldn't let me in on it just yet.

One of the yellow curs that ran around Camp was there, all skin and bones like the rest of us. He'd got himself adopted by some Japs who hung out around that place. He was lying real quiet in the dust, just out of the sun, conserving his energy. Every once in a while he'd cock an eye to see what was passing by. Or maybe scratch for flees, or snap at a fly, or lift his hind leg and lick at his balls. That dog had himself a pretty good life by Santo Tomás standards. Most dogs and cats had been skinned and eaten by local connoisseurs in search of protein. This one never moved out of the shade except to get a scrap from some Samaritan Jap every third or fourth day. They always cursed at him and teased him plenty, but all in all, they treated that dog pretty good.

There was this threesome of sentries there too, up on the porch, sort of lounging in the sun, laughing and discussing things among themselves. They had those bamboo clubs, and every once in a while, they'd kind of rap them against the side of the porch, just to hear that thwack. They called out to the dog a couple of times, but he'd just maybe twitch an ear or slap his tail on the ground. He was too tired to do more. When the dog didn't hop to and come over, one Jap started yelling at him. That opened the cur's eyes and got his tongue lolling, but nothing more. The Jap kept hollering, getting himself angry and sweated up, but it wasn't doing him any good.

One of the others said something and went into the kitchen. After a bit he came out with a piece of raw fish in his hand, bent over and held it out and talked sweet to the dog in a coaxing voice, like that hound was his closest and dearest friend and he couldn't do enough for it. After a while the dog must've sniffed what the Jap had, because he got himself up, kind of stiff-legged and cramped, and limped over to get a taste. Meantime, the other two Japs sort of slipped around behind him and came in on his flanks.

The first one snapped his club down like he was chopping wood, real deft and hard across the dog's haunches with a solid crack that knocked him to the ground as if he'd been shot. When he tried to get himself up, he found his back legs didn't have any life to them, so he could only yelp and whine and snap out in pain and drag himself round in circles. But when he bared his fangs and snarled, the other one cracked him hard across the muzzle. That looked like it had done for the dog, and the others yelled at the Jap for killing it too quick, I suspect.

But it seemed like the dog was only stunned and he got himself part way up again, blood coming from his mouth and nostrils, snorting and shaking his head in a red spray. Then they moved in and started working on him more methodical, laughing and shouting at each other for turns. Oh, they did have themselves a merry time, just whacking away at that dog with their clubs like he was the fiercest enemy they could think of. Finally he lay there without moving at all, blood clotting in the yellow fur and dust. They poked at him, hoping to get a growl or a whimper, but he'd had enough. It took my breath away, I want to tell you. Left me speechless.

Polecat just shook his head and came over and put his arm around my shoulder.

"Come over here," he said. "I want to ask you something." When we got further from the kitchen, he nodded back toward the porch. "What you think's in the big can?" There was this can up on the porch and he knew as good as I did what was in there.

"Don't know," I said. "Food maybe?"

"How'd you know?" Polecat asked.

"I saw them dipping into it. Some kind of sauce or soup or something."

"Then how come you say, 'Food maybe?'"

"What do you want?" I asked him. "What kind of craziness you up to?"

"They put it out fresh every day. I'll be by your shanty after dark," he said. And, oh boy, I thought. Here we go!

"How about Pete and Knockers?" I said, figuring it would be good to beef up our ranks.

"No good. Knockers says his old man's too sick. Pete's mom won't let him out after curfew."

CHAPTER 23

Late that afternoon, those new recruits moved their wood wagons to the edge of the big field and camped themselves down for the night within spitting range of our shanty. I watched them straightening out their stuff for the night, then settling down to have some chow. But it made me too hungry and sad seeing those guys together like that, eating and talking. So after my mom left for the Hospital, I went and sat down at the back of our shanty all by myself where the muddy stream ran under the acacia tree with just a shallow trickle of water. Even there I could hear them chattering away, kind of soft and pleasant, sometimes laughing. And behind that I could still hear the click and clank of mess kits and pots and stuff, so I walked up the path aways, trying to think of something else. I was kind of nervous, to tell the truth, wondering just what we were going to get ourselves into. Finally, when it was getting near curfew and everything was quieting down all over Camp, I went back to the shanty, kicked off my shoes and lay down on my cot, thinking of my old man and missing him. I did that when I got nervous. I guess it was natural.

I concentrated real hard on his face. Gosh, I was fond of him. I never could forget in a million years the way he came towards you. He had a kind of forward lean, real physical, like he was attacking life. Seemed like he just loved every minute. I figured maybe he and some of those other miners up in the Benguet could've become guerrillas, hiding out in the jungles and swamps, ambushing Japs and stuff. Boy, I wished I was with them. That would be the life. Thinking about that made me feel better about going off with Polecat.

Sometimes I'd dream about Dad coming over the top of the wall to rescue us. Lots of people come up with the worst thing that can happen. Like how somebody's going to be tortured or executed when we don't even know where those people are for sure. But when you think about it, that's pretty stupid. My old man was plenty resourceful. He was a very strong person, too, he really was. You give me a choice, I'll come up with the optimistic picture for you. I figure if there's something bad on the program, I'll find out soon enough and then I'll deal with it.

I must've drifted off because the next thing I knew, Polecat was pulling at my foot and whispering my name from the edge of the shanty. It was getting pretty dark.

"Get your dinner pail," he whispered. He didn't have to say anything else, and I kept my mouth shut because I didn't want the Japs out front to hear us. We snuck soft as shadows out the back and up along the path under the trees towards the Education Building. The night had got so thick you could barely make out people when they slipped by. Everybody was moving back to where they were supposed to bed down for the night. It was so quiet I could even hear the frogs singing way over in that ditch along the wall. And even though we hadn't had an air raid yet, there was a blackout all over the city, and on the ground floor of the Education Building the lights were all shaded. That's where a lot of Jap officers were quartered. When we got closer I could hear muffled talking and laughing deep inside.

"Drunk," Polecat whispered. "They're plenty nervous." We walked along slow and casual, swinging our dinner pails like we were just out for a stroll. Nobody was near the Commandant's Kitchen, just a dim light from inside throwing pale yellow squares onto the lawn. No window at the front or back, just a door that was shut. But I heard a Jap voice, kind of far away, chattering inside the kitchen someplace. Then, while we were standing there, straining to make out who and where it was, this bat darted low, right over our heads, squeaking. It was enough to give you the willies.

Polecat handed me his dinner pail and disappeared onto the porch. I backed in close to the shadows and stood still as a tree, looking out, studying the road off to the side. The lid on the can clattered and Polecat cursed. Not loud, but you could sure hear it. I was holding my breath like I had my head under water. But it stayed so quiet, I could still make out the frogs and that little far-off voice talking to itself inside. The voice had me spooked until I finally figured it out. It took me long enough, that's for sure. But there was no other answer for it. It had to be a radio. I felt like a sap, standing there getting nervous over a radio voice, but it'd been so long since I'd heard one.

Finally Polecat reached out of the shadows and grabbed a pail. Then quick he handed it back heavy and dripping with some sticky liquid. It smelled fishy. I handed him the other pail. Then I heard the lid again, real light this time, and he was right there next to me and we were walking together back across the road and down the path under the trees towards my shanty. I was thinking to myself, boy, that was a cinch, we could do this every night, when all of a sudden I saw this big shadow looming towards us up the path, and then I saw the outline of the helmet. It pretty near stopped my heart. In the snap of a finger we'd come full circle from "home free" to "cooked goose."

We just froze there in front of him and Polecat right off gave him this real low bow. So naturally I followed suit. I didn't want to stand out. All the time my mind was racing on what excuse we could come up with for being out past curfew with our dinner pails full of Jap sauce. But before I'd even begun a plan, I heard Polecat saying something real loud and clear in Japanese.

"*Konban wa, Abiko-san*," he said just like he was a Jap native. And both of us stood there like statues for what seemed about a whole lifetime, not saying a word, just bowing as low as we could. Finally there was this low grunt from the Jap and he went on up the path.

"That was Abiko?" I whispered when we got back to the shanty. "What the hell did you say to him?" Polecat set his pail down and started laughing like crazy and trying to hold it all in at the same time. I kept asking him what he'd said, but it took him a full five minutes, I swear, before he could answer. Every time he started to talk, he'd break into the shakes.

"*Konban wa* is good evening," he finally confessed. "And then, Abiko, sir." Well, there's no telling what a so-called friend will do behind your back. All this time Polecat was posing as a Jap-hater, and here he was talking just like he was one of them.

"How'd you know how to say that?" I asked him.

"I figure it'd come in handy," he said, still grinning like the smartest mestizo on the face of the earth.

"Well, you sure fooled old Abiko," I said. "I got to hand it to you there." Then he started sputtering and shaking all over again, only harder, and it took even longer this time before he got himself straight.

"Not Abiko, you sap. Not Abiko."

"If it wasn't Abiko, why'd you say, Abiko-san?" I asked him. And after he told me, I could've slapped myself silly.

"Who's that Jap most scared of? Abiko. Just the name got him worried, I bet. He probably thinking right now Abiko maybe knows us real good. Maybe like buddies." One thing I'll give old Polecat every time, he was as quick a study as you're likely to find for a tight situation. I felt like I'd just tripped over my own two feet.

But, damn, we felt big and heroic. We sat in the dark on the back step of my shanty and slurped that fishy sauce and kept giggling and trying to hold it in until our stomachs hurt. We came pretty close to the hysterics. Guerrilleros. That's what Polecat called us. And he made me swear I'd go with him on another big raid.

"Yeah," I said. "Someday." I was proud as punch. That sauce was so good and rich, it made us kind of sick to our stomachs. So we saved most of it, closed up our dinner pails, cleaned them good outside so the ants wouldn't crawl all over them and put them down under the shanty floor for the next day. Then Polecat slipped off to the Gymnasium so he'd be there in his cot when everybody woke up.

Next morning while Mom was still sleeping off her night at the hospital, me and Polecat did some serious bartering. Those farm boys camped out front were so wet behind the ears they never even thought where we got our sauce, so we traded them even, one dinner pail of sauce for a whole mess of fresh-cooked rice. You should've seen us there with all those crazy Japs around us, smiling and pointing at the sauce and then at them and the rice and then back at us, like we were in some bazaar, until finally we struck a deal. And those guys were pretty nice to deal with, all in all. We still had one dinner pail half-full of sauce and more rice than the two of us could eat in a week, so we went over and fetched the Colonel. And when Mom got up, we had us a real feast.

You consider what we'd been eating along with our lugao on a regular day – worthless greens like telinum and pechay and kang-kong and pigweed. You figure we were so hungry we'd even chopped down a banana tree behind our shanty, sliced the trunk up like an onion and ate it boiled. And all we got out of it was a little bulk and then the runs. Well, you can see what all that rice with fish sauce spooned over it must've tasted like. We just sat there in the shanty, barely even chewing, just letting it melt like sugar in our mouths, smiling at each other like we'd been born again.

The Colonel ate real good and my mom ate good and still nobody said one solitary thing about where it'd come from. They just seemed to accept it like "manna from heaven." That's what the Colonel called it. He said we should be as happy as the Israelites with this unexpected gift thrown in our laps by Providence. The old guy sure had a way with a phrase. Like we were out in the desert somewheres and God was looking after us. I tell you, it made me feel pretty good.

But then I took a good look at Polecat who was grinning at the Colonel like he was nuts. And I figured it out. Here we just pulled off this slick raid and then duped a bunch of Japs into trading for rice, and along comes God and takes credit for everything. The tough thing about being secret at what you're doing is you can't own up to anything. If you've done something good and don't jump on it quick and take the credit, somebody else is going to grab it away. But after Polecat and the Colonel took off, Mom put her hand on top of mine, real soft.

"Look at me," she said. So I looked at her real close. She looked kind of miserable and wrung out, to tell the truth. I have to say it. She was still nice looking, with those green eyes and pale yellow hair bleached even lighter by the sun. She just looked bushed. Kind of dark around the eyes and her hair all sweaty around her forehead. I guess it must've been hard on her, being a parent to me all by herself, since I was at such a difficult age. I guess it was easier for her to be a nurse under the circumstances. "Promise me, Johnny, you won't do this again."

Well, what could I say? First someone took all the credit, then I got all the blame. It was hard enough just to work yourself up to go on a raid without some woman swearing you against it. I guess that's why guerrillas are so set on not having ladies running around on bivouac. They'd never get to do anything. But I thought it over a minute and saw a way out. I figured no matter what me and Polecat would do, it couldn't be just like this time. I mean in some way, shape or size, it wouldn't be exactly this. Right? So I squared myself up, looked her right in the eye and swore to her with all my heart.

"OK, Mom," I said. But she just kept looking at me like she needed something more. Isn't that just like a woman? Always wanting something more. Something exact. It's like she had to see it in writing. "OK, OK. I swear I won't ever do this again."

About then Polecat was starting to sound like the local expert on the Jap morale. Everything that happened was just one more sure sign that they were about to crack. "Look at all this stuff they're dumping in here," he said. He grabbed me one day to show me some big crates of machinery they'd just unloaded at the end of the field across from the Education Building. "You see, you see," he kept yelling. Then he made me go look at gasoline drums they were burying over by the Camp Garden. "Pissing their pants, Johnny," he said. Then they started dragging in these big rolls of heavy wire mesh. "Know what that is? Know what it's for?" he kept asking me. "Airstrip!" he said, real excited. "So they can escape in a airplane. Hah!" Well, they sure were loading a lot of stuff into our Camp.

Polecat started dancing for real when the first air raid came, even though we never saw a single plane and the all clear sounded in less than an hour. Just the sound of the siren wailing got everybody digging in the ground all at once, and if you asked Polecat, that was the best sign of all. The Japs were ordering up work details to build air raid shelters. And all kinds of new Jap soldiers kept rolling in and out of camp like it was vacation time. Then somebody started feeding us rumors that they were going to move us all out of Santo Tomás to some whole new place.

"That's a real good one," Polecat said. "They don't know what to do – run like a dog, fly like a bird or dig like a pig. I tell you this Jap Army's real fucked up."

Me and Polecat built our air raid shelter right under the back corner of the shanty. And it was fine. First we dug out some ground back there, only we couldn't go too deep because the water would start leaking in. Then we went out to the big field where the work crew was cutting squares of sod out of the lawn. We got a bunch of that sod and piled it all around the hole we'd dug to protect us from bombs and such. When we were all through, we put a sawali mat on the ground and crawled down there like it was our secret place. It was good and cool on a hot day. And there was many a night it became our home. It fit me and Mom and Polecat with room to spare. Sometimes we even invited the Colonel to come in and join us.

The Commandant wasn't so lucky. He had a work crew start digging a big hole right out in front of our shanty. It was going to be the special air raid shelter for his car – this big black Packard roadster he had requisitioned from some poor American who'd lived near us out in Pasay. I remembered it from the old days. We sat there and watched while a crew dug and dug to make it big enough and deep enough. Until one day their hole sprung a leak and filled up like a swimming pool. The Commandant came and inspected it and just shook his head and looked sad. After all, it was such a grand plan. An air raid shelter for a whole Packard! You got to admit, that's a scheme.

For a long time that hole just sat there gathering water and mosquitoes. But finally someone came up with this ingenious plan to make it the Commandant's Carabao Wallow. Polecat loved that. "The Official Carabao Wallow of the Imperial Japanese Commandant of Santo Tomás," he'd say very serious and then tickle himself silly.

They chained the Commandant's pet carabao out there – one of those big-horned Filipino water buffaloes – and that carabao made himself right at home and luxuriated in it. Probably the finest time of that beast of burden's life. I mean, to beat out a Packard! Polecat and Pete and sometimes Red would come by just to look at him. They'd ask, "Johnny, how's he doing? He keeping all right?" like I owned him. At night that big fearsome-looking beast made a real special sound. Not big and bellowing like you'd expect, but a small mewing call, like a cat's. It did funny things to your head, that sound. Sometimes I'd wake up hearing it in the night and lie in the dark, dreaming I was back home and there was a cat down in our garden.

CHAPTER 24

About now, you're probably ready for one of the special fireworks I promised. One of those big spellbinder flares that go up and up and kind of explode out of themselves in a way that makes you think you just saw eternity. And it just so happens one of them came along this day when we were all in the middle of English Class. Well, we were really in the middle of "Gunga Din," which had run over from English into Arithmetic because it was our teacher Miss Clark's second favorite poem. Her all time winner was "The Highwayman." She liked poems that went on and on. Sometimes we'd miss out on Arithmetic altogether.

Polecat was doing this big dramatic part, which was to keep saying "Din! Din! Din!" whenever there was a pause in this girl Millicent's reading. She had this real English accent and then Polecat would add this Filipino accent to the Din part. So he'd go, "Din! Din! Din!" And then back in would come this little chirpy English voice saying, "You Lazarushian-leather Gunga Din!" It was a stitch to hear the two of them, specially Polecat, and me and Red and Pete pretty near split a gut. Since he was a mestizo and all, Miss Clark probably figured he couldn't handle much more than just the "Din! Din! Din!" part.

There we were right in the middle of Gunga Din at the Camp School on the roof of the Main Building, when every plane in the whole God damn American Army and Navy showed up. Somebody was shouting outside and everybody ran out into the bright sunlight, leaving old Gunga Din in the dust. We all stood around with our mouths open, searching the skies, our hands shading our eyes, just yelling and pointing.

Then there they came, far off, drawing out of a big white thunderhead, small and silver like a school of fish in the deep morning sky.

When they came closer, you could just start making out some kind of markings on the lower ones, but there were even more above them, and still more above them, little glints of silver you could barely see, with smaller planes darting around among them like minnows. When they got still closer, they broke off into different bunches, banking in the sunlight. My God, it was something to see!

But even with that, there was this one dumb kid from another class standing there, just shaking his head back and forth, sad and forlorn, while all the rest of us were screaming our fool heads off.

"Them ain't our planes," he kept saying like he was at a funeral. "Them's Jap planes."

And Red said, "You're just stupid, kid."

But the kid kept up with "Them's Jap planes." Just shows you how tough it is to make some people happy. Like the Colonel once told me, you show some folks the Garden of Eden and they'll say it looks about the same as Iowa.

But Polecat said he could even see bombs falling. He was dancing there beside me, all sweated up, pointing to each bunch of planes and shouting out their targets. Well, it did get your heart pumping!

"Look at them!" he was yelling. "Grace Field. They're kicking hell out of her." The building shook like an earthquake had hit it, and then you saw the smoke rise in a big black cloud. "Pow!" He slammed his fist in his hand. Then he grabbed my arm and spun me around to the south. "Nichols, Johnny, they're hitting them at Nichols too." He was jumping up and down with both arms around me. "Look over there, Johnny. Sweet Jesus, look at that. That's Nielsen, baby." Now the machine guns were chattering all across the city, and then came the pump of the pom-pom guns. You could see little clouds bursting in and around the planes while they were moving out away from us. But there were no Jap planes up there. Where were the Japs? "No monkeys up there, Johnny. They all run for the trees."

"Din! Din! Din!" I was yelling and laughing, lost in the power of it. My God, there is glory in destruction!

And Red he yelled "Din! Din! Din!" back. But Polecat was having none of that.

"Fuck Din too," Polecat said. You had to love him. He knew when school was out.

By the time the next bunch of planes came over, the siren'd gone off and they'd ordered us all off the roof. We tried to look out through the windows downstairs, but the monitors kept pushing us back into the hall. We had to stay there in the corridor, crowded with everybody in the dark, feeling the bombs rock and shake the building. It got too hot and stuffy in there and everybody was real still and hushed, listening for what was going on outside. I don't like being crowded in tight with a lot of sweaty, nervous people. When it was over, I was rung out and pretty shaky myself. And then we had to wait for about a half-hour in the chow line. But we ran into some luck. The rice that day had a little scraping of fish in it. We took it over to the shanty and sat there waiting for the planes to come back.

They weren't long coming. We crouched by this big tree and watched them. Mom was trying her damnedest to get us to go into the air raid shelter, but we were hypnotized. This time there were dive-bombers too, and they streaked in on targets over Pandacan and the North Harbor. Polecat kept darting out to the edge of the field for a better view, then giving a little jump and running back to yell close-up at us where they'd hit. The sky was so loud with the roar and drone and chatter and the sirens wailing, we could barely hear him. That's when I saw my first P-38 Lightning, with those two bodies kind of glued together, flying along as lovely and proud as an angel. Then we saw dive-bombers go into a cloud of smoke out over the harbor, and all of a sudden one of them caught fire and started to skid downward and screech like a big wounded beast out over the acacia tops. There was no mistaking that awful sound out of the engines and that black smoke trailing off behind. It pulled so hard at you it was tough to keep your eyes clear.

"Help him, God, help him," my mom was praying. And you could see she meant it, her eyes all red around the rims and her hands clutching at her sleeves. I could see in my mind the poor guy in that plane diving right into the flames and burning up. Made me feel hollow. But Polecat was still dancing like it just turned New Year's. "Just one, Johnny. That's the only one we saw them get the whole time."

Wow, that first day was a whopper and it wasn't even over yet. Late that night this big explosion out of nowhere just about knocked me right out of bed. Me and Mom looked out the front of the shanty at this huge red glow lighting the sky. Then there was another explosion and a high leaping yellow flame that kept growing and stretching itself out until the whole horizon glowed red and yellow together. The Japs had their searchlights going too, crisscrossing each other and scraping across the bottoms of clouds. At night it got even more mysterious and wonderful than in the day, drawing you in towards it so you couldn't hardly sleep. You had to keep getting up and looking, afraid you might miss something.

You had to know the very next day was going to be tough times at roll call, all of us just standing and bowing while Abiko got into a whole new set of rules. First off, we learned we were all in very big danger and it was the job of his Imperial Army to protect us. That caught me a little off guard. I was sneaking looks at all the guys round me who were working overtime just keeping a straight face. From now on, he said, we had to go right into our shelters when the air raid sounded. If we weren't in our shelters, bad things would likely happen.

Abiko gave us this very serious lesson in Japanese. He taught us two words. And he got his real deep growling voice on for it too. He kept repeating these two words over and over like we were all morons. If anybody was found outside his shelter during an air raid and a guard said, "*Tomare*," that meant "Halt" and you better stop right there or get your ass shot off most likely. There was just one excuse for ever getting caught out in the middle of an air raid and that was "*benjo*" which stands for "bathroom." He marched back and forth for about two hours, giving us all this hog slop about how we were under their special care and these rules were for our own good.

After roll call was over, seemed like no one wanted to leave the Main Plaza. Everybody just sort of shuffled around kicking at the ground and smiling. There was this one old codger who could barely just stand he was so weak, and he was smiling so hard he couldn't keep his upper plate in his mouth.

"I sure am glad Abiko told us about this benjo place," he was saying. "I figure if it keeps up like yesterday, I'll be pretty much livin' full time at the benjo."

After it broke up and we wandered away from there, Polecat lay down in some tall grass under a banana tree, crossed his legs real comfortable and smiled like a crocodile. I never saw him look so tickled.

"Abiko is one very nice guy," he said. "You never need a papa or a mama if you got Abiko-san. He will love you and take care of you and make sure to protect you from the bad Americans. By golly, he's the best damn Jap I ever saw." He looked so comfortable there, I lay down right beside him. But no sooner was I at rest than he jumped up again like a crazy, whipped out his pocketknife, and started carving a circle in this bare spot of ground. "That's Manila. You're the Japs. You go first, Johnny-san." He gave me this deadman stare like I was his worst enemy on earth.

I played along with him. It was a kind of mumblety-peg we called "territories" or "war." We chucked the knife into the circle, carved up the pie. He always beat me easy at this game, so I was glad to play the Jap side. I groaned real loud like it hurt every time he stuck the knife deep into my territory. When he was all through carving me up, he wiped the blade on his shorts, snapped the knife shut, bowed low to me and said in this super-low voice, "So vely solly, Abiko-san."

Then he whipped the blade out again and held it up in front of my face. "Someday, I'm going to stick this in that Jap," he swore, dead serious. Then he flashed me a crazy grin, like maybe he was joking. Only I knew better. I guess we were all on the verge just then.

No, let me take that back. I hate it when somebody tries to make excuses and smooth over the truth. On the verge, my ass. Like we're supposed to believe we're our real selves only when things go easy and all we have to worry about is going to school. But that's not true. I gave it some hard thought one day. I believe the way you are when there's no food and bombs are falling is maybe closer to your real self.

You take Polecat. As far as I could see, he was thriving on those times. He'd run around checking things out all over the Camp. You wanted to know something that happened inside our walls, you asked Polecat. He was so many places, you never knew where to look. Like the time he just up and disappeared. I mean gone. I looked for him high and low for about half a day and couldn't find him anywhere. I asked Pete and Red, but they hadn't heard a thing. I was kind of scared to ask too many, to tell the truth. You never knew just what he was up to. Then we found out at roll call he and some other guys'd got caught looking at a dogfight after the siren blew and the guards grabbed them and took them to the Jap compound, up front, back of the sawali fence. I didn't see him for a couple of days. And I got plenty worried. Then all of a sudden, there he was, standing right in his regular place at morning roll call, just like nothing happened.

"Jesus," we said, all excited. "What'd they do to you?" But Polecat played it real tough. He should've had a cigarette dangling out of his mouth, he was so tough.

"Games," he said with this funny smile. "Just games. They make us stand at attention on this log and look at the sky. Balance. You like to look at sky, they say, you look at sky. If we step off the log or try to bend our knees, they start bangin' our legs with clubs. Funny monkeys." He showed us the bruises on his shins.

"Boy, how long you have to do that?" Pete asked him.

"Seven hours, maybe eight. Till after dark. Don't worry, I play their games OK. Only that old guy over there he passed out." Polecat pointed out this poor old sickly-looking bird. He sure didn't look too hot. "Fell off and started kicking." But you could tell Polecat was loving it, like he'd just won the game.

And you take Mom too. She was always pretty religious and all, going to mass on Sunday and making sure she had something on her head and genuflecting at all the right times. That was always her nature, only she was moderate about it. But after that first big air raid, she was there for matins every single day, and vespers too if she wasn't at the hospital. Well, what can you say? She needed it, I guess. I think it was that plane going down in flames that did it. It might've been something else at the Hospital or her worrying about me, but I think it was that dive-bomber and the way it screeched going down. That's my theory. It's funny, you would've thought she might have started sooner, when we got separated from my old man. But she waited for that plane. She wasn't fanatic or anything. She just needed to pray a lot. And the thing is, I think that was closer to her real self than any other time I knew her.

Anyway, we got lots of practice finding out who we were. Those raids went on pretty constant for something over four months. It was living on the high wire. Sometimes you'd never even see them but just hear an air raid signal and then far-off explosions and drifting smoke. Sometimes just two or three planes'd streak in and strafe and be gone before you even had time to look up. Sometimes big booming waves of bombers'd come slow and steady like they ruled the world and blast hell out of a whole section of the harbor until you thought nothing was going to be left. And the Japs'd be pumping every ack-ack gun they could muster, shooting about a billion little clouds into the sky. Then fighter planes'd go up and have a go at each other, climbing and banking and diving with that nasty screech, every machine gun going at once.

Sometimes they'd catch us unawares when we were just walking up a path and we'd run like hell along the shanties until we got to a clearing where we could watch. Sometimes we'd jump and cheer until we wore ourselves out. But when the roar and thud of the big planes was too close and awesome and heavy, we'd just lie close to the ground under the shanty, with a toothbrush jammed between our teeth to cushion the impact, and hope the bombs went away real quick.

Then the all clear'd blow and every kid in camp fanned out across the grounds to see what had fallen out of the sky. We picked up these crazy, twisted hunks of metal and called them the Treasures of War. And the more pieces of shrapnel you picked up, and the bigger, the more the other kids envied you. We found some real beauties too – big knife-sized hunks with jagged edges that could cut a man right in two, whole perfect nose cones with all the rest blown away, sometimes strange pieces we could only guess at and that would always remain a mystery. We turned them over and over in our hands and just speculated.

But the best of all fell on my fifteenth birthday. Me and Polecat found this hole behind my shanty and dug out an entire perfect dud. All in one piece. Black and sleek and deadly-looking as any cobra. Still hot from being fired off and whizzing down like death through the air. We cleaned it up good and carried it nice and easy over to the Colonel.

"What the hell you got?" the Colonel said. "Be mighty careful there, boys."

"Can you get the explosive out?" I asked him, but he didn't look too pleased with the idea.

"Why in the name of Jesus would I want to do any such fool thing?" He was standing in the doorway of his shanty and it didn't look like he was ready to invite us in just yet.

"This is a whole shell," Polecat chimed in.

"Yeah," I said. "It's priceless!"

"It looks a whole lot more like it's intent on doing harm," the Colonel said. But we kept after him and after him and finally we wore him down. "I'm only doing this if you swear to fetch my meals for a week," he said. That was slave labor, standing in line a whole half-hour with an extra dinner pail, but it was worth it.

We operated on that shell down by the Colonel's air raid shelter. It was in the back and out of view of the Japs. The Colonel sat cross-legged on the ground with a towel across his lap. First he just looked at it a long time like he was trying to peer inside. Then he attacked it real careful with a screwdriver and a pair of pliers, but mostly just twisting with his hands. He made us stand back so we wouldn't all die at once. He kept talking to the shell like it was his child. "Easy does it, baby. Be nice."

"How you know how to do that?" I asked. "You done it before?" It did seem a little funny, his putting it right in his lap like that.

"You hang around these islands, boy, you learn plenty about munitions. Setting a charge, handling a fuse. Where the detonator goes." He was sweating plenty, but appeared to enjoy it. "Be nice, baby," he kept saying.

"Is it Yank or Jap?" Polecat asked.

"Jap," the Colonel said. He could tell because the threads were backwards when he unscrewed the cap. And there was this tiny symbol stamped in the metal way down on the side. After he took it apart, he boiled out the powder over his charcoal stove, cleaned it up good inside and dried it so it wouldn't rust. "We could use some oil," he said. "But I guess we'll just have to wait for that."

It was always nice and comfortable in the Colonel's shanty. Some of his banana trees'd survived and they shaded the front. We all sat back and just admired our souvenir.

"How long you think before it'll be over?" I asked him. He always had opinions on such things.

"They better not take too long or there won't be none of us here to greet 'em."

"Japs'll throw up their hands pretty soon," Polecat offered up. But the Colonel looked doubtful.

"There's no doubt the Yanks got these Japs where they want 'em. They got 'em in a bear hug and they're ready to squeeze. Every sign says the Jap is a goner and that sounds promising. There's just one little hitch. The more they squeeze, the more the Japs squeeze us. It does put you and me in a precarious position, boys. Mighty precarious." That put a wrinkle in it we might not have been studying. The Colonel was of the opinion that bushido wouldn't allow certain Japs like Abiko to give up all that easy. "I'd say the best policy for you boys right now is to lay low. Layin' low is definitely the best way to keep your scalp."

But laying low was not about to be policy as long as Polecat could put in his two centavos. "Layin' Low" is what he named the little Jap plane that would only go up into the sky after the all-clear sounded. When the sky was full of bombers and fighters, thick with smoke and gunfire, heavy with hell and damnation, that little plane was nowhere to be found. But blow the all clear and allow ten minutes or so of silence, then listen careful and you'd hear him, small as a Singer Sewing Machine, circling around in the sky over Manila like he was king and would reign forever. Folks laughed every time they saw him up there. But Polecat spit on the ground and said in this loud old man's voice, "There goes your big and mighty Layin' Low." And he boomed it out so he was sure the Colonel heard him.

What Polecat wanted was to be sudden and swift. We talked about it a good bit. We figured if Dad and Harry and Southy escaped the Japs and were free, they'd be out there somewheres, acting sudden and swift. Guerrillas. Ready to pounce. "We just wait for our chance," Polecat said. "Then we be sudden and swift." And not too long after that I got a real clear view of just what this sudden and swift thing looked like. It happened when we were out in the big field and nothing over us but blue sky. Not one cloud, just sky.

It came like a dream all packaged with a beginning, middle and end. Three planes – bam! bam! bam! So low they were there before we saw them coming, like they just jumped the wall and were already above us, moving fast. Corsairs. Bent gull wings, gray-blue, a white star, so tight and low to the trees you could see the pilots in the cockpits. Then they banked and lifted and rolled, like birds playing games.

"Jees!" I said. "You see that pilot. He waved!"

"Victory Roll," Polecat was yelling over the roar, pointing. The Corsairs climbed and rolled quick against the sun.

"He waved, for Christ sake! He waved at us!" I felt dizzy, like I was up in the cockpit with that pilot, flying fast over the trees. Then they banked again and dove, strafing something right out beyond the wall.

We were running along after them as fast as we could go, shouting at the top of our lungs, like we were trying to lift off and fly with them, when something funny happened. All of a sudden the starch went out of my legs and I dropped like a rock. The ground just came up and hit me. Whap! My heart was pounding and I was gasping for air like a guppy out of water. Boy, I felt light-headed and weak. And stupid too. Then Polecat was looking down at me from out of the sky like a black shadow.

"You OK?" he was asking. It was all kind of flat and shiny behind him.

"OK," I was saying. "OK. Did you see that guy wave?" I couldn't get off the guy in the cockpit. "It was something, I swear."

"Sudden," Polecat said, making his hand dive and bank like a fighter. Then he was laughing, reaching out his hand to help me up.

"Swift," I laughed back at him and grabbed hold. Then I was OK again. It sure wasn't easy keeping up with Polecat. But there was no way I was going to let him think I'd gone soft. "Boy, I was flying! Did you see me flying?" I asked him, with my arms stretched way out like wings. "Or you too busy watchin' the other guys?" He looked back at me like I'd gone funny on him. He was really looking worried. And just then, while I had him off balance, I tripped him up, kicking his heels together from behind. Then I fell on top of him hard. "Maybe you missed my flying, kiddo," I was yelling in his ear, "but you sure caught my three-point landing."

CHAPTER 25

Well, you know how they generally proceed at your honest-to-God fireworks show. They start off tame, and just when you think this is nice but nothing special, they show you a dazzler just so you know it's worth hanging in until the end. There's a kind of rhythm to it, start small and build, then back off and build again. But sooner or later you know they've got to show you the real goods. And you can always feel it when it starts coming, like two big ones close together and then something real exciting just behind to get the heart pumping.

Some time in January, these other explosions started up all around us, right inside Manila. At first we took them to be bombs, but lots of times they were going off when nothing at all was happening up in the sky. You'd just hear this big boom and then this column of smoke would drift across a stretch of empty sky. There wouldn't be a single plane anywhere. It was a real mystery, so naturally it was followed up by all kinds of crazy rumors. First we heard the Yanks had arrived in Manila, then we heard guerrillas were at work, and then we heard they were bombs after all just with some kind of delayed fuse. We heard a lot of other whoppers too. But it was the Colonel who finally came up with the answer. Only it was so strange when we heard it, we took it to be a whopper too.

"Who's doin' that?" I asked right after two big explosions went off together.

"Japs," the Colonel said. He said it like it was gospel and you know when it's gospel you're not supposed to ask questions. So I came at it from a different angle. I kind of tossed out a lure.

"I thought the Yanks were supposed to be blowing up Manila this time," I tried. "The Japs blew it up when we Americans were ruling here. Now it's our turn." But the Colonel didn't bite.

"It's Japs. They're trying to blow the whole damn thing sky high," the Colonel said. His voice was kind of old and shaky all of a sudden, not his usual loud delivery. But you could tell he wasn't joking.

"How come you know?" Polecat asked. He wasn't buying anything the Colonel was saying these days. Then he got out his knife, went outside and drew a big "territory" circle on the ground. "This is Manila. Here the Japs. The Japs' job's to fight for Manila, try to keep it, not blow it up." Polecat didn't like anybody messing with his ideas.

"Stand in that circle," the Colonel said. "Go ahead, get inside." Polecat finally climbed in. "Now you look out. What do you see?" That was something Polecat could really get into. You could see him just trying to sort it out. But it took him most of a minute to catch on.

"Yanks," he said. "I see Yanks everywhere coming at me." He made big engine noises, sputtered out machine-gun fire. His hands dove and banked like dive-bombers through the air.

"Now think Jap," the Colonel said. "How does it make you feel?" Polecat knit his brow and pondered it. Then he just lit up and smiled his best Jap-hating smile.

"Like a rat in a trap!" he yelled out at us like he'd just cracked the mystery of life. So there you had it. Poor old Manila was now getting it from both sides.

And at night you could really see it. These sudden flashes of light followed by heavy blasts and then huge leaping flames. They said Japs were blowing up storage depots, oil supplies, bridges, big office buildings, just about anything they got their hands on. Every time one went off, somebody was there yelling in your ear what he thought it was. The night sky was lit up with it. Not just on one side, but all around. And with those fires that kept burning bigger and stronger came these huge sparks floating over us, carried by the winds – some of them a couple of feet across – and it panicked the folks down where the huts were thickest in Shanty Town. Everybody was running to the stream behind us to grab a bucket of water just in case a spark landed on his nipa palm roof. I put our bucket out on the back step, just in case.

Then I caught this glimpse of my mom in the shanty. She was leaning on the front rail, looking out at the sky like it was Judgment Day. The fires were doing funny things with her face and hair, all red and orange, shadow and light. All of a sudden she looked so skinny and frail, like a ghost that kind of flaps and shakes in the dark and won't stand still. It gave me the willies just to look at her. I think if I'd reached out and touched her just then I might've bawled. Thank God Polecat came by. I looked down and he was standing there with a bucket in his hand, all sweaty and shiny in that crazy light.

"Hello, we've got our own private fire brigade," Mom said to him. She gave him this big smile. "Mabuhay."

"I help build this shanty," he yelled back. "Nobody's going to burn it down." And you know, I'm ashamed to say it, but it made me jealous. A whole crowd was standing out there on the path, looking at the sparks flying over the big field. The light shifted and rippled across them, like wind playing over tall grass. Seemed like Polecat was out there performing to the audience.

"OK," I yelled back at him. "You just watch the front-half. I'll cover the back." We were like little brats fighting over the same toy. It made me feel just rotten. I know Dad would've bawled me out good if he'd been there. It's a damn good thing Polecat and me never got tested. We probably would've been wrestling over who got to throw the first bucket of water on the fire. But the only real fires were back in a few shanties and the folks there worked together, getting water on the nipa roofs before anything too much was lost.

Well, if that was Judgment Day, the next week was trying hard for the Resurrection. Nothing at all cooled down except when it rained. And everybody kept adding fuel to that fire with more rumors. Then some whole new kinds of lights started flickering and flashing up north across the horizon. And they kept up all night long.

"What you figure they're bombing up there?" I asked the Colonel.

"They ain't bombing nothing," the Colonel said. He sat there real still, like the oracle studying for signs, squinting at those flashes long and hard. "That there's artillery, boy. Big guns."

"You sure?" I asked.

"Look careful," he said. "See what's different about them?" Boy, I felt ignorant. A flash pretty much looked like a flash to me. But I had to answer something.

"Not so big," I ventured.

"That's just distance. But you look out there long enough, you'll see they're all sticking low in the sky, little happening above. And most important, they keep repeating themselves. You see, they're setting there, not flying all around. Just doing what they was built for – old lock and load." Sometimes I figured there was more to that Colonel than you could find in a whole library. "That means the enemy's being engaged on the ground, boy. The Yanks is right here on Luzon and pushing south."

Well, that was a tune we'd all been waiting to dance to. I tell you, it was crackling – the Japs going crazy with the dynamite, the Yanks going nuts with the bombs, and now the twenty-four hour artillery drill. It was enough just trying to juggle it all in your head at one time. And it did seem, if they were that close, even the old codgers could hold out a few more days. But the food just kept getting scarcer and the deaths kept right on piling up – some twenty in a week by the end of January. I think every grown man had the beriberi by now, and the Colonel was starting to hobble around in earnest like he was in some real pain.

Just to show you how things had got, the Camp Doc and the Camp Commandant had a row over the semantics on a death certificate. Mom told me about it. Seems the Doc allowed some of these folks had been dying of the malnutrition, but the Commandant took exception and claimed it was more likely the heart attack. And in a way he had a point, because the heart did stop, but the Doc flat refused to sign a death certificate with that as the explanation. It is curious where folks choose to draw the line. The Japs gave him a couple of days to reconsider and then they made their move and flat out won the argument. They just threw that Doc in the Camp Jail and appointed a new Doc.

The Japs were really acting nervous now, busy burning their papers and killing their livestock like they were on the eve of some great celebration, drinking themselves silly and eating their way through the slaughter house all at once. Somebody set that carabao in front of our shanty loose and this sentry jumped on and rode him hard, trying to cut his throat with a bolo knife and hang on at the same time. He must've seen a movie about the rodeo. It took over a half-hour to do for that poor beast and in the end it wasn't a bolo but a sledgehammer that did the trick. I guess they'd trained those boys to kill men but neglected practice down on the farm. They cleaned out all the supplies in the Jap Bodega, cooking up big pots of rice and roasting themselves big hunks of pig, carabao and chicken. Maybe they were working themselves up for some of that bushido stuff. Like the Colonel said, food and drink can sure help fuel the gumption. There was a lot of shouting and singing going on.

Within a few days we were hearing machine-gun and rifle fire getting louder right in the north of Manila. And all the booming explosions and fires were keeping pace. One afternoon the Japs rolled in a bunch of big trucks and lined them up in front of the Education Building. Then they got busy loading on all their weapons, supplies and such. Sentries kept running back and forth along the paths, weighted down with gear. There were rumors that they might clear out without a fight, and others that they were going to take hostages. The Japs started making announcements over the loudspeakers, telling us to come to the Education Building so they could provide us with protection.

Around dusk I stopped by the Colonel's shanty, just to be with him awhile and watch the sunset. A Manila sunset is almost always worth looking at, but with all the fires, this particular sunset was a mighty ball of red, stretched about a mile wide, like a lantern straight out of hell. The Colonel said, "Don't you be lured in by them announcements, Johnny. They got gasoline drums stored under the stairs in the Main Building. They're scared, boy. Just think, if they plan a retreat, what're they gonna do with us? You can't tell what they might be up to. And tell your mom to stay away from those Japs too." So I went back to our shanty and found Mom lying on her cot in the shadows. I didn't see her right off. She was listening to the battle and waiting for the next shoe to drop.

"That you, Johnny?" she said. "Don't go anywhere tonight. I want you close by in case there's trouble. It could get dangerous." But I was so edgy I could barely stay put. I kept thinking about my old man. Maybe he was out there right now where the machine guns were firing, out past Cemeterio del Norte. Maybe he'd be coming in tonight. I was thinking hard about just how he looked the last time I saw him, over three years ago. I kept trying to picture it, wondering if I was getting it right, if he'd still look the same. I had myself all convinced he'd be there. It was like there was no doubt at all. I wondered what he'd be doing right now if he was in Camp. Not sitting in a shanty, I bet. I was kind of vibrating all over and couldn't stop. Like I was coming down with fever and the shakes.

Mom said she had to get to the hospital. I told her it wasn't right with what was happening. She looked awful tired and the gunfire kept getting closer all the time. I told her how the Colonel'd warned me, but she said a lot of folks were near to dying and needed her there. I was really worried, so I walked her over to the gate that led into Santa Catalina Hospital. The sentries wouldn't let me go further. You had to have a special pass and an armband. None of them appeared too friendly just then. Like they were looking for some excuse to pop someone with a rifle butt. So I had to leave her. I felt crazy as a cat, just twitching all over. So I took a hike down the path under the trees, trying to walk it off.

I was pacing back and forth there in the dark when Polecat came up and grabbed my arm from behind. He never said a thing, just sneaked up on me and pretty near gave me a seizure. Then he said real matter of fact, "You ready?" and it was like telepathy or something. We just went on up the path like we both always knew that's how it would be.

Up where the path met the road, we got in under the low branches of the last big tree, scouting out the Education Building and the road and the trucks parked there. The loudspeaker started to chatter again, telling us to join our protectors. But right in the middle the power must've gone off, because the speaker shut down and all the lights went out at the same time. There was a lot of loud talking, then it got hushed. It was spooky. We could just make out the trucks and a couple of sentries silhouetted way down at the front end of the line. I couldn't see another soul out there.

We picked the truck closest to the trees and snuck in low, keeping it between us and the building. I pushed inside the shadows until I touched metal, then worked my way around to where the canvas flap was loose at the back. Polecat was breathing close beside me. We found a foothold and rolled in over the gate. It was pure black and hard to breathe inside, with a smell of gun grease and canvas that's been stored a long time. We didn't have to think, just felt around on instinct. I took up a position by the canvas flap, holding it open just enough so Polecat could see to dig around. He got busy going at it but was coming up short.

"No damn guns," he whispered. "Where the hell they stick the guns?" I guessed by that Polecat had some pretty big plans for us, but right then we got a little crimp in them. Somebody stepped out the front door of the Education Building just when the power surged back on, so he was lit up by the flash. I couldn't tell for sure who it was, but I had a premonition. Hanging on his belt was a samurai sword. He stood some time in the dark after the door'd closed. Then he started to walk out slow towards us.

"Sh! Jesus, shhh!" I was hissing at Polecat, but he kept on rummaging. "He's coming, shut up!" I was on all fours, scrambling over to him in the dark. That finally got his attention. "He's right out there!."

"Who?" Polecat asked. I didn't say another syllable. I don't think I had any left. We felt our way back and cracked the flap just enough to look out. Just then the Jap lit a cigarette, and in the flare of the match, there was no doubt. "Abiko."

Up till Polecat said the name, I was going along like what we were doing was natural. But as soon as he said it, one half of me thought of another place it wanted to be. But we didn't budge. We just kept staring through that crack. And he kept smoking his cigarette and staring out at the night. Finally he barked something at the sentries and they came a little ways towards him at a trot, answering back. Then he yelled at them again and they stopped and pointed. And they were pointing right at us.

Before I knew it, we'd scrambled up to the front of the truck bed, burrowing under about a dozen layers of stuff in about two seconds. Don't ask me what was going on out there. I left that business to others and lay still as I could, holding my breath and thinking my prayers. Abiko was right out there, real close, saying something. Then I heard the flap tossed back and someone digging around in the truck. I just hoped he didn't reach down and grab me. I figure it all must have gone on for about eternity. Polecat told me it was only five minutes. But I doubt he was any closer to the truth than I was. Finally I heard the flap again and the voices moving further off. I stuck my head out for air, but it was as dark and stuffy as the inside of a sack. I had something in my hand that felt like a wallet. So I stuck it in my pocket.

"You see that?" Polecat asked.

"What?"

"He took something out of that sack. I think it was a grenade. Did you see it?"

"Pretty dark," I said.

"Looked like he was just checking to see if it was there. Then he put it back."

"Well, where is it?"

"Didn't you see? He took it, sack and all." Polecat was at the back gate, peering out the flap again. "See, he's right out there." I could see the pouch pretty clear, slung over Abiko's shoulder. "C'mon, hold the flap while I see if there's more grenades," he said. He dug around some more but had no more luck this time than the last. I think if I hadn't said anything, he'd be there still, digging through everything about a million more times. He got plenty frustrated.

I had my eyes glued on Abiko. He kept staring into the night like he was searching for something. Finally he tossed his cigarette, pulled himself up to attention, clicked his heels together, drew the samurai and did a salute. Not a hand salute, but the sword kind. He brought it up smartly till the blade was right between his eyes, and stood there like a statue for about a whole minute, saying his prayers or giving his pledge – whatever Japs do. What light there was from the sky just danced along that blade. It made hairs rise on my neck just to see it. He could've sliced my head from my shoulders with just one swipe. But after a while he relaxed himself again, sheathed that ugly sword, and went on up along the trucks towards the sentries.

"Let's get the hell out before he comes back," I said. "I don't fancy getting skewered on a samurai."

"Take it easy. There's plenty more here." When I was back out on the ground and had scouted to see that Abiko was still busy on the other side of the trucks, Polecat handed me his bundle. He had it all wrapped up in some netting, and it must've weighed about a ton. I don't know what kind of strongman he thought he'd brought with him. Both of us putting all we had into it just could barely drag it back to the big tree.

"What the hell you got in here, anyways?" I asked.

"How do I know?" Polecat said. "We'll sort it out back at your place." And, stupid as if sounds, we were just about to start down that path, when out of the night came three sentries towards us, huffing and puffing and rattling with a load of gear. That shifted our plans pretty quick.

"Listen," I said. "Maybe we don't need all of it. Why don't we sort it out here and just take what we need." Polecat gave me an argument, but I finally persuaded him. So we dragged it out onto the big field behind those rolls of airstrip wire. We got just as much light out of the sky there as we could back at my shanty.

I can be pretty persuasive. I even got him to ditch most of it. It looked a whole lot more like the Japs' dirty laundry than war booty anyway. Boots and leg-wraps and g-strings and first-aid patches and rolls of gauze. Not a single weapon in the pile. They must've packed in a hurry. Polecat came pretty close to weeping. But after putting himself in certain peril, he wasn't about to accept disappointment right off. He kept going back to what he'd already tossed and reconsidering it all over again.

"If we're gonna be sudden and swift," I told him, "we got to travel light." That's what made him listen. But he still insisted on keeping a few real important items, like this metal ammunition box, a hunk of canvas that looked like it was part of a tent, a cartridge belt with a canteen on it and some camouflage netting. But just when I thought I'd done the trick and got him halfway up to the shanty, he turned around and went back for some damn gauze. I hope I'm nowhere near Polecat when it comes time to pillage and loot.

Soon as we got back to the shanty, we stowed most of the stuff on the ground under the floor without even looking at it. Polecat tried wrapping the cartridge belt around his waist a couple of times, but it slipped straight down around his ankles, having little or nothing to latch onto. So he slung it over his shoulder and across his chest like one of those Pancho Villa bandoleers. He fancied that style and puffed himself up like he was ready to have his picture took. He did come pretty close to a real guerrilla, I had to admit.

We opened up the metal box, full of high hopes for rounds of ammunition, but there was nothing in it but a few capsules of rifle grease and cleaning tools. Polecat was as low as he could get, but he wasn't one for lying around and sulking. He could put a good face on seven-year locusts and a tidal wave.

"God damn! We can use this box for shrapnel," he said. "We'll wipe 'em up with grease and wrap 'em up with gauze. This'll be one hell of a War Chest."

Then we got down to the real prize. I'd forgot all about it and Polecat hadn't even seen it yet. You could've knocked him over when I pulled that wallet out of my back pocket.

"Where'd you get that?" he asked me, real surprised.

"Bottom of the truck," I said.

"How come you never said nothing?" He asked it like I'd done him some real harm, so I told him I was sorry. But when I opened the wallet up, he warmed quick to the occasion. First I pulled out some paper currency. "Fifty Peso Mickey Mouse!" he laughed. "Very good. We can ride in a calesa downtown." Then I pulled out this filmy white thing and he right off began clutching his sides and splitting his gut.

"What is this?" I asked him. I'm ashamed to admit it, but I had no idea. Old Polecat was verging on the hysterics and the palsy all at once.

"Pom-pom," he laughed, jouncing up and down like he was riding the ack-ack gun, but I was still drawing a blank, so he told me, "Make a suksok. You know, fuck." It still wasn't too clear, but right off that thing in my hand seemed nasty and slimy as a snake, so I flung it way out into the night. Polecat was still chuckling at me. "You touch a Jap rubber, you catch a big disease," he kept saying, waggling his finger at me and grinning his fool head off.

But I was already trying to figure out what this other thing was I'd just pulled out, something real delicate looking, all wrapped in cellophane. I couldn't quite make it out in that light, so I went up into the shanty and got down the charcoal stove and blew on the coals till I got them glowing bright enough. Then I gave it a closer look.

"Jesus, Polecat," I whispered. "Come up here quick." It was one of the strangest things I ever saw in my life. When I blew hard on the coals I could look straight through it, it was that thin and fragile. Like the skin you peel off after a sunburn. And hair sticking out of it. "What you think it is?"

"Looks like eyelid," he said. He took it out of the cellophane and laid it along the blade of his pocketknife. I never saw or heard of any such thing. "Looks like top and bottom eyelid."

It sure was weird. The machine-gun and rifle fire kept getting louder and closer, but we kept staring at that ugly specimen. Polecat figured it must've been like a scalp, cut off an enemy, some Filipino or American. But I held it could just as likely be a piece of someone dear to him, like his dad or mom. Some sort of token from a loved one who'd died. We meditated on it long and hard over the coals, just enough to make our skin crawl. Finally, Polecat came up with the answer.

"Remember what the Colonel told us about that shinto stuff? I bet this is from the eye of some guy who looked at the Emperor." And right then, while we were busy looking at that piece of hair and skin, all hell broke loose.

CHAPTER 26

Bam! This big explosion went off right down by the Front Gate. We must've jumped about a foot in the air. We were wired to go off, that's sure. People were yelling up there along the path, and then a sentry came running right by the shanty, hauling ass and clanking to a fair thee well. Across the field shadows were moving fast under the acacia trees.

"C'mon," Polecat yelled and he was out the front of the shanty and sprinting across towards them before I was even out of my chair. Then I was up and after him, and it felt like I was making time fly, but just before I got to the trees, I slipped in a mess of mud and landed on my ass. Then I was on my feet and running again. But the shadows of tanks were already moving big as elephants up along those trees. So I cut back and made for the Main Plaza. Just about everybody in Camp was gathering there and surging in towards the troops, shouting and crying, "They're here! They're here!" Then they shot up some of the most gorgeous flares you ever saw. Bam! Bam! Bam! They burst open like beautiful rockets right over us and then they jumped out of themselves into these big million-watt candelabras. Not just a few of them, but a whole bunch. They hung up there in the night sky like they were attached. Boy, for a time it was bright as day out there. You could see so good you could make out faces and everything clear across the camp. I thought I'd died and gone to heaven.

Those lights were too hot and lovely to look at, and tanks too with big sweeping spotlights and then behind them jeeps and more tanks, rumbling heavy and handsome up the roadway and onto the plaza. My heart was racing so hard it felt like it'd got off track. Then this soldier hanging on a tank turret started yelling at us.

"Get these people out of here! There's gonna be shooting!" But

barely anybody could even hear him above all the shouting and singing. All those folks were delirious, dancing and hugging and kissing
everybody like they were family and singing every damn patriot-
ic tune that came to mind. "God Bless America" and "America" and
"Star Spangled Banner" all going at once, like dueling anthems, so
you just had to leave off thinking and dance and sing yourself. Then I
found Polecat again when the spotlight swept by. I grabbed onto him
and gave him a big hug.

"We're here, kid! Right here!" I yelled at him. But he shook himself loose and then he was grinning and shouting something back,
only his voice was getting swallowed up in all that high-voltage excitement. The soldiers were out of the jeeps now, trying to push us back
and clear a path for the tanks. And amongst us, they looked to be gi-
ants with real handsome looking rifles and uniforms and helmets on
their heads. It felt like the whole world had come to join us there. This
one soldier even gave me a hug and a kiss. I tell you, you could take all
the Fourth of Julys that ever were and ever will be and string them together in a daisy chain and they couldn't stack up to what happened
right in that Main Plaza. "They're real men," I was shouting until my
throat was sore. "Real men."

One tall guy was pretty close to us, with a gold leaf on his collar.

"This one, he's the leader," Polecat was yelling out. "What rank?"
Someone said maple leaf was a major. He and the others were busy
trying to make something out of all that confusion out there, when
in the other direction, the crowd all of a sudden broke open and four
Japs, two civilian and two military, came into the spotlight with
their hands up. They had a couple of interpreters with them and
appeared to want to say something, but that crowd was none too
friendly just then.

"Kill them! Kill them!" they were screaming. Then a couple of
more flares shot off and those poor Japs looked mighty pale and scared
under all those lights. They sure weren't parading their stuff quite the

same as yesterday. Then all at once the time just kind of jumped forward and shot by in a flash.

"Abiko!" somebody cried out. I guess he'd been lurking back in behind the others in the shadows.

"He's got a grenade!" Polecat was yelling.

"Get the hands up!" the major shouted, but Abiko he went for the pouch, and the major he grabbed a carbine from the soldier next to him and brought it down fast firing from the waist without even stopping to aim, and bam! catching Abiko in a burst and spinning him sideways. Abiko just kind of folded up like he was giving us one last bow and sat back hard on the ground and rolled over on his side. Just like that. Quick as blowing out a match.

"Another damned Jap doing the Banzai Dance," the soldier next to me said.

Then I saw the blade gleam in Polecat's hand and heard him yell as he leaped forward and rushed out over Abiko, slashing down at his face. He hacked him twice before they could pull him up and off, knocking the knife out into the dark. Two guys grabbed Abiko by the boots and started dragging him toward the Main Building. The big spot swept by so you could see the blood soaking black out of his tunic and his dark bloody face too, with the big gash across the cheek and the one ear dangling loose from his head. People were rushing in on him now, kicking him and spitting on him. Polecat gave out a war whoop that could curdle your blood.

"You see the ear!" he yelled at me. "I almost got the ear! If they don't grab me, I have the ear!" But that crowd had just swallowed Abiko up. Gone. I never saw him again.

"Yeah," I was saying. "Yeah." But now everybody was singing again and it was too loud to even hear myself. They broke back again to let the first tank through. It rumbled off across the plaza and up the road towards the Education Building, followed close by another.

"Hostages!" someone was shouting. "They got hostages in there!"

The two tanks were moving up along the line of Jap trucks, everybody high-tailing it along the side, yelling out at the soldiers and up at the Education Building.

"Get these people out of here or somebody's gonna get hurt," the soldier was still shouting. Then the Japs started firing down from the building and the crowd broke and ran in a big wave. The tanks moved up under the trees, stopped and turned around slow and steady right across from the main door to the Education Building.

"Get behind the tank so you don't get killed, kid," this soldier said to us.

"Yes, sir," Polecat yelled back at him and we scurried back in there. The turret on the tank over us swung around and stopped. Then the big machine gun opened up with the first burst and you could see the tracers fly out across through the dark in a low arc and splatter off the front of the building in a big shower of sparks. And gosh, I was thinking, I guess this is it. I mean, it must be all over for those Japs and we're still here alive.

"Hey!" somebody shouted from the building. "There's Americans up here too, for Christ sake!"

"Move away from the center of the building," a soldier yelled back. Then, after a few minutes they opened up again, with another shower of bullets dancing off the facade. A squad of soldiers moved in tight behind the tank and sat down with us on the ground. I kept looking at their faces, but there was nobody I knew. They looked tired.

"You come from up north?" I asked, reaching out and touching a soldier on the arm. He was next to me, sitting there with his rifle between his legs and his head leaning up against it, trying to catch some sleep, I guess.

"Lingayen Gulf," he was saying, but he didn't look up. "Heard they were planning to kill you guys."

"Yeah, you take the city?" I asked him.

"Not yet," he said. "Just cut through. What they call a flying column. We got to hold out here until the front moves down." I kept looking around at all the dark, sweaty faces under the helmets, studying each one careful.

"Boy, how's it been?" I asked. "Pretty rough, huh."

"Not too bad," he said. "It's been a lot rougher than this."

"How about that Abiko?" Polecat said.

"He was doing the Banzai Dance. That right, sir? That what you call it?"

"Lots of Japs been doing that, kid," he mumbled, half asleep. "We seen 'em do it plenty all the way up the Marianas. Sometimes they'll do it by the hundreds." It sure seemed funny thinking about Abiko moving towards suicide along with a whole army of other Japs. That bushido was strong stuff, all right. It sure made quick work of old Abiko.

We sat behind the tank with those soldiers for some time, talking to them while the machine gun fired bursts at the building, the bullets glowing fast up and across through the dark and spraying off the stone and plaster just under the second floor. The men in the building shouted out at us again and then the Japs opened fire and shot out the spotlight on the tank. Then it was real dark out there again under the trees.

Someone was crying out "Medic!" and a couple of men ran by hauling this wounded soldier from in front of the tank. He was moaning some, I could hear that, and the medics were shouting back and forth and unbuttoning his shirt and working on him for some time, but then I saw him when they got up, and he was real still and pale and dead looking. They covered him up and took him further up along the trees. That hit me hard, sent a quick chill right through me. I guess I'd been just sort of floating out there on Cloud Nine, and was in urgent need of cold water and smelling salts.

The soldier next to me got to his feet, looking at them take the body away.

"Was that Nuñez?" he asked.

"That's right," one of the medics said.

"Shit," the soldier said. Then he sat down again, just staring off. That's when I finally had to ask him about my old man. I was so sure he was going to be there, you see.

"I don't think so, kid. What outfit he with?"

"I don't know." I mumbled, feeling low and shaky all at once. "My old man was up in the Benguet. Oldfield. His name's Oldfield, same as mine. Japs took the others north. Cabanatuan, maybe."

"Oh, prisoners," the soldier said.

"Maybe they got away," Polecat said. "Maybe they're guerrillas."

"They sent another outfit up there to liberate that bunch," the soldier said. "But I never heard anything about your dad." I felt real funny, that's for sure. I'd been riding just as high as one of those Corsairs and just like that I got shot down. But the thing was I was still keyed up and breathing hard from all those flares and tracers flashing in the night. Just down in the pit of my gut was all dry and hollow. I should've been feeling nothing but the power and the glory, but I was kind of empty. "They don't look like they been giving you much to eat, kid," the soldier said. He reached in his pocket and pulled out this candy bar. Honest, one of those GI chocolate bars. "There you go," he said.

It tasted too sweet and stale and warm and thick in my mouth. I know that's what made me weak. Then the guy put his arm over my shoulder and gave me a hug like my old man used to do. I sure wish he hadn't done that. I don't know if it was the candy or the guy's arm around me or everything else that went on before, but I just let loose right there. Polecat and all the soldiers back behind the tank were looking at me funny, but I couldn't help it.

"Fuck, Johnny! Fuck," I heard Polecat say. And I began to cry. I mean, not just a tear or two or even a little sniffle, but real choking and sobbing. I tried to stop it, but it just got worse. God knows, I sure didn't want it to happen. I felt so ashamed I'd like to hide. I know my old man would've hated to see me like that. But that's the trouble with letting yourself get so high on fireworks. There's always something out there just waiting to bring you down.

CHAPTER 27

I left our shanty early the next morning, wrung-out and mixed-up. The Yank tanks and the Japs barricaded in the Education Building were still at a standoff. I snuck up along the big rolls of airstrip wire to where Polecat and me'd unpacked our bundle the night before. It was just the way we'd left it, stuff scattered all over. Still half asleep, I hunkered down in the middle of it. And there, amongst the junk, I spotted something we'd overlooked in the dark. It lay half-hidden under a leg wrap, blinking silver at me in the morning light. Damn, I jumped! I never figured to find anything like it – a sweet little chrome-plated, six-shot revolver. For a second I could only gape. Then I snatched it up before anybody saw and slipped it quick into my pocket. And just in case somebody *was* watching, I grabbed the leg wrap too.

I headed straight back to the shanty, shaking with excitement, sat down on the back step and let it rest cool and light in my hand, my finger across the trigger. It didn't feel quite like I'd expected. Not so weighty as you'd think for an officer's pistol. More like something George Raft or Cagney might've been packing in a gangster movie. I'd never seen it before, but I knew it had to be Abiko's.

What I felt was some kind of secret power. That pistol was what we'd always dreamed about but could never get our hands on. Something deadly to hold, like the roar of planes, rumble of tanks and tracers in the night. When the sun peeked over the trees and hit that chrome, it lit right up in my hand. It dazzled me just to look at it. But after I sat there staring awhile, it got me nervous too. So I wound the leg wrap around it, stuck it in an old coffee tin, and hid it under the shanty, next to the sod wall of our air raid shelter.

I walked around the shanty thinking about it, then down along the path and back. Finally I took it out again and went over to the

Colonel's. He was busy watching our troops up near the gate, squads coming in from patrols, making their reports, then heading out into the city again. He was always studying. When I put the pistol on the table, he squinted at me a second, picked it up and weighed it in the palm of his hand. He ran his fingers over it real slow, like a caress, the veins standing up on the backs of his bony hands. He snapped the cylinder out to one side, dropped six bullets into his hand, studied them, then put them back, one by one. He checked the barrel, spun the cylinder and clicked it back into place. Then he eased the hammer back and fiddled with something down by the trigger guard.

"That's your safety," he said, holding it up so I could see. "Keep it locked when it's in your pocket."

"What do you think?"

"It's Jap all right. Small bore. Twenty-five caliber, I figure. Probably the same as what they used to execute those three British boys."

"Damn, I'm feeling edgy, Colonel. Fidgety."

"Yeah, you got a right. Things are changin' fast."

"What about you?"

"Done in," he said. "I could use some rest."

I took the pistol back to the shanty, stuck it in the coffee tin and never said anything about it to anyone else.

Even with all the hostages being held in the Education Building, it got to be like a circus in Camp, everybody mingling with the soldiers and marveling at their stuff. "Avenging angels" was what the Colonel called them. The men of the First Cav. Insignia was a big yellow patch with a black slash and a horse's head. "MacArthur's spit and polish boys," a GI from another outfit cracked. Everybody kept gawking like they'd never seen such men before. The girls hung on them and the little kids got under their feet. But what surprised me most was how nice they treated us. Like family.

Sunday morning this tall young captain came by and started chatting with my mom out front of our shanty. He had his helmet off, holding it careful in both hands, a big friendly smile on his face. And Mom was smiling right back.

"Look what this lovely man's brought, Johnny," she called out. There was a bunch of handsome brown eggs nesting in his helmet.

"How'd you like to share a real home-cooked breakfast?" he asked. His hair'd been bleached near white by the sun and his eyes were a washed-out china blue, but crinkled at the edges, like he'd been squinting into the sun.

"Yes, sir."

"Go get the Colonel," Mom said. "See if he has some lard for the eggs."

The Captain beat the eggs in his helmet while I fanned the coals and Mom got the skillet hot. I saw rings layered round the inside of his helmet and figured he must've been cooking in it plenty. "Cooking, washing, shaving and soaking my feet," he told me. "Steel pot's the universal tool." He served up the breakfast of our lives in there. Those eggs were rich and soft and slipped down like warm butter. And the Captain savored every morsel on his tin plate too.

"Don't know how long it's been since I've had a real sit-down meal with civilians," he said, easing back. Then he glanced at the Colonel, looking guilty for having said it.

"Whatever they been feedin' you has done the job, son," the Colonel said.

"Yes, sir," the Captain said, straightening himself when the Colonel addressed him.

"These sure taste different." I rolled the taste in my mouth.

"You've forgotten how real eggs taste," Mom said.

"We had duck eggs last year, but they were fishy."

"These are chicken eggs," Mom said. "Fresh." And she licked her lips.

"Where'd you find 'em?" the Colonel asked.

"North of Novaliches, sir. Filipinos gave us all kinds of things coming down that road."

"You hear anything about Geronimo up there?" I asked.

"The Indian?"

"He means his dad," Mom said. "We think he might be the guerrilla using that name."

"Up in the Benguet," I said.

"No, sorry. But Benguet Province is where the Japs are supposed to be retreating to."

"It's true then," the Colonel said. "About them plannin' to kill us and take some women and kids up north?"

"Hostages?" Mom asked.

"That's why we rushed down, sir," the Captain said. "The Old Man got wind of something about a massacre and put a fire under us."

"Not enough trucks for many hostages," I said.

"Better thank our lucky stars," Mom said.

"You're sure a sight," the Colonel said, looking at the Captain. "I want to say you're all a sight."

"Pardon me for asking, sir, but which Colonel are you?" the Captain asked.

"I'm what they call a Plantation Colonel."

"Thank God," the Captain said and relaxed himself.

The Army put real Chinese cooks from downtown hotels in our Camp Kitchen and started serving up rich stews with Army B rations, mongo beans and the like. It tasted pretty close to "manna." None of us could stop eating. Put any amount of food in front of us and it was gone. I swear, if you'd sat me in a big room packed solid with chow, I could've eaten it all non-stop and licked the walls for dessert.

But our bodies weren't up to handling real food after so many months of gruel. So we kept puking our guts and running for the latrine. That stew cramped us real bad. I suppose even in heaven you've got to shit. I heard the stew actually killed off some old duffer down at the Gym, but I didn't think much about it at the time. Just kept eating. After all, old-timers had been dying by the dozens over the last few months.

Besides, there was too much other stuff going on. Like all that heavy cannon fire in the city, those big fires glowing in the night and the two friends of Jerry's who'd escaped in the dark out of the Education Building by tying sheets together and climbing down out a second-story window. That got us all excited. But an officer was quick to remind us that they still had about two hundred more hostages left up there. Told us to have patience. I guess he knew his stuff. It took two solid days and nights of serious negotiating to get that situation solved.

"Worse than working out a union contract," the officer said. Yanks finally had to agree to let the Japs keep their light arms and walk out free, in exchange for the hostages. Commandant Hayashi even had the gall to demand their very own military escort out to Sampaloc. Pretty crazy when you think about it, our soldiers giving a bunch of Japs protection. But I know it as fact. I saw them all head out Monday morning. Marched out pretty ragtag. One of them'd been wounded and had to ride on another's back. All at once it seemed strange to think we'd been scared of them for so long.

But for all their negotiating, it ended bad for those Japs. I heard they got left off at this fork in the road and old Hayashi chose the wrong way. A band of guerrillas caught them in an ambush and mowed them all down in a crossfire. Well, it sounded true enough. By then I wasn't giving rumors a second thought. You didn't need rumors when there was so much new happening every day.

Like when they shot a couple of Jap snipers wearing padres' robes and trying to sneak into our Camp over the Seminary roof. Like when they caught two more dressed up like Filipino women, with makeup and all. Nabbed them right in front of the Main Building with grenades under their dresses. That wasn't just exciting, it was good for a laugh. We had all kinds of fun with it in the chow line.

"Bini-boy Japs," Polecat snorted. "Wearing the sexy dresses now. Hiding behind the ladies' skirts." See, *bini-bini*'s a girl in Tagalog and bini-boy's what they call a guy who wears dresses. Then Polecat shortened it to "Bini-Japs" and laughed himself silly. He wanted some more revenge, that's all. I guess carving up Abiko just didn't satisfy the urge.

"Where you been anyhow?" I asked him. "You missed some swell scrambled eggs at the shanty."

"My papa died," he said matter-of-fact.

"What do you mean?"

"Died from the cramps. Stew was too much for him, they said." He wrinkled his forehead.

"That was *your* old man?"

"He was tired, very tired," he said, sounding real Filipino all at once, shaking his head. "Very weak. Cramps got very bad. Too much beriberi maybe." Strange how quiet he said it. I figured maybe he'd done his crying already. He just kept giving me that bahalana shrug of his.

"Where is he?"

"Buried over by the Seminary. Just temporary."

"Shit. I didn't know."

"He kept saying how good it felt to be free," Polecat smiled. That got me feeling low and edgy again. It wasn't like I knew the old guy so well, but I kept thinking of Polecat bunking all alone in that sea of old men.

"What you gonna do?" I asked.

"Same as you, I guess."

"You can come stay at the shanty."

"Yeah, sure."

"You helped build it, didn't you. Said so yourself." I never thought to check with Mom. The idea just came to me. Polecat was like family anyhow and I didn't have to worry. She never gave it a thought.

"Just make sure you leave his mattress out in the sun awhile," she said. "And pick out the bedbugs."

Wednesday morning I went over with him to get his stuff out of the Gym. The old guys sat on their bunks, watching us like zombies. Polecat decided on taking his own bunk, but chose his old man's mosquito net. He spent a few more minutes going through his dad's stuff. He took a couple of photographs and a few religious things and chucked them onto his mattress. I was pretty amazed. That sure wasn't like Polecat. I was real proud of him for traveling so light. We grabbed the two ends of his bunk and moved him out. We didn't have to clear it with anybody. No more roll calls, you see.

We'd made it about halfway across the field when we heard the first long whistle and then the heavy crunch out ahead of us. It kicked a spray of dirt way up in the air. I didn't know right off what it was, but I knew enough to hit the ground. It looked like it'd landed smack on our shanty and my stomach seized up on me. But when the smoke and dust drifted, I saw it'd hit just across the path. Then a bunch more came, first that long whistle and then the hard crunch at the end. It was crazy lying under that bunk in the middle of the big field, listening to those shells dropping. They sailed over us and came down like giant steps, crunch, crunch, crunch, striding across Glamourville and past the Education Building and out toward the Camp Garden, smoke rising and people yelling. Then all of a sudden it just stopped.

We grabbed the bunk and ran for the shanty, tripping over ourselves. I dropped my end when we reached the shell hole out front and headed straight back to the air raid shelter. Mom was lying in there, peeking out of the shadows.

"You OK?" I asked, hunkering down to see. She was holding her head, and her eyes were moist.

"Just a *buko* from when I dove in," she said, smiling up at me. "Banged my silly head." Buko's a tight lump on your scalp from when you get rapped hard. It's Tagalog for little green coconut. I rubbed it for her. "Where were you boys?"

"Bringing the bunk. They sailed right over us."

"Bet they scared those bedbugs," Polecat said and Mom just had to laugh.

"Forget your silly bedbugs," she said. "Just flip the mattress and leave it out there in the sun."

Around noon old General MacArthur came into our Camp. Folks all went pretty crazy. They packed the Main Plaza, all cheering and crowding forward to get close, shouting his name. It was about as close to a mob as you're likely to get from a bunch of skeletons. I never got to see much, just the top of his hat going by. He came and went pretty damn quick anyway, as it turned out. Stayed just long enough to let us know he'd returned. Jesus, I was thinking, I hope they don't drop any mortars on us now.

But just after he left, when everybody was strolling along, talking it over and feeling pretty good about it all, the next bunch came in on us. Only there were more this time, and they came quicker, one right on the other. We heard that first whistle and everybody was off and running. I jumped in quick behind some crates and squeezed tight against the ground. Some others crowded in next to me, one guy breathing hot on my neck. Far off, I heard somebody screaming. Crunch, I heard, crunch, so close the ground shook under me, and then everybody was up and running again. So I jumped up too and rushed down the path, right past the Colonel's shanty, like I was rounding third and heading home. Another hit behind me just as I dove into our shelter.

"Damn!" I yelled, my heart pounding. "I don't like it, I don't like it, I don't like it." And Mom was hugging and kissing me like she hadn't seen me in years.

"I hate it when you're not here."

"I don't like it!" I yelled again.

"Don't know what I'd do without you, Johnny," she said real soft, brushing my hair back.

"Yeah?"

"I'm just a sucker for that nose and that mouth and that black hair your dad gave you." She held my face in her hands.

"Really?"

"And don't you dare get a swelled head over it," she said, looking at me ornery. And that started us laughing. I mean, just like kids getting silly and building quick to hysterics. We tried to stop, but we just laughed and laughed until we were crying. It was so stupid. Her hair was all hanging down in her face and her eyes and mouth all wet from laughing. Every time I took a breath and tried to stop, I saw her grin or heard her breathe – something – and it started all over. The shells kept falling heavy all around us outside, but we ended up shaking so hard we could only groan and hold our sides.

Then it stopped. We lay there panting and listening for the next shell to land, but the attack was over. Finally I crawled out and looked around. There was a crowd gathering up towards the Education Building, right where the path forked. Up near the Colonel's shanty. I went up the path, feeling anxious. Somebody'd got hit right at the fork. He must've been running behind me. They were carting him off on a stretcher with a sheet over him. The sheet was all bloody and there was this big pool of blood where he'd been lying. Polecat was there in the crowd.

"Who was it?" I asked.

"Don't know. Young guy."

"Where's the Colonel?"

"Up in the shanty." Polecat shook his head. There was a bunch of people up there, crowded around the doorway. "Must've got up out of his bunk to see what was going on. Cut him right in two."

I wanted to say something, but I couldn't get it out. I felt numb, frozen. I knew I should go up, but I couldn't. I was thinking, Jesus, why didn't you lay low, for Christ sake, why didn't you just stay put? I had to look away across the field to catch my balance. But the field was a mess. They were wheeling artillery across it towards us, stirring up thick clouds of yellow dust.

I wasn't going to cry, I wasn't letting myself go like that again. But I was mad for not making myself go up to see him. I just kept waiting, and when I finally went, they'd taken him away already and there was just all this blood on the bamboo floor. Polecat stood next to me and we kept staring at the blood. Finally we got a bucket, fetched water from the stream and started washing his floor as clean as we could. Not saying anything. Just washing it down over and over. We straightened up the sheets on his bunk. We cleaned some tin plates he'd left next to the clay stove. Then we sat down at his table. Sat there silent. His pipe was lying on the table and next to it was a new pouch of tobacco he'd got off some GI.

We sat there watching the soldiers set up the howitzers. One-o-fives. They set them on a line along the path and then started loading and firing towards the south, swinging the big shells in low heavy arcs up to the guns to lock and load. Then, "Fire!" and the big heavy booms and smoke drifting across and the empty brass casings rolling on the ground.

We sat there until it was dark, watching them fire the guns, seeing the flashes, listening to the sound roll out toward the black trees and back. We didn't talk. We just sat there watching. After a long time we filled the Colonel's pipe and smoked it, passing it back and forth in the dark.

CHAPTER 28

The next barrage came in about eight. All three of us were in our shanty having supper, so we dove straight into our shelter and stayed put until it was over. It came in heavy, but at least we were together. It was better together. When it stopped, me and Polecat went out to check for damages. It was pitch out there, except for the flashes from the one-o-fives and the glow from the fires outside. We went up the path behind the howitzers and they were booming. We were locked tight in a duel to the finish all right, Jap shells coming in, ours going out.

The Main Plaza was so crowded we kept bumping into each other in the dark. "You guys hear? Somebody got killed over at the Gym," Harvey was yelling.

"Guy was hit in the Education Building too," shouted Knockers. "While he was on the crapper."

"With his pants down!"

"Old lady Haverford's dead. Shell landed on their shanty," Finch said. "Daughter's hurt bad too. That's what I heard."

"No kidding," I said. It was always different when you knew the name. "What about the old man?" But nobody'd heard anything about Haverford. For just a moment I thought about Harry sitting with him under the trees out at the Polo Club, watching the son ride his ponies across the green field and felt sorry for the old guy. But there was too much else happening just then.

"The worst's right here," Red said, pointing over at the side of the Main Building, like it was a competition. "Two shells smacked right into those rooms."

"A guy was standing right over there," Jerry said. "His wife was handing him her bag out the window. They were getting out of that side of the building, thought it was too dangerous to stay." But Red wouldn't let her finish.

"Blew him apart and took her whole arm right off," he yelled. "Her whole arm!"

"Jees," Finch said. "What'd they do with it?"

"What?" You had to yell out there to be heard.

"What'd they do with the arm?"

"For Christ sake, Finchy. Concrete flying, ceilings coming down, people dying. And you want to know about her damn arm?"

"Sure, it's interesting."

"Interesting, hell," I said. All at once I was tired of their dumb kid talk.

They were calling for volunteers over the Camp loudspeakers, so we went over. They grabbed Red and Knockers and Finch and sent them to help take wounded out of the Main Building. Me and Polecat and Jerry got sent to the Education Building. It was even darker inside with the power off and the smell of explosives was thick in the hall. They'd set up a clinic in there, with all sorts of wounded coming in from the city.

"We need all these people moved out to the north side," this officer was shouting. He was the head doc, a heavy-set guy with a booming voice and a flashlight in his hand. "Shells are coming in from the south." The ones who could walk started heading out on their own. But most were on stretchers lying along the halls. It was hard to make them out in the dark, but you could smell their wounds all right. There were sixteen of us working the stretchers. We began carrying them out back and lining them up under the sky. There were low clouds riding heavy above us and then breaks with stars shining. A lot of the wounded were in real pain, moaning and calling out. Medics came around, doing what they could, but it was hard to see much, even outside. For all we knew some could've been corpses already.

"What if it rains?" Jerry asked, looking at the sky.

"Rain's a lot better than mortars," Polecat said.

"We'll get ponchos or something," I said. "I bet they got ponchos."

When we went back in for our fifth load, I heard a hoarse voice calling, "Major" real weak. There were plenty of others calling out too, so at first I didn't pay any attention. Then I heard it again, just a whisper. It called out, "Bolo."

"Jesus," I said, bending down in the dark. "Is it really you?"

"Not even a disciple," he said, letting out a little throaty rattle. He laid a hand on my arm.

"God damn!" I was whispering too now. I felt like screaming my fool head off. I mean, how many times do you get to see a man rise from the dead? "Polecat, Jerry, go get my mom quick. Tell her Harry's back!"

She came running with her Red Cross armband on. Before I knew it she was on her knees by the stretcher, making sure it was really Harry and that he was alive and thanking God and heaven and all. Next thing she was working on the major to let us take care of Harry at our shanty. She kept going back and forth between Harry and the doc, till the big guy finally broke down and said OK. So after we got all the wounded out and covered with ponchos, we carried Harry home on the stretcher and put him down at the foot of Mom's bunk. Even in the dark you could tell he was in bad shape. He smelled like an open sore. Mom had us bring her clean water from up the path. She kept washing off his face and propping him up to pour fluids down his throat.

"Now you'll have your way with me, I suppose," he said.

"You're going to be all right," Mom kept saying. "You'll be just fine."

"Don't keep saying that. Sounds like last rites."

"What have they done to you?"

"About everything they could think of. Now, for God's sake, let me be." Mom said his being cranky was a good sign. But she stayed up late worrying over him anyhow.

Finally me and Polecat went to bed. The day'd sure been long. Polecat was off as soon as he hit the pillow. But I just lay there looking out at the sky moving low and threatening and the stars sparkling bright in the breaks, thinking about Harry's coming back from the dead and then thinking about the Colonel's being killed, until I got so happy and sad together I felt sick. We'd got Harry back, which was more than we could've wished for. But we'd lost the Colonel and you couldn't ever beat him for the way he studied and figured things. It was like I felt a sob coming, but it never came.

There was just no way of knowing who was going to make it. I wished I could figure why. All I knew was it had to be luck, because if it was God he was demented and that was no luck at all. Thinking about it, I got this little vision, like a daydream where you're getting pushed out onto the big field before you're ready and told to run. They've already got the machine guns set up and firing. You're running like crazy and they're shooting from both sides. All around you folks keep dropping in the crossfire, but you've got to keep running, because if you go back for someone you're a goner for sure. Damn, you're tired of it. Maybe you'd be better off just standing still and letting them have at you. Sooner or later you're going down anyways. But it's no good. Polecat's always there grinning and shouting at you, "Sige na! Hurry up!"

I heard Harry calling out in the dark. "Major," and then again, "Major." I figured Mom'd finally gone to sleep. "Bring me the chamber pot, would you." I got him the coffee tin we used at night. When I helped him over onto his side to piss, I felt how frail he was. It must've hurt him just to do that, because I could feel a shiver go through him. "Take it across the path and dump it," he told me.

"I'll dump it at the latrine in the morning."

"No, there's blood in it. It'll worry your mom." So I did what he said.

The next morning I could see just how bad off he really was. Not just skinny, but pale as a ghost with some yellow mixed in. He'd been worked over by professionals all right – legs and arms puffed up with the beriberi, lips cracked and bruised, one eye swollen almost shut, gash along the cheekbone. He couldn't get up onto his own two feet or lift his left arm off the stretcher. The fingernails on that hand had been pulled out. Lord only knows what they'd broke inside. Along with that he needed a good bath and some fresh clothes. He smelled worse than when I first met him off that long drunk.

Scrounging stuff was Polecat's talent, so he worked on getting Harry the clothes and toilet stuff. Mom got the antiseptics, vitamin shots, sulfa tablets and skin ointments for his ulcers. He was embarrassed about it, but we scrubbed him down and dressed him up like a baby, even held him over the can while he relieved himself. We spent the next days getting enough eggs and broth and juices into him to make him look almost human again. We even got him sitting in a chair. He was gaining a pound or more a day and would pretty soon be up to one hundred pounds again.

Artillery spotters up on the tower of the Main Building found where most of the shells were coming from and helped our howitzers get the range. It took a few days to knock them out altogether, and in the meantime the Japs managed to kill off some more of our people. Every time they started dropping artillery and mortars on us, me and Polecat had to grab Harry's stretcher and wedge it down into the shelter. Harry was groaning with pain, but he laughed over it.

"Balangay," he said. "That right, Bolo? This is our little wooden boat on the mighty seas?"

"Yeah, boat that brought the ancestors from far away."

"Imagine how close you get to shipmates in the middle of a great ocean, sailing to a strange land. This is our balangay."

"How come you know about that?"

"Fort Santiago. Young Filipino was there with me in a cell where we were so tight we couldn't find a spot to lie down. Fourteen or more with dysentery and one bucket for a toilet that kept overflowing onto the floor. Bugs and lice crawling all over us. It was how we felt about each other when they tortured one of us or took him out of our cell for execution. Our tight little group. 'Balangay,' he called it."

"Why'd they put you in there?" I asked.

"Virgin, I think. She was in the underground."

"She betrayed you then," Mom said.

"Oh, no. They knew about her from the Front Gate, knew she had been bringing me things. Believe me, if she had told them anything, I wouldn't be here now. God only knows what they put her through before they killed her."

"I'm so sorry."

"All I ever gave her was a name and a dress."

"Did they bring you here from Santiago?"

"No, thank God. I'd be dead. Japs shipped me to Bilibid when they decided not to execute me."

"Bilibid Prison's got military, right?"

"Half and half. Soldiers who were too sick to work."

"Did you hear anything about Dad or Southy?"

"I haven't heard anything about Geronimo lately. But a fellow in Santiago knew him. Young kid they captured in the Zambales Mountains. He wouldn't tell me Geronimo's true name. Couldn't trust anybody. All sorts of betrayals going on. We weren't supposed to talk, so I didn't get much. They executed that poor kid."

"Didn't Southy go to Cabanatuan?" Polecat asked.

"They shipped those boys off to Japan for forced labor. Bad business. Japs stuffed thousands into the holds of ships with no food or water." He took a deep breath and a shake went through him. "Look, nothing's sure in this war, but I'm afraid Southy's dead."

"What do you mean?"

"Their ship went down. Americans bombed it."

"They bombed our own guys?"

"The ship wasn't marked, so they had no way of knowing."

"Where'd you hear that?" Polecat asked. There were tears in his eyes. And he looked mad at Harry for bringing the news.

"Over at Bilibid," Harry said. He reached out and put his good hand on Polecat's arm. "Look, I'm sorry, Bolo. I meant all that about balangay. We're in this boat together. I feel rotten about Southy. He was a damn good friend. I would be tickled pink if he walked in right now with that big smile on his face."

The last barrage came in on Saturday. By then the Japs had lost the range, so the damage wasn't so bad. They moved the howitzers out of Camp and started putting up tents across the field. There was more and more traffic in and out of Camp – army, Filipinos, folks from other camps. The area around Santo Tomás was getting cleared of Japs, but the guns were still pounding away south of the Pasig River.

It was then Polecat showed Harry just what kind of shipmate he could be. While he was working his way through those new tents, sniffing around for fresh supplies, he came across a medic with a supply of GI alcohol. Polecat scrounged a whole cupful of that stuff, even got some ripe oranges to go with it. Never told a soul, just mixed it up on the sly and brought it in right before evening chow. He carried it in an army helmet he'd got hold of and made his grand entrance up the back stairs with a big grin on his face and a khaki towel draped over his arm, like he was head barkeep at the Manila Hotel. He poured real careful out of the steel pot – a tin cup for Mom, then one for Harry.

"I'm sorry we have no ice, sir and madam," Polecat said. Soon as Harry sniffed it, his eyes lit up. He sipped at it and let it roll around in his mouth.

"This boy's a born dog robber," he said with a smile. Polecat didn't like the sound of it and made a sour face.

"What the hell's that?" he snarled.

"Biggest and brightest job in the army. More important than general. You keep this up, you'll be skipper of the balangay."

"Is it OK, Mrs. Oldfield?"

"Divine," Mom said.

"Could use a little aging perhaps," Harry said. "But I'm sure it'll have the desired effect."

"What about us?" I asked.

"Two more cups, señor. Time you and the Major came of age."

"Hell, Harry," Polecat drawled. "I come of age long time ago."

Polecat's potion had the desired effect all right. It didn't take much to get us all laughing and talking silly. Hell, it even got Harry up onto his feet. Mom gave Polecat full credit. I don't mean Harry was skipping rope right off. But in another day he was beating me at chess. And in a couple more he was hobbling up and down the path, dressed like a scarecrow in his fresh army fatigues, left arm tucked into an olive drab sling. It wasn't that we weren't used to miracles by then. We'd been watching turnarounds by all kinds of people who'd been assigned to the scrap heap. But even the doc couldn't get over Harry. He said he'd never seen anybody come back so far so fast. Harry claimed Polecat'd discovered the elixir of life. But Mom said Harry'd made a pact with the devil.

So me and Polecat weren't altogether shocked when Harry came to us later that week with a proposition. He told us he'd already cleared it with my mom and made arrangements with the U.S. Army.

"We've got a jeep for the day," he said. "I need you guys to come with me into the city. We're going on a treasure hunt. Meet you at the Front Gate in half an hour."

A half-hour. That gave me just enough time to slip back to the shanty, scoot under the back and get my revolver out of the coffee tin.

CHAPTER 29

When we got to the Front Gate, it was about ten-thirty and starting to drizzle. But the rain was so light, the GIs guarding the gate didn't even bother with ponchos. Harry was signing for the jeep and talking to a sergeant. What surprised me was to see old Haverford standing there. We hadn't even talked to him since we ambushed him that night over by the northeast wall. He was looking haggard and mean, even by our standards.

"Climb in the back, gentlemen," Harry said. "Mr. Haverford has consented to help us in our search." Haverford didn't say a thing. It looked like he didn't really want to be there. I grabbed hold of the side bar and swung in the back under the canvas flap. Harry eased himself up onto the driver's seat real slow. He winced a little every time he tried to use his left arm.

"Keep a sharp lookout," the MP told us. "Especially down near the Pasig. There's still plenty of Japs on the other side."

"Let me drive," Haverford said. "I'm in better shape."

"Never underestimate a cripple," Harry said. "There's more left than you might think." He said it friendly enough, but he didn't look at Haverford. He steered and shifted with his right hand, used his left just to steady the bottom of the wheel. I kept wondering why Harry'd asked Haverford along. Polecat was looking at him funny too. Nobody said a word about his wife or daughter.

We drove out the front gate where that first tank'd plowed through. The ironwork was all bent and hanging off the concrete post. Harry turned right and headed down España. There were troops out along the fence and more at a roadblock down the street.

I felt cool and free, the damp breeze whipping at me as we drove along. It looked like it might even clear. The drizzle eased off and it started to get hot again. But low dark clouds kept pushing in off the bay. Every once in a while, it spit a little rain on the windshield and Haverford had to crank the wiper back and forth. Then all of a sudden it hit me that we were really outside the walls. I got excited and edgy all at once, like I was going into some strange new land. I hadn't been out here in over three years. The guns kept booming to the south, heavy artillery mixed with the chatter of machine guns and the thin crack of small arms. And we were driving right toward them.

Through Quiapo the houses looked OK except for some bullet holes and broken windows, but then I noticed how much stuff there was all over the streets and how the trees'd been broken and stripped of their leaves, like some big storm'd come through. Haverford told Harry to work his way west at the end of España and then left onto Rizal. I saw how bad it really was soon as the buildings started getting bigger. Polecat stared at it with his mouth open. And the closer we got to the Pasig, the worse it got, until there were whole blocks missing, with just piles of broken concrete sliding down into the streets. Then it was open expanse – flattened, crushed, pulverized. Dust was swirling so thick we had to stop to wipe the windshield. Harry was staring out at the destruction, mumbling to himself.

"Where we going?" Polecat asked, but nobody answered.

"Haverford?" Harry asked.

"I need to see my office," Haverford said. "Down on Escolta." That was where most of the business'd been, all the big rich establishments sitting right along the river. Polecat let out a low whistle when we got there.

"My God," Haverford whispered. Only a few buildings were left standing and they'd been shot up bad. "Stop here," he said, getting out and walking ahead of us down the middle of the street, checking each pile of rubble. Harry followed along behind him in the jeep. The further Haverford went, the more hunched over he got. And you couldn't blame him.

"It's a desert," I said. "Full of holes like the moon." Haverford was standing there, looking at this concrete wall. Just a wall, the building behind it was gone. It leaned toward the river. Big, broken slabs of concrete hung from the ends of metal rods. All the rest had slid down into the street. Haverford just stood there, looking up at it.

"This was my firm, my building, my life," he cried out. "Four stories high." He sure made a pitiful picture standing there on his lonesome, wailing at a wall.

Me and Polecat got tired of waiting and walked down by the water. Dark smoke was blowing down river out of Intramuros and across the Port Area. That's where the heavy fighting was going on. But there was a lot more smoke billowing further south towards Pasay and up river past Malacañang. The river was so dark and greasy, it went all multicolored like a rainbow when the sun came out. The tide was running out and all kinds of stuff floated by – hunks of houses and trees and bodies, you name it. It ran like heavy oil. The Pasig never moved too fast. The bridges had all been blown and the far end of Jones Bridge sat way down in the water. But GIs were hard at work on a pontoon crossing. Polecat was looking down at the old walled city.

"Lots of people dead in there, Johnny. Japs been burning the churches and hospitals full of Pilipinos," he said. "GI told me. Just jammed 'em in, tossed on some gasoline and poof! Lots of people."

When we walked back, Haverford was still out there, shaking his head and pacing back and forth. Harry was sitting behind the wheel, looking pale and tired. He honked the horn.

"Let's go, old boy," he yelled. Haverford was slow coming back. "We're going to look for where he hid his car. Lovely Lincoln Zephyr. But he always had a chauffeur with it. I doubt he can drive by himself." "Up a few blocks this way, into Binondo," Haverford said, waving his hand.

But there was so little left to guide us, it took some time to find the right street. We must've made five wrong turns. The clouds broke for a few minutes and the pavement started steaming. Then it rained again. There was too much rubble blocking the way, so we went on foot while Harry waited in the jeep. I didn't see any bodies, but I could sure smell them when the wind was right. They must've been down in the rubble. It doesn't take long for something dead to go bad in the tropics, even in February.

"This is it," Haverford said, pointing at the broken shell of a building. "I'm quite sure. This has to be where the garage is." But the whole first floor was blocked off by rubble. There were just some broken stairs leading up the side to a doorway. At least, it'd once been a doorway. Now it was just a hole. "Climb up there, boys, and take a look." He waved us up the rubble with his hand. Polecat spat in the dust. The rain'd stopped again and when the wind kicked up, the air was full of grit.

"What if your car's in there? How the hell you going to get it out?"

"We'll manage that when we find it," Haverford said without even looking at us.

You could tell his attitude was getting on Polecat's nerves, but there was something about that doorway, something about the mystery of a hole in a wall that made us want to climb up. Maybe, just maybe, we might find something. But as soon as we got inside, the stench hit us so hard we had to step back a second.

"There should be stairs to the right that go down to the garage," Haverford called up. Polecat muttered something in Tagalog and spat again. It took us a while to get adjusted to the dark and the smell. Then we made out the stairs and felt our way down, our shirts pulled up over our noses. Everything we touched was covered by a heavy layer of gritty dust. Above the wall of debris there were gaping holes where the light came streaming in – big rays of light through a dusty haze – like in a cathedral. We were in a pretty big room. The front part was all covered by rubble. But there was no car around, just two dead Jap soldiers. Marines. We could tell by the little anchors on their helmets.

They looked like they'd taken a direct hit. One lay on his face. He'd been tossed in the corner like a rag doll. His helmet'd been blown off and his rifle stock splintered. His legs looked to be headed in a different direction from the rest of his body. The other one lay further back. He still had his helmet on and was staring straight up at the ceiling. Only his eyes had gone a gummy black. Blood ran black from his ear into a hard black pool on the floor. Flies swarmed all over his eyes and mouth and up into his nose. It was ripe in there, let me tell you, and stifling hot.

Polecat snatched the Jap's rifle. That one was in pretty good shape, even had the bayonet attached. He pulled back the bolt, took a look into the chamber and then slid it forward again. He adjusted the webbing and swung it up onto his shoulder. Then he bent down, unbuckled the cartridge belt and gave it big yank, rolling the body over onto its side. That made the flies swarm and buzz all around us and the stench hit so hard I gagged and headed quick up the stairs.

"Don't you want something?" Polecat yelled.

"Just some air." We passed Haverford on our way back to the jeep.

"Well, was it there, boys?" he asked. "Did you see my Zephyr?"

"I'm not your God damn boy," Polecat spat. "Go see for yourself."

"Just bodies," I said. I was still gagging. I couldn't get the smell out. I took a big swig of water from a canteen Harry'd brought, but the taste stayed in my mouth. Then we headed west towards the North Harbor. I figured our chances were slim to none on finding anything down there. But I should've known better than underestimate Harry.

"We near Tutuban Station?" he asked.

"Just a bit up here," Haverford said, waving his hand again. He waved it like some old lady shushing pigeons. Soon as Harry got his bearings he headed down a street called Azcarraga toward the water. We were a lot closer to the heavy fighting in Intramuros now. The sound of rifle fire sounded like it was just around the corner. Harry took a right and looped back a ways to the north. We came across a squad of GIs heading down the street, working both sides.

"Hello," Harry called out to them. "Any of you seen a big, tall sign – Three-B Beer, BBB beer, something like that?"

"There's nothing tall down here," a GI said.

"You looking for a brewery or something?" the squad leader asked.

"I just remember the sign. Need it to get my bearings."

"I could sure use a brewery right now," the soldier said.

"Matter of fact, I did see something, mister," another called out. "A big B lying next to some corrugated roofing back there. Great big B. Didn't see three of 'em, just one. Back up on the right."

"Hell," Harry said. "I'll take one-B beer. I'll take two-B beer. I'll take any damn beer at all." And everybody laughed.

"You find a brewery, you give us a call, y'hear."

We drove on and sure enough, we found the end of this big metal B sticking out of the rubble. Must've been six or more feet tall. Harry got out and stood in the middle of the street, lining himself up with the spot and then looking back down towards the bay. A breeze was blowing off the water. He held up his good hand with his fingers crossed and walked down the street into the wind, checking all the rubble piled high along the south side.

Some stray dogs came up the street towards us, about five of them, trotting along aimlessly, sniffing the air. Ugly, mangy-looking curs. Wonks, I was thinking. When they got near Harry, one of them wagged his tail and veered off from the pack. Harry turned and held out his hand and the dog sniffed at it. But pretty soon they moved on again, looking for some food, no doubt. I hadn't seen dogs since the ones in Camp got eaten.

"I think we're near the mother lode," Harry said. He turned the jeep around, drove down the street about a hundred yards and pulled in tight against the rubble. He turned off the ignition and slid out. "Anybody want to look for treasure?"

"There can't be anything left in this," Haverford said. "Just a waste of time."

"We won't know until we look, will we." Harry started climbing slowly up over a high pile of broken concrete. He looked spent but was energized by the search. Me and Polecat were right behind him and then Haverford. The sun was out strong now and it was getting good and sticky. From the top of the rubble, we looked down on a row of collapsed buildings. Harry heaved aside a hunk of corrugated metal and started sliding down the other side.

The tin roof had collapsed, but the bottom half of the building was still standing, with a window and a back door showing. The window was cracked and a big wedge of glass had dropped onto the ground. It felt eerie being there, so I reached into my pocket and felt my revolver. I noticed Polecat holding on tight to his rifle too. Harry tried the door, but it was locked. He looked in the window, then grabbed a rock and banged out the rest of the glass.

"You think you could climb in there?" he asked Polecat.

"What's in there?"

"Treasure," Harry said. I cupped my hands, Polecat handed Harry his rifle, took one step up, grabbed the sill and swung in before Harry could ask twice. "Watch the glass," he warned, but by then Polecat had the back door unlatched. "Welcome to Christmas 1941, gentlemen," Harry said and we walked into the bar just as Haverford was coming over the top of the rubble pile.

Like the garage, it was thick with dust, and as soon as we stirred it up, we started choking on it and coughing. The floor was littered with hunks of concrete. The counter ran down one side and behind it there was a wide shelf with a bunch of bottles still standing on it. Harry couldn't stop smiling. He picked a bottle off the shelf and blew the dust off it.

"Mr. Gordon," he said, thumping it down on the bar. Next, "Mr. Dewar." Then he hauled down something dark and round and wiped it against his shirt. Without the dust it was shiny black ceramic with some white Chinese writing on the side. "And this, friends, is my old pal Barney Jenkins." With that he kissed the urn. It was like we'd climbed into a tomb.

Harry was just blowing the dust out of four glasses when Haverford walked in. He went straight for the bottle of gin like he owned it, unscrewed the top and was on his way to guzzling it when Harry grabbed it out of his hand.

"Manners, old chap. This is a moment worth some ceremony." He poured a little scotch into the glasses. "To Barney Jenkins," he said, raising his glass. I took a sip, but didn't swallow right off. I just rinsed it around my mouth to get the dust out. It burned some but it felt clean, so I let it trickle slow down my throat. I felt grimy all over, but the scotch got rid of the dead taste that'd been in my mouth since the garage.

Harry served up another round and the effect was pretty much as magical as with the GI alcohol. We were going at it in silence, but we were smiling more. Even Haverford started to warm up some. Polecat began to get sentimental and teary-eyed.

"Southy Jack," he said.

"What about him?" Haverford asked.

"Oh, didn't you know?" Harry said. "He's dead."

"That so?"

"Yes, that's so," Harry snapped and took another sip of scotch. After a while he said, "I always thought there was something fishy about the way Southy got pulled out of Camp, didn't you?" Harry said. "He was no more military than you or I." Haverford looked at his glass. "Discovered something in Fort Santiago that might interest you, Montgomery. Learned a couple of very interesting things."

"Really," Haverford muttered.

"Japs threw a young fellow in our cell who'd been captured up in the Zambales mountains. He'd been betrayed by his fellow guerrillas, some Huks. All we had left in there was loyalty. In the end, that's all that's left. I didn't recognize him right off because his face was so badly bruised and swollen from beatings. You know how it is."

"Like that English sailor they executed," I said.

"They tortured him pretty much every day until he was finally executed. We all agreed dying must have been a relief. One Jap there loved working on him. Tied his hands behind him and hung him up by them until his arms were pulled out of the sockets. Same way I got my bum shoulder. Jap hung that poor kid up like that for hours and then punched him in the face or kicked him in the balls."

"There was a good bit of that," Haverford said.

"Oh, yes, a good bit. But when I was trying to comfort the kid in our cell, he recognized me. I would never have known him in a million years. You see, Montgomery, it was your son Roger."

"My God, Barnes."

"When they were taking him out to cut off his head, he asked me to tell his father that he had died like a man. Kept his word. He spit in that Jap's face, Montgomery. I doubt he had any teeth left, but he spit blood in his face."

"Stop it!"

"No, I'm afraid I can't, Montgomery, because Roger was my cellmate, my comrade, you see. Remember those fine polo ponies? They ate them up in Zambales. Had to slit their throats and roast them to keep the guerrillas alive." Boy, I was feeling bad for Haverford. Even Polecat looked confused. I didn't like him much, but I couldn't figure Harry being so cruel.

"The other thing I learned there was about Southy. I learned who was running over to Yoshie in the night and trading info for favors." Harry looked at us and then I saw how stiff and mad his face was. The scar along his cheekbone'd gone chalk white. His one arm hung in the sling, but the right hand was clenching his glass like he wanted to smash it. "Remember, Polecat? Remember those shadows in the night. You told us about them. But I was too stupid to figure it out. I had to hear it from another poor bastard who was about to be executed." Then he looked at Haverford and his voice was just a whisper again. "I knew it was fishy, Yoshie fixing on Southy's name, but I couldn't believe it was you, Montgomery. Did you forget you were a God damn American?"

Haverford broke out the back door and was running across the flat ground when Polécat caught up to him. He tripped him from behind so he went down hard, scraping the side of his face on a block of concrete. When he rolled over and looked up, his face was already starting to bleed.

"Get him off me, Barnes!" Haverford was yelling. Polecat had the rifle down so the point of the bayonet touched his throat. The mestizo was screaming in a high-pitched voice I'd never heard out of him before.

"Taksil," he was yelling. "Traitor." And all kinds of Tagalog I didn't know. All I knew was I had to do something fast. But it was already going through my head in ice-cold clear thoughts even while I was running forward. The pistol was in my hand and I brought it down slow so Polecat could see it close, and at the same time I was leaning over Haverford and shouldering the rifle aside. I knelt on the son-of-bitch's chest with the chrome muzzle up tight under his nose, hard against his upper teeth, yelling at the top of my lungs.

"You fuck, you're gonna get yours, you lousy shit." But that was just for show. Just to get everybody's attention. Then I yelled out to Polecat, "Give me a day, Polecat. I need a date. What's Filipino's Day of Independence?" You see, just like a charm my old man's mom popped into my head and Southy telling me how she set up her execution days.

"What the hell you talkin' about, Johnny?" I could feel Haverford's body shaking under me. His eyes were closed and he was whimpering.

"Give me Independence Day," I was yelling, trying to sound tough, but my voice was breaking all over the place. "God, I know you know that, for Christ sake. The date the Americans promised."

"July 4, 1946," Polecat said. Good, I thought. That was more than a year off.

"All right, all right," I whispered. "You got that, mister Polo Club asshole? You remember that day. Don't dare forget it. No matter where you are, no matter what you're doin', that's your last day. Think about July Fourth night and day. Just think about it and sweat. Because my old man's Ben Oldfield and Geronimo takes care of those who kill his friends."

Then I got up and walked away. Man, I was shaking like a leaf, but I'd done it. I'd turned it all around. I just knew Polecat was right on the verge of killing that old fart and he just wasn't worth it. Now we all had time to think about it and cool down. I did it for Polecat and I did it for me. I did it for all of us. We had other things to do with our lives. I went back into the bar, put my pistol on the counter and took a good hard swallow of scotch.

When we left, Haverford was still lying there.

CHAPTER 30

It wasn't far from there to the docks. We loaded a few bottles in the back of the jeep. I sat up front holding Harry's glass, Polecat sat in back holding the urn. He made me take the front seat, called me "King of the Guerrilleros" and said that stuff about execution day was the best he'd heard. Truth was, my revolver had the safety on through the whole damn business. Some guerrilla!

We were sitting on this wharf, looking out across the bay at the Mariveles mountains. It was about four o'clock and out past the wrecked ships and the burnt-out docks the sunlight and shadows skipped across the bay. Harry poured some more Dewar's in his glass.

"To Southy," he said. And "To Virgin," he said. And "To Roger." And "To the Colonel," he said. "To every poor bastard who's dead from this." His voice was weak and tired. The way he looked, I wondered if he could drive the jeep back to camp.

He took the top off the urn and asked me and then Polecat to reach in and take a little ash and let it run through our fingers so the warm air would send it swirling out over the water.

"Think of each one hard and feel them pass through you and it'll feel better."

"And my mother too," Polecat said.

I thought hard, like with Southy hitting the light bag, and it was something, I swear. You just try it with someone you love so much who's dead. It reaches right down into you and they leave you but never go away.

And I was thinking that there were three kinds of dying in this war. There was the one like the Colonel where it happened in front of you and you knew for sure he was a goner. Then there was the one like Southy, where you heard he'd been loaded onto a ship and that all those guys were now somewhere on the bottom of the ocean. You didn't see it, but you were close to sure it was true. But the other kind was my dad. You didn't know anything, you could only hope there'd be a miracle and he'd show up whole like in the Second Coming. And from then on each day would be different. One day you'd see clear how he was lying in a ditch somewheres, flies crawling across his face, his eyes gone gummy black, and the next day how he was running with you down a back street in Pasay, full of life. You'd all be together and it would be like you wanted. And maybe that was the hardest death of all.

But when I reached into the urn a second time, I felt something hard in there. Somebody once told me when they cremate you there's always some bone left, and they had to crush it. And I thought, shit, it's Barney Jenkins' bones. But when the rest had run through my fingers, I held it up so I could see and blew the dust off it and it shined in the sun.

"What is it?"

"That one's an emerald. But there are more. Some I'll take back to Los Angeles for Barney's widow."

"Who else knows?"

"Only Virgin knew. She took a few for the underground. She told me which ones. The rest are still in there with Barney." Then Polecat reached in and pulled out another. It was a whole lot bigger.

"And what's this?" he asked, blowing on it. It caught the sun and gleamed like a star.

"That, gentlemen, is our money in the bank," Harry answered. "It's what will keep us going until we find Geronimo."

WILLIAM REESE HAMILTON spent his childhood in North China and the Philippines, where he and his family were captured and imprisoned by the Japanese Army for over three years in Santo Tomas Internment Camp, Manila.

His education includes bachelor and master of arts degrees in literature, and a mixed bag of experience which includes factory worker, lifeguard, ordinary seaman, English teacher, counterintelligence agent, Romanian interrogator, advertising copywriter and creative director. He left a fast-paced career in New York advertising for a remote colonial village on the coast of Venezuela.

His work has appeared in over twenty print and online publications, including *The Paris Review, The North American Review, The Adirondack Review, StoryQuarterly, Review Americana, Puerto del Sol* and *Eclectica Magazine.*

Made in the
USA
Columbia, SC